Playing Games

Also by Huma Qureshi

In Spite of Oceans
How We Met: A Memoir of Love and Other Misadventures
Things We Do Not Tell the People We Love

Playing Games

Huma Qureshi

sceptre

First published in Great Britain in 2023 by Sceptre
An imprint of Hodder & Stoughton
An Hachette UK company

1

A CIP catalogue record for this title is available from the British Library

Hardback ISBN 9781529368741
Trade Paperback ISBN 9781529368765
ebook ISBN 9781529368758

Typeset in Sabon MT by Manipal Technologies Limited

Printed and bound in Great Britain by Clays Ltd, Elcograf S.p.A.

Hodder & Stoughton policy is to use papers that are natural, renewable and recyclable products and made from wood grown in sustainable forests. The logging and manufacturing processes are expected to conform to the environmental regulations of the country of origin.

Hodder & Stoughton Ltd
Carmelite House
50 Victoria Embankment
London EC4Y 0DZ

www.sceptrebooks.co.uk

For Laurie

One

Mira is sitting on her unmade bed with her back against the wall, her laptop balanced on outstretched legs, ankles crossed, twirling a piece of her hair around her finger. She's staring at the homepage of a playwriting prize, the banner across the top of the site counting down, announcing there are two hundred and twelve days left until the submission deadline in November. Whoever designed the website has done it in such a way that the numbers flick from side to side every fifty seconds, as if they are dancing. Without realising that she's doing it, Mira counts the seconds until the numbers travel across the screen again in their stilted way and when they do it feels satisfying, like scratching an itch or figuring out a magic trick. She's doing this, staring at the numbers and counting to fifty in her head, and deliberately avoiding having to think about the play she both does but doesn't want to be writing, when her phone, which is somewhere on the bed by her bare feet, begins to vibrate.

Mira looks over the top of her laptop and then, using her toes, inches her phone towards her. She glances at the screen with low-level dread. She's wary of a ringing phone, wishes people would just text instead, even though the only person who ever calls is her older sister, Hana. And sure enough, it *is* Hana.

Mira hesitates but she knows that if she doesn't answer, Hana will only keep on trying.

'Hey, Han. What's up?'

Mira cringes at her painful attempt to sound upbeat.

'What are you doing?' Hana makes the question sound like an accusation. This is how Hana naturally speaks, the way she begins more or less every phone conversation, but still it startles Mira and makes her feel like she's being quizzed by a strict headmistress.

'Not much—'

'Because if you're not doing anything, you might as well come over for dinner.'

'Okay?'

'You have weekends off, don't you?'

'Um, yes—'

'So, I mean, you don't *have* to. I'm just saying, the option's there, if you want. If you've got nothing better to do. Don't feel obliged or anything.'

The sound becomes muffled, as though Hana has covered her phone with her free hand or the cuff of her sleeve. Mira hears her say, '*What?*' in an irritated way to her husband in the background, and then, 'I *am* being nice!', before Hana comes back on the line.

'Samir says to tell you he's making his *famous* spaghetti.'

Mira pictures Hana raking speech marks through the air with her fingers for dramatic effect, this being a thing Hana does. She makes the same gesture whenever she asks about Mira's job in the café, or her writing. It seems impossible for Hana, an Oxford graduate and a practising family lawyer, named one to watch in a *Financial Times* special report on legal services, to take anything Mira does seriously.

'Personally, I wouldn't say his cooking is worth the journey, but if you want to—'

'You do know that you could just ask if I want to come over for dinner, like a normal person. You could just say:

"Would you like to come over for dinner?"' Mira rubs her forehead. 'You don't have to go on and on about how much I don't have to or how you wouldn't bother if you were me. Like, that makes it kind of a backwards invite, which defeats the purpose of asking me over in the first place.' She makes a little gesture of impatience with her hands, her fingers exploding like tiny fireworks in the air.

There's a pause before Hana replies in an irritated way, 'Obviously I'm asking if you want to come over for dinner. That's exactly what I've just said.' She laughs. 'I mean, what do you want exactly? A gold-embossed invitation? For Samir's spaghetti?'

'No. Just—' Mira closes her eyes, rests her head against the wall behind her. 'Nothing. Forget it. Sorry, I'm tired.'

She opens her eyes. The dancing numbers on her laptop screen taunt her. In theory she has ages to finish writing this play – she has two hundred and twelve days – but she finds writing hard, even though it's the only thing she wants to do. She hasn't written anything new for months. She feels the familiar, finger-wagging guilt of failure.

Her play is supposed to be about a woman in her early thirties whose life has not turned out the way she expected. The woman is unable to sleep and takes to walking around the city in the early hours, delivering a monologue on her life's seminal moments and turning points thus far. It was only after Mira wrote the first scene that she realised that she was writing about herself, and so she's been trying hard ever since to make stuff up, in order for it to be less predictable, more original.

Since January, Mira's been going to a playwriting group that meets every fortnight on a Thursday evening in the basement of a local bookshop on Crouch End Broadway.

It was her New Year's resolution to take her writing more seriously. She's lost count of the abandoned documents on her desktop, pieces of writing that never make it beyond a first or second draft. The teacher, Dominic, talks often about the importance of the question 'what if?' to help them push their ideas. So Mira's been thinking what if, at some point, the woman lies down on a pavement for an as yet unspecified reason only to decide life feels better that way, and what if she doesn't get up, in spite of all these passers-by tripping all over her, and what if one of them, a man, lies down too, and then one by one all of the other passers-by follow suit, holding hands like paper dolls. She thinks there might be something in the idea, but she has no clue how to make it work in practice. She doesn't even know what to call her lead character, although she does at least have a title. *Pavements.* But in total she has written maybe the first two scenes of the play, and that has taken nearly four months.

It doesn't help that she finds Dominic, a working play-wright and occasional actor, so distractingly handsome. It's not just that he's so good-looking; she loves the way he talks about writing and that he's not pretentious about it. He's kind too, remembers everyone's names, thanks them all for their contributions even when, sometimes, those contributions are quite rubbish. Mira is pretty sure that everyone in her playwriting group either wants to be him or is in love with him. In her more rational moments, she's aware her infatuation may be nothing more than another form of procrastination. But still, she spends no small amount of time wondering what it might be like to kiss him when he's talking about narrative theatre.

'By the way,' Hana continues. 'Someone – and by "some-one" I mean Samir – messed up the online food shop again, so we've ended up with far too much for the fridge. You can take the extra if you like. We won't get through all of it.'

'Hmm.' Mira's not really listening. She's scrolling up and down her screen, flicking between *Pavements* and the Hadley Prize website.

Every fortnight, Dominic picks a student to read a scene from their work in progress and asks the others to offer critiques. It's her turn to read next and she's dreading making a fool of herself. She'd set aside this weekend fully intending to edit or write a new scene, but it's just not happening. She feels like the play is supposed to mean something, knows that people can't lie down on a pavement for no good reason, but can't attach anything she believes to it. She thinks perhaps it could be argued that she's saying something about domino effects and stillness, the connection between strangers, but she isn't sure if she's trying to be that clever. She just likes the thought of all these people lying down and not getting up again. Mira would do it herself if she could. She's lost count of the hours she's spent after work staring at her computer screen, begging her brain to think of something. She wishes she could call her mother, talk to her about being stuck, ask for advice. Her mother was an artist herself, never gave up drawing and painting, even though at times she too despaired. She would have understood Mira's frustration at the creative process. But Mira can't talk to her: her mother died eleven years ago.

Mira worries that she's being ridiculous to even consider entering the Hadley Prize, an award that has launched the careers of many contemporary playwrights. She's certain she's not talented enough. She scrolls through the biographies of last year's shortlist; they've all been writing seriously for years. But she dropped out of a degree in theatre writing after her mother died. For Christ's sake, why is she even bothering, sitting here, torturing herself by looking at the website, again and again?

'Well?' Hana interrupts Mira's thoughts. 'Are you coming then?'

It's Saturday afternoon and Mira can sense from the growing number of unread messages on her phone that her friends are busy making and confirming plans to go out later. She's already said she can't come, but she knows they'll try to persuade her to join them. It's not because she doesn't want to, she'd do anything to escape her flatmate, but she needs to focus. And anyway, she can't afford to go out. She thinks of her bank account and the notification she got this morning warning her that there were not enough funds to cover her direct debits this month. And there is barely any food left in the fridge. The prospect of a proper meal in Hana's beautiful house suddenly seems vital, even if it means contending with Hana's self-importance.

'Sorry, Han,' Mira says. 'I'm just shattered. Tell Samir spaghetti sounds good. I could be there, maybe, seven? Is that—'

'Fine but don't be late. I hate eating late.' Hana hangs up.

Mira takes her phone away from her ear and looks at the screen. Even though Hana always hangs up without saying goodbye, Mira is taken aback by how abrupt she is.

For the next three hours, Mira tries hard to write something, anything, to add to the play. But it's not working. When it's obvious she's fully squandered her day, and she isn't going to get any sort of writing done, she starts searching through the messy pile of clothes flung over her chair for something fresh to wear to Hana's. She's sniffing and discarding items, dropping them on the floor, when she hears a shriek of laughter coming from the living room.

Mira rents her tiny room from a French girl, Lili, whose parents bought her the flat in Hornsey and are financing her Masters in marketing. Lili has a new boyfriend and he's around all the time. They act like teenagers, kissing as if they've just discovered it, slobbering all over each other in the shared living spaces. They're always home, filling up the flat with tinny music and bottles of cheap wine. Now Mira hears another burst of Lili's terrifyingly high-pitched laughter ringing through the walls, followed by a thud, then another shriek. She quickly grabs her toothbrush from the bathroom, along with the old T-shirt she sleeps in, making sure to slam the bathroom door loudly behind her. She wraps the toothbrush in the T-shirt and sticks it in her backpack and then texts Hana.

Lili + new boyfriend doing my head in. Okay if I crash at yours tonight?

She doesn't wait for a reply, just slips her phone into her back pocket and starts searching for her keys.

Hana's house is in Muswell Hill, a brisk twenty-five minutes' walk away, in a prettier and more expensive neighbourhood than the one Mira lives in. Hana and Samir bought their house, a period property, first, and Mira moved nearby six months later when her lease was up. Mira remembers texting Hana the link to Lili's flat along with the name of the road:

This one isn't far from you . . . what do you think?

Hana had texted back:

???????????????????????
Are you serious? Is there nowhere else in London you
could possibly live?

Though Mira hadn't expected Hana to clap her hands with
glee or squeal about how they could go round to each other's
houses to do each other's hair, she didn't think it was asking
too much for Hana to try to be slightly enthusiastic about
it. She had taken the room anyway: it was cheap, and she
needed somewhere to live. Staying at Hana's for one night
here or there was all right but living with her for any longer
duration of time was not an option. They'd briefly tried that
before and it had gone badly, the two of them at each other's
throats the whole time.

In fact, they don't see each other that often; still, Mira
finds it reassuring to know Hana is there, in spite of how
annoying she is. There's a familiarity with Hana that
Mira doesn't have with anyone else – not that she would
ever tell Hana this. It's not that Mira is lonely – she has
a phone full of friends – but lately she's been feeling far
away. Her old friends from school and university, the ones
she kept in touch with after she dropped out, are settled
in their lives in a way she isn't yet, with steady jobs and
partners and nice places to live. It seems like every day,
someone's getting engaged or falling pregnant. She's not
desperate for either of these things but each time someone makes another life announcement, she feels further
and further adrift. Hardly any of her university friends
are interested in playwriting anymore, and they think it's
funny that Mira still is.

She has other friends, better friends, met through the patchwork of employment she's had over the years, the jobs on the side that help her get by while trying to write. These friends understand; they, too, have something else creative they aspire to. Molly is writing a novel while working part-time as a college administrator, and Shay does temp work to fund her documentary filmmaking. The three of them met four years ago, when they worked front-of-house at the Screen on the Green; they're the ones who want Mira to come out tonight. Sometimes they go out dancing and Mira ends up going home with some guy who isn't right for her because they're the kind of friends who don't tell her to stop. But more and more, that's not what Mira wants.

Sometimes, when Mira goes over to Hana's, and Samir isn't around, Hana and Mira collapse on the sofa in front of something mindless on television. Times like these, Hana lets her facade drop and the bickering grinds to a halt. They watch *The Good Wife* and *Grey's Anatomy* and other shows Samir deems girly, shows they are far too embarrassed to admit to other people they enjoy. In rare moments, Hana jokes around and is funny. When it's like this, everything feels easy. The way it was when they were little. It's not as if these moments happen all the time, and Mira knows they aren't exactly profound, but they take her back, still mean something. Being with Hana is so difficult. Except for when it isn't.

Mira finally catches sight of her keys, half-hidden behind a picture frame sat atop the chest of drawers that serves as her wardrobe. The frame contains a family photo, taken on Hana's tenth and Mira's eighth birthday – they were born on the same day in August, the twenty fifth, only two years apart. In the photo they're wearing matching dresses their mother bought for them from a department store, the kind of ugly dresses girls might have worn as bridesmaids in the eighties. Their mother had hung it in the hall of their old house, right by the front door. It was the first thing anyone visiting would see, and Hana always hated it, tried to hide it whenever her friends were on their way. Even now, on the rare occasions Hana deigns to visit Mira, she pulls a face when she sees the picture, asking Mira why she can't just put it away in a drawer. But Mira has had it for so long now, she barely notices it anymore.

Two

Hana is in the living room watching television – one of those property shows, another guilty pleasure – when her phone buzzes with a text. At first she ignores it – she doesn't often have time to do nothing, to watch television, put her feet up, just be at home like this uninterrupted. But her phone buzzes again, reminding her of the unread message. It's Mira:

Okay if I crash at yours tonight?

Hana presses her lips tightly together. It has been an especially challenging week and she is completely drained. It's not that she minds Mira coming over for dinner tonight. She actually likes seeing her, even if she doesn't always show it. She simply prefers Mira in small doses, that's all. This is the first weekend in a while that Hana hasn't brought home work from the office, and she has plans for Sunday morning, to go for a swim or a yoga class, maybe even stop at the farmers' market. Of course, she could do those things with Mira, but if she's seeing her tonight, that will be enough. Tomorrow, Hana wants to be by herself, in her own space. Ever since their mother died, Mira has taken up such an awful lot of Hana's headspace. With Mira, there is always something to think about: is she okay? Does she have enough money? Has she lost her job yet? Is she seeing someone, and if so, who? And are they normal and good for her? And what exactly is her five-year plan for her life, anyway? Sometimes Hana simply can't help herself from asking Mira these questions. Someone has to check how she's doing.

Hana reads Mira's message again. Her instinct is to just say no, she can't stay over, but then she catches herself and hesitates. It surprises her, sometimes, how mean she can be to Mira without even trying. So, she types:

Fine but bring your own things.

Last time Mira stayed over, she forgot her pyjamas and helped herself to Hana's expensive designer ones from the clean laundry basket without asking. Hana didn't realise until Sunday morning, when Mira came down to the kitchen for coffee still wearing them. Hana was outraged, but both Samir and Mira found her reaction funny. Samir told Hana to chill out, they were only pyjamas. The fact that he said this, that he used the words 'chill out', the kind of casual lexicon Hana hates, only irritated her more. What Hana couldn't explain to either of them was that neither the pyjamas nor Mira's selfishness was the point. It's that Samir rarely takes Hana's feelings seriously. And that hurts her.

Hana sets her phone face down on the coffee table and, almost immediately, picks it back up, tapping into an app. Restless now that she has been disturbed, she's deliberately looking for something. A friend of hers, someone she went to university with, had posted a photo of a pregnancy scan along with the caption: *Some happy news! Baby number two coming soon xx.*

When Hana first saw the post, yesterday evening, on her way back from work, her cheeks turned hot, and her hands shook with a quiet fury she hadn't anticipated. At home, she slammed the front door behind her and when Samir asked her what was wrong, she glared at him and spent the rest of the evening sending angry emails to the juniors on her team, asking them why certain things she'd asked for had not yet been done.

After they'd got married, six years ago, when Hana had just turned twenty-seven, she'd agonised over when the right time to have children would be, taking her career into account. She was a planner, had always been seen since she was young, much to her artistic mother and sister's bemusement, and so it felt important to think about the matter sensibly, and not leave it up to chance. She wasn't in such a rush; she'd always assumed she would have children one day, but she'd also seen women miss out on promotions while they were on maternity leave, and she didn't want that to happen to her. So she decided to wait until she had built up her practice and was established as a senior associate, and more likely to be considered for partner or legal director. Eventually, having done her research, she concluded that if she could just wait until she was thirty-five, and nearly eight years post-qualified, then she'd have made a name for herself and proved her worth at her firm.

It wasn't just about work though. It was also that Hana was determined to do things differently from her mother, who had raised her and Mira single-handedly. Up until her death, she'd worked part-time as an art teacher at a local adult education college, earning very little. Yet Hana knew her mother had creative ambitions as an artist, which never really materialised into any tangible success. Hana loved her mother. She did, and she took care of everything after her death, but for as long as she could remember she'd always vowed to make better life choices than her mother had. For Hana, that meant getting all the other pieces of her life in place first – career, house, husband – before any babies.

Hana had read articles online about the rise in popularity of fertility MOTs, and though she took exception at the use of the acronym, and its implications, she agreed it made perfect sense to take advantage of the technology and science available. The more knowledge she had about her own fertility, the more empowered she would feel about her choices. So, before her twenty-ninth birthday, she made an appointment at a clinic for a fertility scan where a consultant sonographer told her that her ovarian reserve was absolutely fine and that her babies would come one by one, like 'buses', whenever she was ready. Hana remembered laughing at the expression he'd used, relieved. 'I hope not two at once!' She was joking but she also didn't want to leave it too long between pregnancies, certainly no more than two years, so that she could have her babies and then get back to work, picking up where she'd left off.

She firmly believed motherhood would not interfere with her career once it was established. Plus, she quite liked the idea of a relatively small age gap, the idea that her children would grow up close together. Like her and Mira. When they'd been little.

The closer she got to her thirtieth birthday, the more Hana discussed with Samir the pros and cons of waiting to get pregnant. The way she talked about it was always matter of fact. All the while, Samir promised he was on the same page as Hana, that whenever she was ready, he'd be ready too. She felt lucky to have a husband on the same wavelength as her, who respected that her career was as important to her as his was to him. Samir had recently left a job in fintech to run his own algorithmic trading consultancy, something Hana had encouraged, not least because he'd run the figures past her, showing her his financial projections.

Samir also pointed to their friends with children, how regimented their lives were, how they could never have an uninterrupted conversation, were always complaining of being so tired. He joked about how it might be good to put off the sleepless nights, to have a little longer without the extra responsibility of a baby. And Hana agreed. Nevertheless, she had teasingly pointed out that Samir was eight years older than her, that studies had proved the production of sperm was slower and less efficient with age. He told her not to be impertinent as he tickled her onto the bed and offered to prove to her just how efficient he could really be.

Then, last summer, when Samir's parents were visiting from America, his mother had asked, one night, at dinner, if there was something wrong with one of them. If not, could they hurry up, because she was impatient to have grandchildren like all of her friends. She'd pretended she was joking but Samir had seen the look on Hana's face. He'd told his mother that it was none of her business, that she was being inappropriate. Hana thought she'd never loved him so much as she had in that moment.

That same evening, when they were alone, Samir told Hana he'd support her whether she wanted children sooner or later, or not at all. The 'not at all' part made Hana's ears prick up, and she went from loving him to being furious. In her head it had always been a case of *when* they'd have children, not *if*. Had Samir been honest about how he really felt? They argued about it for days, whenever his parents were out of earshot. She asked him what he'd meant by it, demanded to know if he'd even wanted to have children in the first place, given that he seemed so laid back about it now and, one might say, ambivalent. Samir had mocked her use of the personal pronoun 'one' and replied that Hana was being ridiculous. He'd asked her to stop putting words in his mouth and reading so much into it when he'd only tried to be understanding and had only defended her to his mother in the first place.

But then, three months later, while she was away over-night at a work conference, Hana woke up in the early hours with cramps: she was bleeding on the sheets. At first, she thought it was her period, a little overdue. But when she counted back the weeks, she realised she'd never been this late before. By morning, the bleeding had got heavier, the cramps more intense; she felt uneasy and made an excuse to miss a breakfast meeting, something she would never nor-mally do, pretending there was an emergency at home. At the train station, she bought three packs of maxi pads – she could feel herself soaking through. On the journey home, she panicked when she felt something inside her shudder.

From the train, she called the doctor's repeatedly, trying to explain what was wrong, grateful that the carriage she was in was long and empty so nobody else could hear. Finally, she convinced the receptionist to give her an appointment that same day. But she didn't call Samir, not from the train, because she didn't want to, not without being sure what had happened. She didn't know what she would say, or how to say it.

The doctor who saw her, an older man with a bulbous nose and thin black wire glasses, tested her urine sample and looked at the dates of her last period on a little circular calendar. He said, he couldn't be certain, but she was most likely five to five-and-a-half weeks' pregnant and experi-encing a chemical pregnancy.

She had looked at him blankly, having never heard the term before. His estimate of the number of weeks stunned her, and for a split second she didn't understand that he was saying she wasn't pregnant anymore. 'Most women confuse chemical pregnancies for a late period,' he explained, a touch wearily. 'But now that women can track their cycles so closely, with these apps, it means we're diagnosing very early miscarriages that, in the past, we wouldn't necessarily have needed to see a patient for. But it's very common.'

It was only when he said the word 'miscarriage' that she finally confronted what she'd been trying to avoid; that she was losing a pregnancy she hadn't even realised she was carrying.

The doctor smiled at her, his hands upturned. 'It will simply feel like a heavier than normal period. Most women, we tell them not to come in, but I gather you very much wanted to. Still, it's nothing to get too worried about. It'll pass. All right?'

He turned to the computer and began typing, then asked if this had been a planned pregnancy. When Hana said no, he replied: 'Well, that should lessen the blow.' At least she now knew she could get pregnant if and when she wanted to, he added. Hana had said, 'Right', thanked him and left, completely numb.

At home, Samir came downstairs when he heard her key in the door, surprised to see her back so early.

'I started bleeding.'

She felt disorientated, taking off her coat and her shoes, had to reach out and touch the wall to steady herself.

Samir looked at her blankly, not understanding.

'I've been at the doctor's,' she continued. 'It's called a chemical pregnancy—'

Samir's eyes widened, his mouth fell open.

'—I'm not – not pregnant. I mean I was. I guess. But I probably only was for a few weeks. I didn't know. It's a . . . miscarriage. I'm miscarrying.'

Samir stood where he was in the hallway for a moment, frowning, and then as if he suddenly remembered where he was, he went to her, put his arms around her. 'Fuck. How . . .? What . . .? Are you okay?'

'I don't know.' She pulled away. 'I'm tired. I have really bad cramps. It will pass but—'

She sat on the bottom of the stairs and put her hands over her face. He sat next to her, rubbed her back. She told him she needed a shower; he said of course and helped her up the stairs. Her legs hurt so much, pain thundering up and down her thighs, that she couldn't stand and so she sat instead, watching the water run pink as it mixed with her tears, shivering despite the shower's heat.

When Hana came out, Samir was sitting on the bed with his laptop in front of him. He'd pulled the duvet partly back and she could see he'd covered the mattress with towels. The sight of this made her want to cry all over again. He helped her inch her way into bed, pointed to the cup of sweet tea he'd made for her and the painkillers left on her bedside table.

He sat beside her and showed her his laptop screen. 'I did some reading. Apparently it's really common. It's nothing to worry about, honestly,' he said, unconsciously echoing the doctor's words earlier. He put his arm around her. 'I know it feels awful, but it's probably for the best.' He meant it consolingly, his voice soft and sad, his cheek resting on the top of her head, but all Hana could feel was cold.

'Right,' she said. 'We weren't ready, were we?'

He squeezed her shoulder, asked if he could bring her anything else. She told him no, she just wanted to sleep. Eventually the cramps subsided and by morning, the bleeding grew lighter, kept getting lighter, until it was gone. And that was it.

Hana went back to work two days later and didn't tell anyone about it. What was there to tell? She'd only been pregnant for all of a handful of weeks, and she didn't even know about it. It wasn't a longed-for pregnancy, so what was there to mourn? It was easier not to say anything.

Or so she told herself.

Hana and Samir didn't talk about the pregnancy again in any great detail – there wasn't much to say. Life went back to normal, like nothing had happened. At work, she was so incredibly busy, she barely had time to think about it. Yet it was always there in the background, low like the hum of a fridge. Often the sadness hit her while doing ordinary little things like washing the dishes or brushing her teeth or looking for a band to tie her hair up with. If only, she began to think. If only. If only she'd known she was pregnant. If only she'd taken the right vitamins and not eaten all those brie canapés at that conference – as if that somehow explained what had happened. If only. She lay awake at night and wondered what would have happened if she'd never lost that pregnancy. She panicked in case the sonographer who told her she was so fertile got something wrong.

That was six months ago. Hana will turn thirty-four in just over four months. If she'd had a healthy pregnancy, they'd have chosen a buggy, bought a Moses basket and baby blankets by now. There are times Hana looks at herself sideways in the mirror, passes her hand over her stomach and can barely comprehend the possibility. If she thinks about it for too long, she begins to feel dizzy. Sometimes she's sure she's overreacting, doesn't have the right to feel so upset. Other times, it's too real. Something was there, then it wasn't. The vastness of all these thoughts catches at the back of her throat and can, at times, make it hard for her to breathe.

Now she inhales deeply. Hana searches for the photo of the scan her friend had posted. The property show is still on in the background on the television. She no longer feels the sharp rage, but when she sees the little fuzzy picture there's an odd pulling sensation inside her. She straightens up and clears her throat as she scrolls through the comments, her thumbs poised to write her own response.

Amazing, so happy for you, she says to herself in an exaggerated, slightly sarcastic way, making her eyes wide, presses post. There, she thinks, it is done. She puts her phone back face down on the coffee table. She mutters under her breath and then briefly covers her face with her hands.

'What's that, babe?' Samir asks, as he wanders in from the kitchen.

'Nothing.'

'I thought you said something.'

'No. Just, this house – it's amazing.'

She points at the television screen and clears her throat again. Samir leans against the doorframe with his hands in his pockets and looks absently at the television for a moment. A couple are renovating a dilapidated barn in Cornwall; it had, they said, always been their dream. The wife is recovering from cancer and the husband had promised he'd build it for her himself. Just before the break for advertisements, the presenter comes on screen and gestures towards the wide expanse of the half-renovated house and says this is the most beautiful show of love he's ever seen.

Tears spring into Hana's eyes. This has been happening recently, her eyes welling up in reaction to certain emotional triggers. It alarms her, because it's unlike her not to be in control of her feelings. She starts blinking to stop her tears from spilling. She doesn't want Samir to notice. But she needn't have worried. He isn't watching her. Instead, he points at the television: 'That guy! Honestly, he's so over the top. I don't know how you can stand to watch this shit.'

He turns and goes back to the kitchen and Hana watches him out of the corner of her eye, still blinking stupidly quickly. Then she picks up her phone to text Mira again.

By the way just letting you know I have lots to do in the morning so I'll need you to go early.

She runs her fingers through the end of her ponytail, smoothing down her hair again and again, concentrating on her breathing. Until she feels more like herself.

Three

Mira arrives at half past seven. When Hana opens the door, she looks at her watch and tells Mira she's late.

'I couldn't find my keys,' Mira says. They hug awkwardly, leaning into each other clumsily, Hana patting Mira's back in a perfunctory way. Samir comes into the hallway. He's barefoot, with a tea towel flung over his shoulder. He leans forward and kisses Mira's cheek.

He points at Hana and then says to Mira, 'She's like a small child, she gets grumpy when she's not fed on time.' He winks at Mira, and she smiles back at him.

Hana narrows her eyes and crosses her arms. 'As if you'd know anything about small children anyway,' she says to Samir.

Samir makes an expression as if to say touché and turns towards the kitchen. He whips the tea towel off his shoulder and swipes at Hana's backside as he passes, a move which Hana ignores. Mira takes her shoes off and then follows them into the open-plan kitchen.

'God, I'm starving,' she says. She goes over to the hob where Samir's stirring his famous sauce. 'This smells so good. Thank you for having me.'

She's talking to Samir but Hana answers. 'We weren't doing anything tonight and you know what Samir's like when he gets going in the kitchen. Cooks far too much. Loses all sense of proportion and gets carried away. Story of his life. Anyway, how are you?'

Mira picks up a baguette that's lying on top of its paper bag on the kitchen worktop and breaks the end off with her fingers, the crust rustling and splintering into crumbs. Samir tips the spaghetti into a large serving dish. A cloud of steam bursts into the air.

'Tired. Busy. Usual.'

'Busy? Doing what?'

'Work,' Mira says defensively.

She leans on the countertop, licks the tip of her index finger and presses it into the crumbs that have fallen, then puts her finger in her mouth. Hana nudges Mira out of the way, sweeps the crumbs off the counter with her hands, then dusts her palms off over the bin. She begins roughly cutting the bread on a board, tossing the rounds into a basket.

Mira goes around to the other side of the kitchen island, positioning herself out of the way, and starts talking again. She explains that she's in charge of opening Flora, the small independent café where she works, every morning now, during the week. Even though she knows Hana doesn't see the appeal of the job, Mira genuinely enjoys working there. It's popular, because of its artisan coffee, cakes and pretty aesthetic. Best of all, Mira finishes every day at four p.m. and has weekends off, which gives her time for her writing. She's also now the first one there at seven, an hour before they open to customers, the extra responsibility meaning more pay. She doesn't actually mind the early starts though it's taken some getting used to.

'—Seven?' Hana's tone is incredulous.

'Yes.'

'*You?* You're really awake that early?'

Mira ignores this and carries on talking. 'Plus, I'm, you know, writing my thing. It's taking up a lot of time.'

Samir gestures to Hana to pass him the plates so that he can finish laying the table, but Hana waves her hand at him, telling him to wait.

'What *thing*?' Hana asks.

Mira makes a pained face. She doesn't really want to talk about it, but as she was the one who brought it up, there's no hiding.

'Just this th . . . my play.'

'Oh. *That* thing. Oh yes, I remember now. How could I forget. Your "group" thing,' and the way Hana says 'group' makes Mira feel self-conscious, as if she has an addiction.

Mira never intended to tell Hana about her playwriting group, knowing that she'd have opinions about it, because she always has opinions on what Mira does. But there'd been a night, two months ago, when Hana happened to call three times while Mira was at her class. When Mira finally rang back on her way home Hana made a big show of asking what Mira could possibly have been doing not to have answered.

'—I was in the middle of something.'

'In the middle of what?'

'Just. Something.'

'Why are you being so secretive?'

'God! Hana! Why are you so interested? Fine. I was at a writing thing.'

'A what?'

'An evening class. A group thing. For writers. People . . . who want to write plays.'

There was a pause and then Hana said, 'But Mira, writing plays? I thought you were done with that—'

'See, this is why I don't tell you things—'

'I thought we agreed, you were going to forget about all that. Look for a real job—'

'Excuse me, *we*?' She laughed derisively. 'Also, I have a job. I like it, and I'm good at it, so thank you but—'

'*No*. You have a temporary job until you find something else, like a *real* job that makes *real* money,' Hana insisted. 'Are you really going to serve people coffee and croissants for the rest of your life? Did we or did we not grow up in the same house?' She paused, took in a deep breath. 'You saw how hard it was for her to try and make a living out of something creative. I'm not saying never write again, I'm just saying . . . at least if you're going to pay for an evening class, invest in something that could actually be helpful. You dropped out of a theatre writing *degree*—'

They had kept going then, talking all over each other without listening to what the other was saying. Mira said Hana was being unfair, she knew the reason she had dropped out of her degree was because of how hard it felt to do anything after their mother died, not because she was lazy. Hana said yes, but that was years ago now and wasn't it time to grow up, stop dreaming she'd make a living out of making up stories about people who didn't exist? Didn't she see, she was making the same mistakes as their mother, who thought being an artist would magically pay the bills? Mira said then that if to settle down meant to live a life as boring as Hana's with a job as boring as Hana's and to marry the first man that came along who seemed interested, then she could think of nothing worse. Hana had seemed more insulted about the comment about her job, which she loves with a passion, than she had about the one about Samir.

25

They hadn't spoken to or messaged each other for about three weeks, until Hana finally texted to say she was clearing out her wardrobe.

Do you want to come round and see if there's anything you want before I drop things off at the charity shop.

Mira knew this was about as close to an apology as she was going to get, and because she wouldn't say no to some of Hana's expensive clothes, she texted back: *okay*. They haven't spoken about this particular argument since.

Samir tells Hana and Mira to stop talking, and to come and sit down at the table and eat. He starts serving, passes Mira a plate heaped with spaghetti and says, 'Yeah, I remember you said you were busy writing. You were entering a prize, right? What's it called? The Hadley something?'

'The Hadley Prize for Playwriting.' Mira's touched that he remembers but also unsure why he does.

'How on earth do you know all this?' Hana's looking at Samir with a perplexed expression.

'She told me,' Samir says simply. He takes a bite of spaghetti and, still chewing, carries on talking. 'One time, when I was in Flora. You weren't there,' he adds, turning to Mira. 'I looked it up actually, after you first mentioned it. It sounds great. Quite prestigious. Huge prize fund, thirty grand or something.'

'God, no!' Mira puts her fork down, mortified. 'That's not why I'm entering. I don't expect to, you know, *win* or anything.'

Hana frowns. 'Why would you bother to enter if you didn't think you stood a chance at winning?'

'Because I just want to . . . have a go. Something to work towards.' It's true, but she hates how pathetic she sounds.

This is exactly what Dominic had said, when he encouraged her to enter. That it would be good to set herself a deadline. To challenge herself. Show she could finish something she started. And to feel proud of it. They had been standing outside on the pavement during a break in that evening's writing group. He had smiled at her, his hair ruffled by the wind, and said he had faith in her. She looked up at his face out of the corner of her eye. She had believed him; but repeating his words now, she realises how unrealistic it sounds coming from her.

'Oh. So, you mean, like a goal,' Hana says, helping herself to bread. It comes across more than a little patronising.

'I get it.' Samir smiles. 'I think it's great you've got something to focus on and work towards.'

Hana nods emphatically and this time Mira looks at her like she is being weird.

'What?' Hana says. 'I'm being *supportive*.'

'I didn't say anything.'

'But don't do yourself a disservice,' Samir says. 'You've got to believe in yourself. You'll stand just as good a chance at winning as anyone else who enters.'

'How would you know?' Hana looks at him. 'You've never read anything she's written!'

'I have, actually,' Samir says.

'What? When?' She turns to Mira, who is sipping from her glass. 'Why would you show him your writing, and not me?'

'Why do you think? Besides, he asked. You never do.' Mira sticks her tongue out, to which Hana screws up her nose.

'Anyway,' Samir says. 'It was really good, what you wrote. A really touching piece. What do you call it when it's one person?' He concentrates, trying to remember the word.

'A monologue,' Hana and Mira say at the same time, catching each other's eye.

'Jinx,' Mira says quickly, and she curls her little finger into a hook, the way children do.

Hana ignores her and leans back in her chair. She lightly raps the tabletop with her glossy painted nails, thinking. 'I remember some of those plays you used to write at school. They were so weird. There was this one—'

'No, Hana, no.' Mira raises her hand like a warning.

'—about some girl that turned into a, what was it? A pigeon? How did you even come up with something like that?'

'It was existential!' Mira cries, and then she picks up a piece of baguette from the basket and throws it at Hana's face. Hana ducks, covering her head with her arms, and the movement makes all three of them laugh.

Hana sits up and clears her throat. 'Sometimes I think I might write something,' she announces, brightly.

'Is that right?' Mira says.

Samir groans, 'God, no, please.'

'What?' Hana sounds so affronted, Mira and Samir begin to laugh. 'Why is the idea that I could write so funny? I could write something if I wanted to.'

'Okay,' Samir says. 'So go on. What exactly would you write about?'

'I have plenty to write about. The stories I hear from work. The gossip. Marriages can get so ugly.'

'But it's unprofessional,' Samir says. 'You'd be breaking client privilege.'

'I'll use a pen name. And obviously I'd change their names.' Hana nudges Mira's arm. 'Or I could just tell you everything and you could turn it into a play. Your talent and my access to all the salacious details.'

'My talent? Oh, really now? Is that what it is?' Mira's bemused. 'I thought it was a complete waste of time.'

'I never said that!'

'Unstoppable talent,' Samir says loudly over the two of them, with a grin.

Mira rolls her eyes, but smiles. She doesn't mind the banter. She stretches her legs under the table and glances around Hana's handsome Shaker kitchen, with its dark blue painted cabinet doors, marble counters and scented candles alight on the side. She's relieved that she's here and not in her bedroom, trying to drown out the sound of Lili and her boyfriend or still staring at her blank computer screen.

Samir pushes his chair back and gets up to refill the water jug. Hana leans towards Mira and says, 'Go on then, Shakespeare. Tell me what you're writing about now.'

Mira twirls her fork around on the plate. 'I'm not sure. It's complicated. Look, could we please just talk about something else? I know – let's talk about your favourite subject. Let's talk about you!' She makes a rainbow shape with her hands near Hana's face.

'Ha, ha, funny.' Hana smiles in a fake way, showing her teeth, and swats Mira's hands away.

'Hey.' Samir ruffles Mira's hair. He's standing behind her chair and she twists to look up at him. 'If you're stuck with what to write about, you could write about me!' He brightens, as if he thinks he is seriously onto something.

'Yeah, because your life is so interesting,' Hana laughs, shaking her head. 'I mean just look,' she gestures around the dining table, 'at the fascinating life you lead.'

'Actually, I think my life would play out wonderfully on the stage. My youth, specifically. It could be a coming-of-age play. But nothing too serious. I don't like things that are too serious. It would have to be funny.' He sits back down at the table and motions to Hana and Mira to pass him their glasses.

'But Samir, darling,' Hana says in a deliberately slow and affected way. 'People would be laughing *at* you, not with you.' She reaches across the table and pats his hand.

'Tragic ending though,' he says in quick counter-attack, his hand darting out from under hers. 'Since I end up married to you and all—'

'Nice,' Hana says.

Mira reaches across for a second helping. 'Honestly, you two are a comedy unto yourselves.'

'—It could be about the trials and tribulations of growing up first generation.' He snaps his fingers, as if this is a genius idea that's never been written about before. 'You know, your immigrant parents always telling you what to do.'

'Our mother never told us what to do,' Mira says. She is proud of this. Their mother was considered unconventional. She was passionate, impulsive, fell in love with their father, whom she met at a festival, although Mira and Hana never knew him. She divorced him when Mira was three and Hana was five, and raised them on her own, all while pursuing her dream of being an artist. She never once cared what other people thought about her, never criticised what Mira and Hana wore or told them not to hang out with boys the way it seemed other parents from similar subcontinent backgrounds did. It's one of the many reasons why Mira can't understand why Hana is the way that she is, so proper, given that they weren't raised with the usual expectations to pursue sensible careers, settle down and not have boyfriends.

'Sure, but your mom was one of the cool ones,' Samir says. 'Most of us, we lied to our parents and felt guilty about it.'

'Honestly, it sounds boring to me,' Hana says. 'Same old story.'

Mira nods. 'Sorry Samir, I'm with Hana. I hate when people write that first-generation culture-clash kind of thing, as if it was the same for all of us.'

'No, but imagine it for a second,' Samir pushes. 'The story of life growing up as a young Brown boy—'

'Let me guess, trying to reconcile his culture with his sexual frustrations.'

'No, Hana, not exactly. But a play that makes light of it for a change. Usually that stuff is always so serious. But I'm thinking a sweet, simple comedy about familial expectations. Just a city boy, born to desi parents, living in New York State–'

Hana taps the tabletop again and starts humming the introduction to a familiar tune. Her forehead wrinkles as she focuses, searching for the lyrics. 'Wait, how does it go?'

Mira sits up straight like she's at a pub quiz answering a question in the music round. 'Oh, hang on . . . I know, I know.'

She hums the opening bars and then it comes to her. '*Just a city boy . . . Livin' just to find emotion!*' She jubilantly hits the table with her hand and continues singing. Hana points at Samir and laughs.

'Witty,' is all he says.

Hana searches for the song on her phone, connects to the wireless speakers and presses play. Mira starts singing tunelessly on purpose and Hana laughs, joins in.

'Right, settle down now, the pair of you.' Samir says, unimpressed. He rolls his eyes, but the sisters can't stop laughing. 'Okay, very nice ladies.' He stands, his chair scraping the kitchen tiles. He starts clearing the table, still talking, saying things like 'but seriously' and 'that's not funny' or 'can you just put the volume down', but Hana and Mira are still laughing and the song is playing loudly and no one is listening to him anyway.

Four

It feels so good, so unexpectedly good, to act stupid and mess around in the kitchen with Mira, making fun of Samir and singing along to Journey. Hana realises she hasn't laughed like this, so freely, in a very long time. For these few minutes, while Mira is singing so passionately, deliberately acting over the top, clutching at her chest and making exaggerated hand movements, Hana forgets the sadness which she's been trying so hard to hide.

She's glad Mira's here, though she doesn't feel the need to explicitly say it. Then again, it occurs to her that the fact she feels better right now may not even have anything to do with Mira. It might just be that having someone else in the house is the distraction she needs. It was a relief, to talk about Mira's play over dinner, instead of it just being her and Samir winding each other up as usual. Hana makes a mental note to ask their friends over and do this kind of thing more often.

As the music fades out, and Samir finishes loading the dishwasher, Mira suggests they watch a series on television, a romantic musical comedy that Mira sometimes watches late at night when she's supposed to be asleep.

'It's hilarious,' she tells her sister.

'Okay, but you have to promise not to talk all over it like you normally do,' Hana says. She turns to Samir. 'Do you want to watch it with us?'

'God, no. Romantic musical comedy? It sounds awful. I'd rather eat my big toe.'

'Suit yourself.' Hana shrugs. She tidies a few things away on the kitchen counter, setting the oversized pepper mill in its place by the induction hob and straightening up the row of cookbooks on the shelf. Satisfied that everything is where it should be, she says to no one in particular, 'I'm going upstairs to get changed. I'll be down in a minute.'

She looks across at Mira, whose head is inside one of the cupboards. 'What are you doing?'

'I'm just looking for something to eat—' Mira's voice is muffled.

'You literally just had something to eat. You had *three* bowls of spaghetti. How can you possibly still be hungry?'

'I just fancy something sweet.'

Hana goes over to where Mira is standing and lightly hits her arm. 'Stop rearranging everything. You're making a mess. There's an order to everyth—'

'I'm not rearranging anything. You've got nothing unhealthy to eat anyway. What's wrong with you people?' Mira is still rummaging hopefully.

'If you hadn't made fun of me,' Samir says, 'I'd tell you where I keep my secret stash.'

Mira's head pokes out the door. 'Oh, go on.'

'No,' Samir folds his arms.

'Please?'

'No.' He shakes his head emphatically. 'No!'

'Honestly,' Hana mutters, on her way upstairs. 'You two are like children.'

Hana goes straight to the ensuite attached to the master bedroom and pushes her hair back with a towelling headband before smearing cleansing lotion over her face. She's rubbing the cleanser in ferociously when she sees Samir through the partly open door, reflected in the mirror. She squints at him. He comes into the bathroom and opens one of the drawers in the vanity unit.

'It's nice to see you two getting along,' he says.

'What's that supposed to mean?' Hana replies, still rubbing at her skin.

'Just. Sometimes you're a bit hard on her.'

Hana runs the hot water tap and holds a flannel under it. She turns the tap off, squeezes the flannel and then holds it over her face, breathing in deeply, pressing it to her skin. Slowly she wipes the lotion off and then she rinses the flannel and repeats. Samir is still searching through the drawer next to her, bumping against her leg. She wishes he'd get out of her way; her skincare ritual, this time alone, is sacred to her.

'No, I'm not,' she says finally, looking critically at her reflection.

He stands up straight and looks back at her through the mirror. 'You are.'

'I'm not. I'm not hard on her. It's just how I show her I care. She knows that.'

Samir laughs. 'Ah, tough love. The de rigueur choice of parenting.'

He goes off on a tangent, telling her about one of his business partners who has an eight-year-old son. His wife is apparently panicking, insisting their son be tutored for the eleven-plus at no small cost even though the exam is still three years away, on top of all his hundreds of other extracurricular activities.

'So?' she says as she carries on with the rest of her elaborate routine, patting a thin cream under her eyes and squirting various serums on her fingertips.

'What do you mean, "so"? Don't you find it a little ridiculous? He's eight, and she's prepping him from now. She's acting as if it'll be the end of the world if he doesn't pass this exam. He's just a kid.'

'She only wants him to have the best chance. I can understand that.'

'Well, I would definitely not be that pushy.' Finally Samir finds what he's looking for, an unopened nasal spray, and he sits on the edge of the bathtub, fiddling with the packaging. 'Mind you, it's nice what you did for Mira, ordering the extra groceries. But I don't know why you pretend every time like I messed up the order. Sooner or later she will realise you're making that up. You should just tell her outright that you worry about her, and you'd like to help her out.'

Hana watches him in the mirror.

'I don't want to make it into something bigger than it really is,' she says, briskly. 'It's just groceries.'

'I think she'll appreciate it. You two. You're just so—'

Something about the way he says this reminds Hana of a scene from years ago, another conversation about Mira in another bathroom. It was when Hana introduced Mira and Samir for the very first time – they'd met up for lunch at a gastropub in Islington. Hana had been nervous about it, certain that Mira would be embarrassing on purpose. Samir had already told her about his sister, Natasha, stories of their childhood summers spent on Lake Michigan, building dens and going sailing together. Sometimes Natasha phoned him from New York, where she still lived, and they spent hours talking, making plans to meet up on holidays, saying how much they missed each other, complaining about their mother, signing off with 'love you'. The whole thing, their entire sibling relationship, was unimaginable to Hana. When Hana and Mira talked on the phone, one of them almost always hung up on the other.

Before the lunch, Hana sent Mira a list of all the things she explicitly couldn't talk about. Naturally Mira mentioned everything on it: how Hana's eyebrows had once been a monobrow, how her favourite teenage pastime was to tidy her wardrobe . . . Hana kicked Mira's ankles under the table several times, but it was obvious Samir was enjoying it.

Later, Hana and Samir were standing next to each other in his bathroom, in the flat where he then lived, brushing their teeth before bed, when Samir said how nice it was that she and Mira were so close. Hana frowned at his reflection in the bathroom mirror as if he'd just said something in a language she didn't understand. She held her hair back and spat in the sink, and then straightened up, still frowning at him, unable to fathom where on earth he had got that idea from – concerned that she had inadvertently given him the wrong impression.

'No, I don't—' Hana started. 'We're not really that close. I wouldn't say that. No. I don't think so.'

Samir had just smiled at her with a stupid look on his face and rubbed her back a little patronisingly, as if he knew something she didn't, as if he was just humouring her.

Now as she watches him carefully in the mirror, the memory of that day falls away just as quickly as it came. Out of nowhere, she says, 'Allegra's pregnant again. Due September. Put the scan online for everyone to see.'

Samir is quiet for a moment. He wipes his nose with tissue paper, then starts faffing about with the spray. He sniffs. 'That's nice,' he says, eventually. Studying the white plastic tube, he reads the instructions, even though he must surely know how to use it. He doesn't say anything else.

After a minute Hana turns to face him. 'Nice. Yeah. It's very *nice*. Just lovely, isn't it—'

'Han,' Samir looks up at her from his position on the edge of the tub. 'It *is* nice, actually—'

'If it's so nice, then why can't it be us?'

He gets up and throws the tissue paper in the bin. He puts his hands on the sides of the sink and looks at his reflection in the mirror.

'Han, I don't know what you want me to say.'

After a moment, he walks out of the ensuite and into the bedroom. Hana darts behind him. Samir crosses over to the bay windows to draw the curtains and she stands in the middle of the room, watching him. The way he does this, so slowly, the way he just walks away from her when she is looking for him either to make her feel better or retaliate makes the muscles in her back tense.

He sits down on the antique chaise Hana keeps in front of the window, a dainty piece of furniture she's had reupholstered in tea-pink velvet, and pulls off his jeans. Hana watches him try to fold them and thinks how ridiculous he looks sitting in his boxers and socks, his hairy legs almost offensive against something so pretty and delicate. After a few attempts he gives up and squishes his jeans into a roll instead.

'I want you to tell me that it'll be us,' Hana says. 'I want you to tell me that you want to start trying properly for a baby.'

Samir scratches his head. 'We've talked about this,' he says, quietly. Then he looks at her. 'We said we wouldn't rush. I thought you wanted to wait. Until you were eight years post-qualified and all that. What happened to that plan? I thought you were ambitious.'

'I am ambitious,' she snaps back. 'It's not impossible to be ambitious and also want a baby. And besides, that was before last year—'

38

'So maybe that's another reason not to rush. Maybe you need to be, I don't know, in a better place or something. Clearly, you have some issues.'

'*Issues?*'

'I mean, you never talk to anyone about how you feel about things. You haven't told anyone else about the miscarriage—'

'You never ask how I feel,' she hits back, 'and besides, you were the one full of bullshit platitudes. "*It's for the best*", "*it's very common*"—'

'That's not fair, I was trying to make you feel better.'

'And that's not even what this is about! Look,' Hana moves towards him. 'When we got married, you said you'd stand by me whenever I was ready to start a family. I said, we'll start trying when I'm thirty-five. I'll be thirty-four in four months' time. It's not that big of a deal to start now instead of next year, is it? I don't understand why you're so dead set against trying sooner rather than later, when it will so obviously increase our chances—'

'Your odds of getting pregnant aren't just going to disappear on your birthday. I'm pretty sure it doesn't work like that.'

'That's incredibly insensitive.' She glares at him.

'I'm not trying to be insensitive,' he says quietly. 'I get that you're worried it might happen again. But at least you know you can get pregnant now, and even that doctor said just because it happened once, doesn't mean it'll keep happening. And that fertility MOT you took—'

'Fertility *scan*. I'm not a car.'

'Fine, the scan then, didn't the results say how healthy you are and—'

'That was years ago. And it doesn't matter how healthy you are. Case in point.' She gestures at her body.

'Well, we'll get another MOT then.'

She doesn't say anything.

'Han, listen—'

'No, Samir, *you* listen. I don't want to delay things another year. And you shouldn't either. You're forty-one. Did you know that there's a higher risk of autism when the father is older? The longer we wait, the more rushed we're going to be, and I don't want to be stuck in three years' time having to go through IVF just because you—'

Samir's mouth drops open. 'Wait, what are you talking about autism and IVF for? Where has that even come from? You're just making blanket statements now. In my last job there were women in their forties getting pregnant like all the time—'

'Wow, well, in that case! Scientific research right there. And I suppose you asked them, did you, whether they conceived naturally? Did you have an in-depth discussion about their fertility then?'

'God! Hana!' He sighs loudly, puts his hands in his hair, then drops his arms to his side. 'Look, there's so many things to consider here. I'm running my own consultancy. I'm expanding. It's a tricky time for me. And I need to be sure we're in the right place financially, because I know you're not going to be happy with just sending the kids to state school, and you'll want that goddamn tutor, the same way you wanted this house in this neighbourhood, and the extension, and the loft conversion. And somebody has to pay for it. Someone has to pay for all of this.' He gestures at the room.

'It's not like I'm just sitting here spending *your* money all day!' Hana laughs mockingly. 'I earn my own salary. I work for one of the best city firms. So don't try to belittle me. Besides, that's such a redundant, ridiculous argument. You make shit loads just sitting upstairs on your bloody bean bag. Don't pretend like this is about money. It's not. You're just clutching at straws now.'

'Okay, fine. Fine. Forget it. Forget I said anything.'

Neither of them speaks.

Hana sits on the edge of the bed, picks at a loose thread on the throw. Samir comes closer and kneels on the rug in front of her, taking her hands in both of his.

'Look at us.' His voice is softer now. 'Don't you think it would be good for us to just have some time to ourselves, to get back on track? Stop all this arguing, before we leap into this?'

Hana looks at him sideways, the expression on her face conflicted. Samir moves his hands lightly upwards so that his palms are resting on her forearms, but she stays motionless. He goes on regardless. 'Maybe we both need a break. We should go somewhere. Travel. Be spontaneous. We could go to Paris . . .' He smiles weakly at his own suggestion.

She pushes his hands away. 'I've been to Paris. I don't want to go to fucking *Paris*.' He's infuriated her so much that she's raising her voice. She inches further up the bed away from Samir, clasping her knees to her chest.

'Well, not Paris then,' he carries on. 'Rome or Sydney or the Maldives. Anywhere. We could go wherever you want. We could be spontaneous, we wouldn't need to plan, throw caution to the wind—'

'We'd still have to plan.'

'What?'

'We'd still have to plan, if we wanted to be spontaneous. Not that we ever are,' she adds.

'You know what I mean.'

'Yes, but *you* wouldn't know. Who do you think organises our holidays, Samir? Who do you think organises everything? I'm the one that keeps things going in this house like clockwork. You never plan. It's always me. I literally do everything. That's why this whole thing is so absurd; you keep saying I'm not "emotionally ready",' she mimes speech marks, 'or this isn't the "right time", but I'm the one who is going to be doing everything anyway. What difference does it make to you?'

'Don't be like that.'

Hana gets up and stands square to him. 'I know what you're doing. You're stalling. Why can't you just be honest with me? Just tell me. Do you even want to have children at all? Are you deliberately leaving it until it's too late?'

'That's not fair. I'm not saying never, I'm saying not now. I've never said never.'

'You'd better be telling the truth, Samir. If you're not, I swear to God, I will take you to court and I will—'

'Hana! Please! Enough with the divorce threats. Cool it, all right? Just because you're a divorce lawyer, doesn't mean you can joke about it, you know it's actually hurtful—'

'Do you want to know what's really hurtful?' Hana asks bitterly. 'Having to beg my husband to want to have a child with me.'

Samir looks at the floor, pinches the bridge of his nose between his fingers. He crosses the room over to the chaise and grabs his jeans, yanking them back on.

'I can't talk to you when you're like this.'

He slams the bedroom door as he leaves – which neither of them realised had been partly open all this time.

Five

Mira wanders into Hana's living room and stands at the bay window, closing the shutters. There's a woman walking past on the pavement outside and she catches Mira's eye. Mira smiles; the woman smiles back. It's likely the woman thinks this is Mira's house and she's just closing the shutters as she would every evening. For a minute, even though the woman has gone, Mira plays along with the fantasy, imagining what it might be like to live in Hana's house. She does this sometimes. It's a harmless indulgence, but she'd be mortified if Hana ever found out.

Even though they have very different tastes, Mira can appreciate how beautiful Hana's house is, with its subtle palette, elegant furniture and considered finishing touches. The overall effect is restful and soft, which Mira always finds surprising, given that Hana is neither of those things. Hana is so particular about her interiors that she refuses to hang up any of their mother's artwork because she says it doesn't match her style. Instead, the drawings or paintings that were kept are stashed in a cupboard under the eaves in Hana's loft conversion. Occasionally Hana grumbles about them taking up space and reminds Mira she has to take them, especially since Hana, who doesn't spend an awful lot of time reminiscing about the past, wasn't keen to keep them in the first place.

Now, Mira turns on the large urn lamps on the side tables one by one and idly trails her fingers along the books on the shelves in the alcove, without really looking at the titles. Hana doesn't read fiction and almost all of her books are to do with legal matters. Naturally, Mira has no interest in them. She moves towards the mantlepiece, with its carefully curated collection of framed photos from Hana and Samir's wedding. Mira picks up one of the frames. It's a black-and-white photo of Hana sat at the top table, looking up at Samir as he grins, holding the microphone for his speech. In the photo, Hana's expression is dreamy, her chin resting in her hand. In reality, Hana had been a nightmare on her wedding day, stressed about everything running late, and taking it all out on Mira. She sets the photo down and then falls backwards onto Hana's sofa, the fabric the colour of emeralds. She puts her feet up on the coffee table, runs her hands over the green velvet and then slips her phone out of her back pocket to check her messages.

Molly has sent a selfie of her and Shay at a bar on Upper Street. They've sucked in their cheeks and pressed their faces together, a ghoulish purplish light about them. She looks at the picture and smiles, texts back a heart and three sizzling hot flames. But she doesn't feel any regret at not being there with them.

Out of habit, she opens the dating app on her phone, the one Molly insisted she sign up to after her last relationship fizzled out in an unspectacular way. She scrolls through a few profiles, but she's not really paying attention. She doesn't know why she's even looking; she's not had much luck with it. She's so tired of meeting up with guys who invariably look and sound nothing like their profiles in real life. There are so many unspoken rules about dating, like trying not to look too keen or not replying to a message too soon: she finds the whole thing exhausting. All she wants is just someone to come home to. Someone who might cook for her. Someone to quietly bring her cups of coffee while she sits at a desk and writes. They'd go out to the theatre; they'd watch foreign films. She doesn't feel like this is asking for the world, and yet she's had no luck finding anyone who might remotely live up to this.

She thinks about Dominic. She imagines what a quiet night in with him might look like and she smiles, curling her legs up beneath her. She knows, because he's said so in their writing group, and also because of her own late-night online searches, that he lives fairly locally, on the other side of Crouch End, where it borders with Highgate. She's even spotted the back of him once or twice in the Co-op (for a while in her text messages, these were referred to as SODs, 'sightings of Dominic') and another time in Waterstones, but in spite of all of her and her friends' detective work, it's impossible to know if he's single. His one social media profile is set to private and even though Molly has tried to steal Mira's phone to send him a request to follow, Mira's not yet done it herself, in case he doesn't respond.

Her crush on Dominic at least adds a little decoration to her life. It is no exaggeration to say that seeing him every other Thursday evening at playwriting group is the highlight of her fortnight. For ninety minutes, she gets to look at him, listen to him talk so beautifully about dramatic exposition or the rules of scene writing. During the break, she positions herself casually near the hot drinks table, waiting for him to come over, which he always does. She looks forward to every single conversation over their lukewarm teas, no matter how banal, filing away each tiny detail that he lets slip, like the fact he prefers sushi to pasta or that his favourite colour is forest green. She stores the snippets of information to go over in her head when she's making coffees at work. If he smiles at her or holds the door open or pulls a chair out for her, she wonders if it means he likes her. Sometimes, she's convinced he does. They make a lot of eye contact. He's very smiley. Last week at the end of the group, when he stood at the door saying goodbye to everyone, she could have sworn he touched the small of her back as she passed.

Every now and again, Mira checks his profile, just in case he's changed his privacy settings, although this has never happened yet. She's doing this now, looking him up, when she becomes aware of raised voices coming from upstairs. She ignores it; Hana and Samir often argue. But the voices get louder. Mira sits up. She swings her feet off the coffee table and enters the hall. Standing at the bottom of the stairs, she looks up, hesitates, then walks part way up the stairs. From where she is, she can see, through the banister posts, that their bedroom door is open. She can't hear exactly what they are saying but she catches flying words from their argument.

Sometimes Hana and Samir's outbursts are funny and sometimes they feel like a performance, almost as if they put it on or do it on purpose for her sake. Mira has come to think that maybe this is just the way Hana and Samir work, a kind of twisted expression of their love. But this sounds more serious than a tantrum. Hana's shouting now. Her voice sounds like it's been snapped in two. Mira concentrates. She hasn't heard Hana like this before.

She walks quickly up the rest of the stairs and stands in the doorway of the spare room, further along the landing. She keeps listening, trying to catch up and fill in the gaps of what she's possibly missed. She hears Hana say something about Samir being insensitive and a mention of IVF, and then she hears Samir say it's a tricky time. Hana shouts, 'I don't want to go to fucking Paris.' Mira hears movement, heavy footsteps that sound like Samir's, so she quickly ducks into the room and closes the door as quietly as she can, just as the other door slams.

She runs through what she's heard in her head, filling in the gaps with her own assumptions. It is not surprising to Mira that Hana wants a baby. When they were little, Hana was the one who looked after her dolls like they were her babies and stuffed a pillow up her top and wrote down names she liked for her future children. The idea of having a baby has always seemed so far away to Mira, even if every now and again some women's magazine or opinion piece will tell her that her time is running out.

But with Hana, Mira had just assumed that children were a given. She could see Hana with two perfect, most likely very photogenic children, enrolled in an expensive prep school since the day they were born. Somewhere at the back of her mind, Mira half expects that every time Hana calls, it will be to tell her she is pregnant. She is sure that when the time comes, there'll be a big baby shower that Hana will get stressed about, and Mira will have to make small talk with Hana's uptight lawyer friends. Knowing Hana, she'll make Mira serve the canapés. She has wondered a few times why Hana *hasn't* had a baby yet, but she's never asked, because it's not as if they talk about these things.

It hasn't crossed her mind before that problems in Hana and Samir's relationship might be getting in the way. They've always bickered, but it's never seemed serious. Now she thinks of the little swipes and off-hand comments between Hana and Samir and how they've been sharper than usual lately.

She remembers an incident from a couple of months earlier, when she'd come round. Hana had been excitedly telling Mira about a legal podcast she'd been asked to appear on to talk about rising divorce rates, when Samir interrupted and said that he could think of nothing worse than listening to Hana's voice so close in his ears. 'Can you imagine?' he'd said to Mira, and then he shook his head and let out a long puff of air. Mira had just smiled, she was interested in what Hana was saying, but Samir went on. He said how sometimes at night Hana's voice regurgitated itself in his head and stopped him from sleeping. Mira remembers it had felt unnecessarily cruel. 'Okay,' she had said, still smiling but glancing at Hana. 'A little harsh though, don't you think?' She could tell Hana was upset by the way she looked straight ahead and kept brushing her hair behind her ears.

Mira lets out a long breath. She feels for Hana, she really does. She thinks for a moment about crossing the landing, knocking on Hana's door, to see if she's okay. But it's not as if Hana will talk to her. As far as Mira knows, she rarely talks about her feelings to anyone, always somehow managing to keep them in. After Mira dropped out of university and briefly moved into Hana's house share, they'd argued constantly and their arguments inevitably ended the same way – Mira would accuse Hana of being unfeeling and emotionally repressed, refusing to talk about their mother's death, and Hana would call Mira immature, too emotional and directionless. It embarrasses Mira to think of this now, knowing that people process things differently.

She stands in the spare room, not knowing what to do. It would feel weird to go downstairs and put the television on and pretend like she hasn't heard anything. It would be even weirder if she saw Samir – she's not sure where he is. Or she could just stay where she is, take a nice long hot shower, help herself to Hana's fancy guest toiletries and thick expensive towels. She could listen to a podcast in bed or read the novel stuffed in her bag or just browse her phone and look up Dominic's actor headshots. The more she considers it, the more appealing it seems. She's about to turn on the light for the ensuite, her finger on the switch, when she stops.

'Oh, for God's sake,' she whispers, before leaving the room, crossing the landing and quietly knocking on Hana's door.

Six

The bedroom door opens. Hana looks up from where she is sitting up on top of the covers, her arms wrapped around her knees.

'What?'

'I just thought I'd . . . I just . . . I heard—'

'You heard nothing. Everything's fine. I'm fine.'

Mira crosses the room, sits down beside her. 'Han,' she touches her shoulder, 'I only wanted to see if you're okay.'

Hana turns to look at her. 'I said I'm fine.'

Mira laughs a little sadly. 'You're clearly not fine! It's okay not to be fine.' And then, softly, 'You don't have to be fine all the time, Han.'

Hana's eyes fill up and as she stares into the blurry space behind Mira's head, she thinks of times that she has pretended she is stronger than she really is, flashes of her life appearing in quick succession like a trailer to a film. For a moment she rests her head on her forearms. Then she quickly lifts her head up and says, 'I'm fine. Or maybe I'm not. But I will be tomorrow . . . Ask me tomorrow.'

Mira smiles. Hana sniffs.

'No, seriously, I'll be okay. It's nothing. Just a silly argument. A misunderstanding, nothing I can't fix. Couples fight all the time.' Hana laughs in an embarrassed way. 'I should know. I spend my days trying to fix things for them.'

Mira squeezes her shoulder. Hana glances across at her sister. She reaches up and touches Mira's hand, then presses her lips together sadly. It's not quite a smile, but it's an acknowledgement.

'Do you want to, maybe, come down and watch that show to take your mind off things? I can make you a cup of tea?'

Hana shakes her head, no. She moves her hand away, and Mira does the same, standing.

'Okay. Well, if you need me, just shout.'

After Mira has pulled the door shut behind her, Hana covers her face with her hands. She cries and cries and cries.

Professionally, Hana knows how to manage people and she knows how to win. She is a brilliant lawyer. She cares about her clients, tells them that she is there for them, will help them leave their marriages with dignity. When her clients aren't sure if they are doing the right thing, or wonder if they are jumping the gun, Hana reassures them that people leave each other for a lot less. A trade legal directory once called her a rising star, praising her cool head and charisma. It said: 'Hana Faizan is an exceptionally gifted lawyer who fights every one of her clients' corners with her straight-talking and remarkably sharp intellect. In even the most difficult of cases, her opponents end up eating out of her hand.' When the rankings were published there was a little celebration in the office, cake and Champagne and elderflower cordial – the whole team had done well. It was around about that time that the rumours, that Hana might be up for partner-ship sooner than usual, started.

At home, she read out the write-up and Samir said, frowning, 'I'm sorry? Exceptionally gifted? Remarkably sharp intellect? Am I missing something here?' And she'd punched his arm, hard, before he fell about laughing and tried to kiss her. Later he looked it up online and printed it off. He stuck it in the downstairs bathroom until Hana said, 'Very funny,' and took it down.

Because of all this, because she fights for a living and because she's so outstanding at getting her own way, it feels like a personal failing that she can't seem to win with him. Samir's the trickiest, most stubborn opponent she's ever had. He's certainly not eating out of her hand, and she's definitely not got a cool head around him.

The argument they'd just had wasn't new. They've been doing this for months now, ever since the miscarriage. Each stand-off followed by a brief return to normality. She hadn't thought that Samir would have the energy to keep on going like this. There's so little that seems to bother him, and he's never been stubborn before; if anything he is maddeningly laidback. He doesn't mind when friends change their plans for dinner last minute or if their flights get cancelled. He'll just shrug and say there's no point wasting energy on things you can't control.

But being in control matters to Hana. Though she knows there are certain things she may not be able to plan for in her pursuit of motherhood, she still feels like there are so many things they can both do to at least give themselves the best chance – especially after the chemical pregnancy. She came off the pill after the miscarriage. When Samir asked why, she told him it was because it was giving her migraines. But really it was because she wanted to be ready to try. They use condoms on the increasingly rare occasions they have sex, but she's already started taking the right supplements, tracking her cycle more diligently, exercising more and reducing her caffeine intake. She's swapped Samir's coffee for decaf, hidden the cigarettes that he claims only to smoke socially, although when he realised, he told her to stop policing him. Sometimes Hana wonders what's happening to her own dignity.

It feels like such a waste of time, all this back and forth, all this time they could have just been having sex, increasing their odds of her falling pregnant. She used that line on him too: wouldn't you rather be having sex right now instead of going around in circles? To her horror, he'd replied: 'No, not really. Believe it or not, I'm not in the mood right now, Hana.'

When she wakes the next day, Samir has already left for his habitual Sunday morning run, and she remembers, slowly, that he crept into bed in the middle of the night, and also that Mira stayed over. That she's still here. Hana feels an urgent need to set the morning straight, like the act of shaking out and then smoothing down a bedsheet. It irks her that she cried a little in front of Mira, that her closely held privacy cracked in front of her sister. She hates crying in front of anyone.

After their mother died, Mira used to cry all the time, on tube trains and standing on corners of pavements, calling Hana at work in tears. Hana tried to be patient but, privately, she couldn't believe Mira had such little self-awareness or self-control; she thought it so typical of Mira to want to make a scene, to show everyone her emotions, all the time, everywhere. Sometimes Hana wonders what it would be like to be so open, and she's not sure if she would find it a relief or a nightmare.

But now, on a very basic level, it annoys her that Mira is here, that she asked to stay the night in the first place. Yes, Hana is aware she's being completely irrational and unreasonable and that she's taking out her feelings about Samir on Mira. It's hardly complex psychology, to recognise this. But the thing is, she doesn't care. And so Hana barges into the guest room, clapping her hands.

'Come on! Wake up.'

She violently pulls up the Roman blind, flooding the room with pale spring morning light, and starts collecting Mira's things, setting them straight. Mira groans and rolls over in bed, presses a hand over her eyes.

'What time is it?'

'Time to get up,' Hana snaps. 'I've got a lot to do today. You'll have to get going soon. And tidy up before you leave, please. You've left your clothes all over the floor.'

Mira grunts, sticks the pillow over her head. Hana strides over to the bed and yanks the covers off her sister's body, throws the pillow onto the floor, her hands shaking.

'God! What the hell is wrong with you?' Mira sits up and pushes Hana away with one hand. Hana stares at her. 'Just calm down, won't you? Jesus, Hana, you're insane. What's got into you?'

Hana leaves the room, eyes stinging, the door wide open behind her.

Seven

Mira flops back down in bed, bewildered. It's far too early to deal with Hana's mood swings. This is why being with her is so impossible. Mira can barely believe that for a short while the night before, she actually *wanted* to see Hana, even enjoyed her company. Or that she was bothered enough to be worried about her after the argument with Samir.

Mira fumbles for her phone on the bedside table. She's disappointed when she sees that there are no new messages from her friends, nothing entertaining or gossipy to distract her. She lets her phone fall onto the mattress. She yawns, covers her face with her hands, takes a long inhale as she stretches her arms over her head and then exhales, staring at the ceiling. Mira thinks again about what happened last night. Right now, she's still too annoyed with Hana to feel sorry for her, but she can see that Hana's outburst was nothing to do with her, and everything to do with Samir. She wonders where he is, if he stayed or if he went out last night, and if so, what time he came home. Whether he slept in their bed or upstairs on the futon in his office.

It's such a familiar storyline; a couple arguing late at night, one of them storming off and leaving the other crying. She must have read, and watched, scenes like this a thousand times. Another thought comes to her; a memory of a play she had watched a few years earlier. It was about a marriage slowly falling apart in the aftermath of losing a baby. Mira remembers she had felt as if she were holding her breath all the way through, watching the couple move around each other thinking unspeakable thoughts, their love twisted into something terrible and devastating and tragic by the end. At times she'd had to blink back the tears she'd felt prickling her eyes.

The man she went to the play with kept clearing his throat and shifting in his seat beside her. During the interval, he laughed in her ear, saying, 'It's all very serious, isn't it?' Mira didn't see him again, can no longer remember how it ended with him, only that it did. But she does remember leaving the theatre that evening, wishing she too could one day write something that moved an audience so deeply, wishing she could write something as beautiful but also as sad and as profound as this play.

She thought about the play for weeks afterwards. She read everything she could about the playwright, her inspiration, her story to success. But her flurry of enthusiasm only left her deflated. She often feels like this when she's impressed by someone else's work, or hears the success stories of people younger than her, their plays being picked up for festivals or turned into films – instead of feeling motivated, she becomes convinced nothing like this would ever happen for her, because she's so obviously incapable of ever finishing or achieving anything.

But now she sits up in bed instead, her arms wrapped around her knees, and thinks: 'what if?' That's the question Dominic is always pushing them towards. The context of that play was entirely different, of course, and Mira has no idea, really, of what's going on with Hana and Samir, but it occurs to her that the idea of exploring a marriage in which one partner wants children and the other doesn't, and a couple's general inability to talk about their feelings, might make an interesting theme to explore. She reaches for her phone, types a note to herself, quickly setting her thoughts down.

She stops typing and rests her head on her forearms. She thinks about another guy she once dated when she was twenty-five, and how one night they went out for dinner with several of his old friends in Clapham. He hadn't introduced her to anyone. He didn't even sit next to her. When she'd attempted to make conversation with the people on either side of her, they showed no interest. She might as well not have been there. All evening, she'd tried to catch his eye. She had felt so lonely then.

She doesn't feel sad thinking about this now, she's hardly thought of this person since, can't even remember his name now, but the episode comes to her, and she wonders what it would be like to capture that same feeling of loneliness in words. She thinks how someone might show it on stage. She types everything she's thinking about into her phone in a stream of consciousness. She goes on and on until finally she writes: *could there be something in this?*

She looks around the room and then quickly gets out of bed, energised. In the bathroom, she stands under the shower and turns the question 'what if?' over and over in her head. An image comes to her of two people in a room, only they feel quite far away, like she's looking at them through a telescope. She closes her eyes, but it's hard for her to see them. She remembers an interview she once read with a novelist, who said the image of one of her characters just popped into her head fully formed while she was loading the dishwasher; when Mira read it she scoffed, but also very much wished the same might happen, just once, for her. She squeezes her eyes shut again, tighter this time.

She wills the two people, the two characters, in her head to come closer, to show themselves to her, but it's no use.

She steps out of the shower, gets dressed and makes the bed. Then she sits on the edge of it, just thinking, trying to keep her frustration in check. She glances at the notes on her phone and suddenly wonders what she's even doing, this half-baked idea; it's entirely stupid. She's already got her hands full with *Pavements*. But she can't stop thinking about the way Hana says she's fine when she clearly isn't; how Hana's default reaction is to hurt someone else when she's hurt herself. She thinks about how Hana is such a perfectionist, so highly strung. Even as a teenager, if ever they went away on a family holiday, Hana would insist on repacking their suitcases just to prove the efficiency of her packing technique. It's never occurred to Mira before, how interesting it is to observe her sibling as a writer would, to notice her quirks as character details. In a way, Hana's a gift of a character study. If she wanted to, Mira could write pages and pages about her, fill entire notebooks with the throwaway comments she makes and the way she behaves.

Downstairs, Mira calls out, 'Hello?' But there's no one in the kitchen or the living room and the car on the driveway is gone. So Hana really did leave and Samir's still out on his run. It's not the first time Mira has been in Hana's house on her own – Hana always asks her to pop in and check on the house when they're on holiday – but she doesn't normally linger any longer than she has to. Today she does. She sits in Hana's kitchen, drinking Hana's coffee from Hana's mug, surrounded by all of Hana's things. When Mira daydreams about living in Hana's home, she does it for fun, a little game she plays in her head. But now, she sees things differently. All of Hana's things, the painting

58

of clementines in a bowl, the ceramics bought on honeymoon in Italy, they appear to Mira to be like objects on a set. Everything telling a story. And it occurs to her that a story is exactly what's happening. Here it is, playing out in front of her eyes – a story about love and marriage, expectation and disappointment, two people wanting different things, just waiting to be written, to be grabbed, daring her to want it enough to try.

Eight

It's late on Sunday afternoon when Hana opens the front door, her arms full of shopping bags. Samir appears in the hallway.

'Hey, where've you been all day?' His tone is intentionally bright, although he's got a sheepish look on his face, the one he always has when they've argued.

Hana's been to lots of places since she left the house this morning – the gym, an eyebrow threading bar, a café, the supermarket, the organic food shop, another café, the bookshop. She's actually been very productive, and this has kept her mind off things, but she doesn't tell him any of this. She just slips off her shoes and looks at him with an angry expression.

'I made that stuffed chicken you like, for dinner. With those crispy roast potatoes,' he adds, hopefully. She ignores him and hangs her bag up on a wall hook.

'And I nipped across to Flora, got some of that cheese-cake you like—'

'Stop it,' she says. 'Stop acting as if everything's okay.'

'Hana.' He tries to pull her arms, to gather her in towards him like she's a piece of rope, but she keeps resisting. 'Hana. Hana, stop! Stop. Listen, I'm trying to talk to you. Last night was awful, and I'm trying to talk to you. Would you just—'

'Can I get past please?' She tries to squirm through but he blocks her way again.

'God, Han! You don't make it easy, do you?'

She twists her lips, crosses her arms and taps her foot, impatient.

'I would just like to talk calmly about this,' he continues. 'I did a lot of thinking last night—'

'Oh, so that's what you were doing until two in the morning was it? Out "thinking"?'

'Okay. You're angry about that. I understand. I shouldn't have just left. I should have told you where I was.'

'I thought you weren't coming back—' She shoves his chest.

'Hey, hey,' he reaches for her hands, but she steps away. 'Babe, I'm sorry, okay. I said some hurtful things—'

'Right.'

'—And you did too.'

'I hate it when you call me "babe".' She pushes past him. He follows her.

In the kitchen, she looks at the plate that's not been put in the dishwasher, the crumbs that haven't been wiped away, the chopping board still out. She tidies everything away quickly and then fills the kettle with water and flicks its switch. She takes just one mug out of the cupboard and sets it down on top of the kitchen island between them sharply, staring straight at him. She raises her eyebrows as if to say, *what?*

'Hana, please.' He rubs a hand over his head. 'I'm as tired of this as you are. Look what it's doing to us.' He gestures at the space between them. 'I don't like what it's doing to us.'

She makes a rolling motion with her hands, telling him to get to his point.

He looks at her calmly, leans forward on the kitchen island. 'It's very hard being married to you—'

'Thanks,' she says bitterly.

'—because you're amazing and beautiful and much cleverer than me. Sometimes it astonishes me that you even want to have a baby with me, of all people, in the first place.'

She looks at him in disbelief. The kettle clicks off and Hana turns away from Samir to pour water in her mug and fetch milk from the fridge. When she opens the fridge door, she notices that Mira hasn't taken any of the extra shopping.

'And? Your point is?'

He straightens, clasps his hands together and says, 'You're right, I promised you, I gave you my word, that whenever you felt ready to start a family, we would. It's not fair for me to go back on that – and maybe I have been stalling.'

'Why?'

'Sorry?'

'Why are you stalling?' She pours the milk, stirs the tea.

He laughs, caught off guard. He rubs his hand across the side of his face. 'Well. I guess I'm nervous. It is a big step. You've always been better at this grown-up stuff than me.'

Hana doesn't respond. When she does, her voice is calm. 'You're forty-one. You run your own business. You'd think you'd be used to being an adult by now—'

'Listen, Han. My point is that I hate seeing you this upset and this angry all the time. I would do anything for you not to be this upset. And I did some reading last night, about some of the stuff that you said, about the risks with men being older and whatever. I would never forgive myself if there were problems further down the line, because of me.'

'So, what then?' she says coolly, standing across from him on the other side of the kitchen island.

'So, you're the smartest person I know. That remarkably sharp intellect, remember? So, I guess what I'm saying is, you're right.' He shrugs, lifts his hands and then drops them, letting them settle on the work surface. 'You're right. I've been unreasonable. It doesn't matter if it's this year or next. It's still a baby. And we both want that.'

'And?'

'And there's no point waiting. That's what I'm trying to say.'

Samir goes around the island to her then, looking for an embrace, but she pushes him away, hard, in the stomach.

'Do you mean that?' She's holding him at arm's length, scrutinising his face. 'Do you *really* mean that?'

'Yes,' he says. 'Yes, I mean it. Let's do this—'

'And you're not going to change your mind? Or tell me I have issues? Because, my God, I hate it when you say that—'

'*I* have issues. Everyone has issues—'

'And you're not going to pretend like all of a sudden we can't afford it?'

'I'm sorry, Hana. I was just . . . I don't know. You were right,' he looks at her, his face earnest. 'I was clutching at straws. Desperately clutching.'

'Can I get all these assurances in writing?'

He laughs. 'Han. Only you would say that. Would you come here now?'

'I'm not even joking,' she says, pushing him backwards again.

'Of course not,' he says. 'I wouldn't expect anything less.'

And then, to stop her from talking, he hugs her into a headlock and kisses the side of her head.

'Stop it,' she laughs in spite of herself. 'Stop it,' she says again, trying to pull away.

'Hey,' he holds her even tighter. 'Anyone would think—' but he doesn't finish because then she puts her arms around his waist, hugging him back. She feels his solidity as she leans into him, pressing her head into his chest, and begins to cry.

'Hey,' he says, softly now, the bravado and the teasing falling away. 'Hey.'

He kisses her forehead, runs his hand across the top of her hair. Leaning back against the kitchen island, he shifts his legs so that Hana's standing between them. They stay like this for a moment, Hana allowing herself to be held. Then Samir growls comically, nuzzling her neck like an animal, and she can't help it, she laughs. She gives in to the moment and lets him continue.

Nine

When Mira gets back to her flat after leaving Hana's house, she goes straight to her bedroom, straight to her laptop and her notebook, both of which are still lying where she left them on her bed. She doesn't take off her jacket or her shoes, doesn't bother to check whether Lili and her boyfriend are in as she usually does, doesn't even close her bedroom door properly. Instead of preparing the scene from *Pavements* for the upcoming class critique, she opens a new document and starts typing quickly, copying the notes she made on her phone.

As she writes, ideas rushing, a vague outline of a scene begins to form in her head. She jots down a few details that could possibly, eventually, help to set a scene: a couple, sitting in a kitchen, a retro-style fridge in the background and a light hanging low over a dining table. She imagines the couple and what acts of passive aggression they might engage in, one of them wiping down the kitchen counters in an exaggerated fashion even though the other has already done it. She hesitates, unsure of where to go from this feeling, drawing her brows together, trying hard to remember something. She feels restless, desperate, like she's blindly reaching out in the dark, grasping for a light switch. She knows she is so, so close to something. She tastes the fizz of anticipation on the tip of her tongue.

She taps her fingernail quickly in the space beneath her laptop's keyboard, urging herself to think, think. What was it Hana had said?

'I don't want to go to fucking Paris.' She says the words out loud as she types. She reads the words back, this time louder and with feeling, pretending it really is a line from a play script and she's the main character.

'*I don't want to go to fucking Paris—*'

'And why not?'

Mira jumps and turns. Lili's standing in the doorway, licking an ice lolly. She's dressed in her pyjama shorts and a camisole, along with a pair of sheepskin slippers.

'What's so wrong with Paris?' Lili asks, her tone defensive.

Mira squeezes her eyes shut briefly.

'I didn't mean it like that, okay? I'm just working on something. Would you mind, please, shutting the door for me?'

Lili snorts, mutters something in French about English people and pulls Mira's door shut, louder than necessary. A few seconds later, Lili puts on a song, some hideous house track from the late nineties. The volume is louder than necessary, high-pitched repetitive beats like a thousand little fists knocking hard on the paper-thin walls. Mira groans and rummages in her backpack until she finds her headphones.

She tries to refocus. She reads the line she's written again: *I don't want to go to fucking Paris.* It's what Hana said, word for word. She sits with that thought for a moment. When she left Hana's house this morning, it felt urgent to write something down. But is it writing if it's what Hana said? But no. No. She's overthinking it. She's only making notes. So what if Hana said something about Paris? Big deal. It sparked a thought and Mira wants to know where that might take her. That's all. It could be nothing. She saves the document.

It could be nothing. But it could be something.

She presses her fingers to her lips, thinking. There it is again, that restlessness, the desire to write, the feeling writhing like a small animal under her skin. Her writing has felt so stale lately that it's a relief to remember it's possible to also feel like this. She shrugs off her jacket and takes off her shoes and sits cross-legged in the middle of her bed, pulling her laptop towards her.

She spends the next two hours flitting between writing down ideas as they come to her and reading essays and articles and blog posts online with titles like 'My husband doesn't want children anymore' or 'I want kids but my partner doesn't'. She loves this part, when she can research and write down her ideas freely without committing to them, knowing that nothing has to be perfect, that no one else will ever have to see this wild, disorganised mess of hers.

She lands on an agony aunt column where a thirty-year-old woman has written in for help because her boyfriend says he's not sure if he wants children, but she doesn't want to miss her chance. The agony aunt writes back: 'Your boyfriend can't give you certainty. But your need for certainty is important. You're very clear that if you didn't get to be a parent you would feel you'd lost some infinite thing. It takes real hope, self-possession, and confidence to believe in this. You should treasure this feeling, and you're entitled to defend it.'

Mira reads the piece and lets out a little gasp when she's finished; she's more moved by it than she expected she'd be. She imagines Hana's desire and despair, the pain she must be feeling. Mira closes her laptop. She's not thinking about her writing now. She's thinking of Hana. She should text her, see that she's okay. But she's still annoyed at her for this morning, how she treated her, suddenly wanting her gone; that was entirely unreasonable. It occurs to Mira that maybe, maybe if she writes this play about one woman's desire to be a mother, it might, just maybe, speak to Hana in some way. After all, she thinks, isn't that what writing is about? Shining a light on the complexities of life, offering, if not the answers, then some kind of reassurance in seeing oneself? Mira raises her eyes to the ceiling and laughs, stretching out her arms and curling her back, feeling done for the day. She's reaching so far and, by God, she knows it.

At work the following day, Mira pays close attention to every couple that comes in, trying to listen in on their conversations, wondering what their backstory is and what they're not telling each other. She stares so intently at one couple that Angela, who works with her, nudges her and says, 'Hey, do you know them?'

'Sorry? Who?'

The following Thursday, Mira is late for playwriting group. She rushes to lock up at Flora and runs for the bus, swearing to herself as she does. On the way, she brushes her hair with her fingers, checks her makeup, using the camera on her phone, and then rushes into the bookshop and down the stairs to where they meet.

'Sorry! Sorry!' Everyone else is already there, sitting in a semi-circle on plastic chairs, notebooks open on their laps.

'Mira,' Dominic greets her with a smile. 'You're here, thank goodness. Just in time.'

She doesn't know what he means by 'thank goodness' and she's embarrassed by the extra attention. She smiles tightly at no one in particular as she makes her way to the one remaining empty chair positioned to the far side of the semi-circle.

'So,' he says. 'We were just wondering what you were going to read for us today.'

With a little intake of breath, Mira remembers just as she sits down that it's her turn to share her work. She's been so distracted with this new idea, she hasn't prepared anything, or even brought her laptop with her.

'Oh, my God! I'm so sorry. I completely forgot. It's just been so busy, and I . . .'

She stops talking. She feels everyone in the room looking at her and she's not sure but she thinks she hears someone tut.

'Hey, it's totally okay,' Dominic says kindly. 'This is a relaxed group; there's no pressure. And also, sometimes life gets in the way of writing. You can't apologise for that. Maybe tonight we should talk about that, you know? Like how to balance time for writing when life is spinning so wildly around you.'

A few people murmur in understanding. He looks around the room at the others. Mira wishes she could say something to get his attention back again.

'Is there anyone else who'd like to read something?' he asks. Without thinking, she interrupts.

'Sorry, Dominic, I know I forgot to prepare a piece to read, but I have actually been brainstorming a new idea. It's nothing, really, just a theme that I'm interested in exploring. But the thing is, it was sort of inspired by something a . . . friend of mine is going through. I overheard her say something quite emotive and it stuck with me. And I just wondered what your thoughts are on using someone else's real-life situation, or something they said, as inspiration?'

She can hear herself speaking and she can't believe what she's saying. Ordinarily she would never tell anyone when she's writing something new, and now she's just announced it not only to the man she's had a crush on for months but also to a room of approximately fifteen relative strangers. Her face suddenly feels very hot. But it surprises her, reassures her, when a few people around the room nod, obviously recognising what she's saying.

Dominic looks at her attentively. 'I hear you. Interesting. I'd love to know what your friend said,' he says in a gossipy way that makes everyone laugh. He leans forward, his elbows resting on his knees, so that he can engage with the group. 'So, let's see, you overheard something that someone said and it's inspired you to write something, which is very natural, I'd say. But I understand the lines can feel blurred. I'd say that's also very natural.'

'Don't they say everything is copy?' one of the other regulars interjects. Someone else laughs.

Dominic nods. 'They do. And writers do write about real life all the time. I know I do. Ideas can come from anywhere, and you all know I'm always going on about that – being open, not letting the flicker of an idea pass you by, whether it's something you read in a news story or something someone says.' He pauses and looks directly at Mira, talking with his hands.

'For me, Mira, it's not about "taking" something from real life and putting it on the stage. Whatever you write will be yours the minute you put it into your own words. Our job as writers is to tell a story. And at some point, we have to be brave, and take leaps that feel uncomfortable. And maybe writing should make us feel uncomfortable, ask questions of us, push us to go deeper. I'd say if it's not easy, then it's a good sign.' He looks around the room meaningfully. 'All we can do as writers is tell stories as honestly as we can. It's the truth, the emotional truth, that connects with an audience, and that's what you want,' he says. He looks straight at her. 'Does that make sense?—'

Mira gazes back at him, distracted by the way that he's rolled his sleeves up and the sound of his voice and the shapes his mouth makes while he's talking.

'—Mira?' he says. 'Does that help?'

She snaps out of her daydream, taken aback by the directness of his question.

'Oh! Ah, yes. It's, um, really helpful. Thank you.' She smiles at him, while playing absentmindedly with the hairband around her wrist.

Dominic nods, then rubs his palms together. 'Right, so anyone want to add anything to that or shall we move on? Anyone else up for volunteering to read a scene from their writing today?'

In the end, three people read their work out and there's a different energy in the room as a result of the spontaneity of the session. The time passes quickly. At the end, Dominic says, 'Right, well, thank you, Mira, for forgetting to bring your work in.' She laughs louder than necessary, feeling like a complete idiot.

On her way out, he touches her arm lightly and tells her not to worry, again, about not bringing a piece in and that if she ever wants to go over what they talked about today in more detail, he'd be really happy to. She looks up at him brightly. All she can think about is how badly she wants to kiss him. She smiles widely and tells him, thanks, she'd really love that.

Ten

After they make up and eat the dinner that Samir had prepared as his culinary peace offering, Hana begins tidying the table. Samir tells her to stop. He says he'll take care of it, that she should put her feet up, and then he shoos her out of the door towards the living room. He's trying very hard, Hana can tell, so she does as he says, leaving him to it without complaining or reminding him not to forget to clean the sink. She lets that go.

In the living room she sits with her feet tucked beneath her in the loveseat by the alcove on the far side of the fireplace. She feels exhausted; her strongest desire is to go to sleep, but it's still only early evening towards the end of April, the sun not yet set. With the lights off in the living room, it's darker inside than it is out and from where she is sitting in the shadows, she can see the watery sky through the strips of the shutters in the bay window, the daylight preparing to fade away. The blossom tree outside their house is already blooming, a spectacle of pink; she feels a touch of disappointment, knowing that in a matter of weeks the petals will have fallen to the ground, the colour spoiling like rotten fruit.

She looks around her, taking in the spines of the books she rarely has time to read on the shelves, the violet-coloured handblown candlesticks received as wedding gifts, the cluster of photos on the mantelpiece, the gold-framed mirror above, the muted abstract paintings on the wall opposite. She considers it all, thinking about what it was like when they first moved here, and how she's transformed it, filling it with all of the things she loves. It's been a strange day. She feels spun around, like the room is rotating, and just then, she's struck by the sensation that she's outside of herself. In that moment the image of her slightly younger self appears, standing in this very same room, only the decor bare and neglected, an estate agent telling her the property would make an excellent family home. She had fallen in love with the house despite its run-down condition, convincing Samir that they could turn it into something beautiful. And they did just that. Hana wonders why it's always her having to convince Samir to take these big leaps with her in life.

She blinks twice to clear the blurriness that fills her eyes. The image disappears and her surroundings come back into focus again. She laughs a little, feeling silly, unsure when she got so sentimental, hopes that now they can start to plan for the future in a tangible way, then all these emotions, which are so very unlike her, will subside; although who knows what her hormones might have in store as things progress.

A family. They are going to start a family. Her head rattles with hypotheticals, like pills in a bottle, too many to think about. She needs to relax. She needs to stop overthinking. She should probably just check her phone. She should look at her work emails and her calendar to prepare for the week, it is, after all, what she normally does on a Sunday evening. It'll snap her out of this strange pensive mood. But she just can't bring herself to do it. Her eyes still feel heavy, tired from crying last night.

The memory of the night before summons up Mira. She's tried not to think of her sister all day, but now she does and she flinches at how horrible she was to her this morning, flinging the sheets off her like that. Hana closes her eyes and taps her forehead to alleviate the tension in her face, her fingers like hammers. She'd be so embarrassed if anyone other than Samir, any of her friends, ever saw the way she can be with Mira, how she is sometimes as hard as stone. She doesn't mean it, never has done; it's only that something comes over her sometimes. And then there's the remorse afterwards. She's never known why she finds it so hard to apologise, or to admit how much she cares for her younger sister – how much she loves her, how, truth be told, she'd do anything for her. But it is how it is.

She can remember when she told Mira that she hated her the very first time. She was eight years old and Mira only six, and they were arguing in the car. Hana burst into tears moments after she'd shouted it, a delayed reaction to the situation but also to the overwhelming feelings of guilt and anger that swamped her like a too big jumper. She'd regretted her words as soon as she'd said them, but it didn't stop her from ever saying them, or being mean, again. Right now, she feels ashamed for taking out her feelings on Mira this morning. But it's not as if Mira doesn't do this too. She does. This is the way they are with each other; it's a dance they do. They love each other, annoy one another until they hate each other and then feel bad about it and so they pretend like nothing ever happened, start again, and love each other all over.

Hana picks up her phone and types out a message:

Hi. What are you doing? Just wondering what the name of that show was you mentioned yesterday, the one we were going to watch. Also, by the way, you forgot the extra groceries, I'll tell Samir to drop them off if you let me know when.

It's not the way an apology might be defined in the diction-ary, but this is Hana, making amends. At the last moment, she adds an *x* for a kiss and presses 'send'.

Samir comes in, carrying two mugs of tea, one in each hand. He sets one down on a shelf in the alcove just behind her. He forgets to use a coaster but she doesn't say anything. He comments on the growing darkness, turns on the side lamps and sits on the green velvet sofa. He reaches for the remote control but doesn't switch on the TV. Instead, he takes a sip of his tea and says, 'So, when does the magic happen?'

He wiggles his thick eyebrows at her suggestively, ridicu-lously. She knows he's being stupid on purpose to make her laugh and it works.

'Don't call it that,' she says. 'Because if you keep calling it that, there will be no magic.' And then in a softer voice she adds, 'I don't know, I'd need to check. And anyway, I'm on my period so it's not happening anytime soon.'

'Check?'

She looks at him impassively. 'Well, yes. There's only a very specific window in which . . . wait, do you not know that?'

'Yeah,' he says, 'sure, I do, but I don't know the fine print exactly.'

Hana nods. She remembers how surprised she'd also been to discover, not even all that long ago, that there were only a tiny number of days a month in which she could actually fall pregnant, and how complicated it felt to work those days out. It was new to her then and she was quite indignant that no one had ever told her this before, that no doctor had ever mentioned it, no teacher back when she was a teenager and all they were taught in her girls' school was to not have sex at all. Even the terminology irritated her – 'to fall pregnant', as if the whole thing were just an unlucky trip over the kerb of a pavement. It astonished her how anyone got pregnant at all, when the likelihood of it happening was in fact so slim. It seemed unbelievable – *miraculous* even. She envied the stories she heard at weddings and dinner parties, when pregnant friends or friends of friends would blush and say with their hand on their stomach, it wasn't planned. How could it not be, when there were such precise demands?

Now, Hana uncurls her legs, twists behind to reach for her mug and crosses the room to the sofa where Samir is, setting the mug down on the coffee table in front of them. She sits down next to Samir and folds his hand into hers. He puts his arm around her, a surprised expression on his face. She looks at him analytically, curiously. She touches his face, her eyes moving slowly across his features as if she is studying him.

'What?' he says, with a little laugh but Hana doesn't answer. Instead, she rests her head against his chest and closes her eyes. It's been so long since they've shown each other any sort of tenderness. The constant arguing, the vitriol of all the things they've said in anger, which they both did and didn't mean in those moments, has taken its toll on both of them.

'Hana?' Samir says softly, resting his hand on her hair.

'Hmm?' Her eyes are closed.

'I'm sorry if I made this harder for you than it needed to be.'

She takes a minute to reply. 'That means a lot,' she murmurs into his chest.

He plays with her hair. It feels nice. They sit like this for a few quiet minutes and then he adds, 'I didn't know you were on your period.'

'Hmm, started today.' She yawns and curls closer into him. 'So we'll have to wait until after, figure out when I'm ovulating.'

He nods. 'Are you okay though? You don't need any painkillers? I can get you some.'

'Not yet.' She likes that he's asked. He hasn't done that in a long time either.

'Okay. But just let me know if you want any.'

He continues twirling her hair and stroking the side of her neck with his fingers and then after a while he murmurs, 'So, do you think maybe because you were about to come on, that's partly why you were as upset as you were last night?'

She opens her eyes, puzzled, and then slowly sits up, trying to understand the meaning behind his question.

'No.' She's looking at him, still processing what he's just said. 'No, I was angry and upset because you said, we both said, hurtful things. I wasn't just feeling emotional because of my period, if that's what you're trying to say. And if that is what you're trying to say, it's somewhat patronising—'

'No. No, of course not,' he interrupts quickly. 'That's not what I meant. I was just wondering if *maybe* it made things, made *you*, feel worse. I know that sometimes happens for you—'

'Samir, please.'

'—No, I don't mean anything by it, I'm just saying.'

She sits forward on the edge of the sofa. 'And if the only reason we argued last night was because of, say, PMS, would that change anything for you? Would it make you backtrack on your decision to want to start trying?'

She's not angry and she's not shouting but there is a definite edge in her voice. She wishes she didn't need his reassurance so much, but what she really wants is to triple check that Samir is absolutely certain and that he won't change his mind. She was only half joking when she asked earlier if she could get his agreement in writing.

'Hana, no.'

'Because you can't just blame how I feel on hormones. How I feel, how I felt last night, was real. Is real. Does that make sense to you? Because I need it to make sense to you, Samir, I really do.' She looks down at her hands and takes a deep breath.

'You were right,' she says quietly. 'What you said last night, about us fighting all the time. It's not good. I'm tired of it. I don't want to keep doing that anymore.' She shivers a little.

'Han, I don't either—'

'So can we just try? To be nicer? Kinder? If we both want the same things, it shouldn't be so hard, should it?' She's aware that she says this line sometimes at work, trying to placate the solicitor on the other side to reach a negotiation.

Samir leans towards her and takes her hands in his.

'Of course,' he says. His face is serious, very unlike him. 'That's all I want, Hana. All I want is for you to be happy, to make you happy. And I'm so sorry if you've not been happy lately because of me. I understand that now, and I can't tell you how bad I feel about it, about all of this, about how you must have been feeling all this time.' He raises his hand like a question mark in the air, then drops it.

Hana trembles. For the first time in a long time, she feels an invisible connection to him, like they're holding two ends of a rope, willing the other to pull in. She studies him slowly again, her eyes passing over his wide forehead, his thick eyebrows, the long lashes she's always secretly coveted. She realises she believes him. He wants to make her happy. He wants what she wants. They both want a baby. It can really be that simple. So, she nods, unable to speak. Samir reaches for her hesitantly, as if he's not sure if she wants him to hold her, though she does. She really does. Instead, he places his hands lightly on the sides of her cheeks.

'Hana?' His voice is teasing. 'Did I hear you say that I was right? Like, if we just rewind a little bit. You did say that, didn't you? You said, "You were right." So can I get *that* in writing?' His eyes are shining, and the intensity of the moment dissolves.

But Hana doesn't mind. She clamps her hand over his mouth.

'Stop it, you idiot.' She's laughing. 'You're so childish. We have this big moment, finally we're talking like adults, and yet you still—'

He bites her palm. She withdraws it with a gasp, but she's only pretending: it doesn't hurt at all. He smiles at her, his whole face wide and open, and pulls her towards him. Her hands fall into the thicket of his hair. Though she's so sleepy, blurry with exhaustion and all these emotions, she feels, in this very precise moment, so entirely happy, so grateful for him, for this house, for their marriage, even the constant back and forth between them. For all of it.

Samir kisses her. She laughs once more, her mouth opening in response to his, and she feels as if they've found each other again.

Later, they go upstairs to bed. They move around each other in the bathroom, brushing their teeth, getting undressed, Hana making room for Samir and not minding like she usually does when he accidentally gets in her way. In the bedroom, Samir closes the shutters and draws the curtains.

He slides into bed while Hana pats in her various serums and creams. Then, she goes to her side of the bed and gets in and, adjusting the duvet cover, says to Samir, 'I wanted to show you this.'

She holds out her phone and Samir moves closer, his face gently resting on her bare shoulder. She taps into the app that tracks her cycle.

'Look. So this is how we can check when it's the right time to, you know. This is the calendar, see the red squares? That's for now, because it's the start of a new cycle. And then you see this? This little sun icon, that's when I'm ovulating. Twelve days from now. It's clever, see?'

'Very,' he says, laughing a little.

The screen on her phone brightens. There is a new message notification. Mira's name and the first few words of her message pop up.

'What's Mira saying?' he asks.

'I'll read it later,' Hana replies, dismissing it. 'So, they say the best thing to do is to do it every other day, in the "fertile window".'

Samir laughs again. 'Can't we just do it when we want to?'

'No. It doesn't work like that.' She taps out of the app and brings up a page on a medical website titled 'How to Get Pregnant' (she's read this before). She quickly familiarises herself with it again, then clicks back into her app.

'So, we start trying five days before ovulating – so that's here.' She counts backwards from the sun on the screen. 'That means we start in a week. From here to here.' She taps at the dates on the screen.

'Wow. Seven days. In a row?'

'No. I said every other day.'

'Wow,' Samir says again.

'Okay?'

'Okay!'

'So will you remember that? Next week?' She taps out of the app and into her work calendar. 'I don't think I've got anything on after work so . . .' She turns to face him and gestures at his phone, plugged in to charge on his bedside table. 'Do you want to check if there's anything in your diary?'

She's being serious, but he laughs.

'I'm not sure you can timetable good sex, Han. Especially seven alternating days of it.'

She raises an eyebrow at him.

'What?' he asks innocently.

The look on his face is so impish that she smiles in spite of herself. This is what she loves about him. She's always loved about him. She chose him because he made her laugh, and in making her laugh, he made her life lighter. Until the jokes started to come at her expense, along with the arguments. But she won't think about that now. She puts her phone on to charge and turns off her bedside light. A new beginning.

The following week, Hana doesn't bring any extra work home and Samir doesn't go to the gym. He cooks for her every evening instead. One night, while they're watching television, he strokes her hair and kisses her neck and then not long after, they go up to bed together. After they've finished, Samir murmurs, 'I love you.' It's been so long since either of them have said it that it surprises her. It takes her a moment to say it back.

Eleven

'So, it's a date, right? He wants you to stay later. So it must be,' Molly says. It's a Saturday morning and Molly and Mira are browsing the rails of a vintage pop-up shop in King's Cross. Molly is considering herself in a mirror, holding up a floral dress with a huge lace collar. She looks at Mira, who is sifting through a mismatched selection of tableware on a shelf. The week before, Mira had emailed Dominic and said she'd love to take him up on his offer to discuss the subject of borrowing from real life in writing. He replied and suggested she stick around for half an hour after their next session. It wasn't exactly what she was hoping for.

'—Hardly. "Why don't you stick around for half an hour?" does not sound like a date to me.'

'It's not dissimilar to some of the messages I get from the men I meet online, to be honest,' Molly says.

'We won't even be going anywhere. We'll just be in the bookshop. I can guarantee you, all he'll want to talk about is playwriting.'

'Ah, to find a guy who's creative and passionate about the exact same thing as you, and also moderately successful in his chosen field. I mean. That's just the worst.'

'Stop,' Mira laughs. 'You know what I'm trying to say.'

Molly shakes her head. 'I don't actually . . . Look, you've liked him for ages. And there's obviously some chemistry, you can't have just imagined the whole thing. You're going to be alone with him in the basement of a bookshop for half an hour. He's asked you to be there. Don't waste the opportunity.'

Mira pouts but drops the subject. Molly turns her attention to trying to convince Mira to spend the rest of the day with her, even though Mira has already told her she can't – she has to get back to her writing. She hasn't done anything substantial on *Pavements* for nearly a month. The last time she checked the Hadley Prize website, there were one hundred and ninety days left until the deadline. It's still a lot of time, but when she thinks about it, she panics, already lamenting the progress she could've made and hasn't.

Mira picks up a plate and runs her finger over the wavy rim. It's one of a set of six. They are lovely pieces. Made out of thick milk glass, opaque like icing, a pretty pale celadon, they remind her of a set her mother used to have; they called them their party cake plates, taken out at every one of their birthdays when they were young. This happens sometimes; stumbling upon an object that without warning reminds her of what is missing. It's been eleven years since her mother died and her grief is not as raw as it once was. It's still there, but the weight is lighter, softer. What she feels right now, holding the plate, is a bittersweet nostalgia. She's back in her childhood kitchen, the plates stacked up on the table, candles and matches on the side, her name and Hana's spelt out in sprinkles on top of a cake.

'Why are you looking at those? For all your opulent dinner parties?' Molly teases.

'Something like that,' Mira says quietly, putting the plate back. Before leaving the shop, she snaps a photo of them and sends it to Hana, quickly typing: *do you remember these?* Hana doesn't reply immediately, but when she does she says: *Party plates! Where did you find them??* And not for the first time, Mira feels a small relief. Even if they don't always understand each other, at least they have this. Whatever this is.

Outside, Mira says it's time to go. Lili and her boyfriend are supposed to be going to Margate today, said they'd leave in the afternoon and they'll be there until Monday. They've never been away together before and Mira intends to make the most of having the flat to herself.

Back home, Mira clears a space at the small two-seater dining table in the living area, moving piles of post over to the kitchen counter. She hates that the flat is so messy, would love for it to be neater, but between waking up so early to open Flora during the week, and then being so tired in the evenings, tidying up in her limited spare time is the last thing she feels like doing. Besides, it's not even her mess, which is largely confined to her room: it's Lili's. She wishes, not for the first time, that she lived somewhere that felt beautiful and inspiring; a room of her own with an actual desk, perhaps a handsome mid-century piece, or maybe something more minimalist and modern, made of birch ply. For now, this will have to do.

She sits down, opens her laptop and clicks into *Pavements*. She skims over the last page, trying to familiarise herself with the rhythm. She's got as far as her main character lying down on the pavement. People are shouting at her, telling her she's in the way, that she has to get up else they'll fall and hurt themselves. Mira lets out a long exhale; she's been stuck on where to go from here for such a long time. She cringes reading back her work. It feels so tedious and overly laboured. The characters are so mean, nobody cares about whether the woman lying down might get injured;

they only care about themselves. She wonders where this has come from, what it might mean. Quite abruptly, she closes the document and opens the one called *New Idea??* instead.

When she reads over her notes, she feels a tremble run right through her. This idea feels so much more real than *Pavements*. She reads the quotes she's collected and copied and pasted from all the articles she's read about couples wrestling with their different wants, their failure to communicate or to communicate too late. There's something so tragic about this. She's struck by the fact that most of the relationships she's read about didn't survive – not because the people involved had fallen out of love, but because they had to choose what they really wanted for their lives and put themselves first. It's maddening: if only they'd been upfront about what they each wanted sooner, they'd have been spared all this grief, but then they'd never have fallen in love. And isn't it better to have loved than not? But, if you love someone, would you not want to try to compromise? Then again, where is the compromise on having children? Is it even possible? Mira holds all these questions in her head, wanting to understand. If she could write characters for this piece, surely she'd care about them in a way she no longer cares about the characters in *Pavements*? She realises that this is the play she wants to write.

She pushes her laptop aside and, in her notebook, quickly sketches out a little map for the stage. What if the whole play took place in the couple's home, with each act or scene in a different room? The audience would follow the characters from room to room – living room to kitchen, bedroom to spare room – bookmarked as the future nursery for the child one of them wants, which the other uses as a dumping ground. She likes this idea, it feels symbolic of sharing a life together, but also being trapped by it, with nowhere they can go to escape the problems they must face.

She remembers back at university they had discussed a stage adaptation where three sets of actors all played the same couple, only at different ages in their lives. In one scene, the younger couple were placed at the front of the stage but the audience could glimpse the older couple in the background, in a way that was described as haunting. Mira had loved that detail, and it comes back to her now. She's not intending to follow her couple through their life – that feels long and complicated – she knows she wants only to stay in this particular period of their marriage, but she's gripped by the notion of having more than two actors to play the same couple.

She thinks about how she could modernise the concept, by the actors being of different backgrounds, their identity rooted in their shared roles of husband and wife rather than anything else. She loves this idea, the idea that anyone might then see themselves in this couple, her couple; that the experiences of their relationship might in some way be seen as universal. It occurs to her that if she does this, she won't have to specify their heritage, in the way that she's always felt she's expected to, because of her own ethnicity. And maybe this means she won't have to risk her characters being interpreted purely on background alone; this used to happen all the time, at the workshops she took part in at university, her professors making all sorts of assumptions about the sorts of plays she ought to write. It feels thrilling to her, inventive and so incredibly freeing, to be able to tell a story, like this, in this multi-charactered way. She knows she might come back to this in a day's time and rip out all the pages, decide everything she's done is pointless. But in the very moment, in the seconds of it, she's struck by the fragmentary delight of her ideas and she feels as if she's flying.

She turns the pages of her notebook, looks up at her laptop, and then back at her sketch again. And then, she thinks about Hana. Mira scrolls through the document and reads what Hana said, or what she thought she heard Hana say. But it's not about Hana anymore. It's something else, or at least it could be: it could be something poignant, about relationships and the painful similarities of human experience, if only she could manage to write it that way. It reminds her of something Dominic said, that the moment she starts to write her words will take over, regardless of where the idea came from. And Mira's intentions aren't to sensationalise, she wants to treat this subject with tenderness. She opens a new document. She looks back at some of the details she'd written before – the couple, the kitchen – and her basic story outline. Her hands hover over the keyboard for a few seconds. She stretches her fingers and then she begins to write.

All week, she writes quickly, snatching time on her breaks and when business at Flora is slow. She writes on her phone, glued to her screen. Angela glares at her to put it away when a customer comes in, and it takes Mira a moment to remember where she is. It's obviously far from perfect, and she's only written a handful of pages, but it's a start. And the more she writes, the more it begins to feel real. One day, in her bedroom, she tears a sheet out of her notebook and writes the deadline of the Hadley Prize in the middle of it along with the words 'You Can Do This!!!'. She underlines it three times, feeling cheerful, and then sticks it up on a blank space of wall above her chest of drawers.

She gives her characters names: Adam and Natalia, the kind of crossover names with origins in many cultures, which suits her entire concept. She never even managed to come up with a single character's name for the other play, *Pavements*. But now Adam and Natalia feel like people to her. Their different shapes move in front of her, like she's outside, watching them through the windows of their house.

By the time Thursday comes round again, Mira can't wait to see Dominic, and not just because he makes her feel giddy but also because she's genuinely excited to discuss her new work with him. She's forgotten how just a few weeks ago she was so disappointed by his suggestion she 'stick around' for just half an hour to talk. She spends a long time checking her appearance in the bathroom at work, smiling at her reflection in the mirror and smoothing down her hair and fixing her makeup until Angela bangs on the door and asks her what the hell she's doing in there. Mira leaves Flora early and makes it to the bookshop on time, for once.

'Hi!' she says enthusiastically.

A few people have already arrived; one of them, an older man, is helping Dominic unstack the chairs and set them out in a semi-circle. Dominic looks up at her and their eyes meet. She sits down, looking around the room at everyone, smiling and asking how they've been even though she never usually does this. She opens her notebook to a fresh page, clicks her pen several times; she's excited for this week. Once the full group has assembled, Dominic comes to the front and sits down like he usually does, his legs outstretched. Today he's talking about dramatic rules and plot construction.

'It's really quite simple,' he says. 'Your story has a protagonist and he or she wants one thing. Your story begins when something happens, and that event sets something else in action, or creates a reaction. Cause and effect. It's a game. And that's it. It really is as simple as that. Your story now exists.'

They go on to play a game, making up events at random and then seeing what the knock-on effects might be, a sort of he said–she said; it's fun and everyone joins in, but it's also useful, a simple way of breaking story down. Everything Dominic says makes so much sense and this week, Mira pays attention to what he's saying, not just how he looks when he says it. By the end of the session, Mira feels energised, knowing she can apply all of it to her own work, reassured that she's doing the right thing.

She lingers at the end, slowly putting her notebook and pen back into her bag and spending a long time looking at her phone, as if she is reading something important. She doesn't want to make it obvious to the others that she's staying to talk to Dominic because she doesn't want anyone else to get the wrong idea and stay and talk to him too. But Dominic is peering into his phone, frowning. She's not sure he's noticed she's still there. She tilts her head to one side like she's peeping round a corner and says, 'Shall I give you a hand putting the chairs away?'

He looks up and smiles again, and tells her there's no need, that apparently someone from the bookshop will sort it out in the morning.

'Right,' Mira says.

'But, thank you, for asking,' he adds. 'It's very sweet of you.' He turns away and starts packing up his own things.

Mira is confused. 'So,' she starts.

He smiles at her again and raises his eyebrows in question. 'Did you . . . was there something—?' He puts his bag on his shoulder.

'Oh!' Mira says. He hasn't remembered that he'd asked her to stay. She feels her face suddenly turn warm but still she smiles brightly. 'No, no. I mean, just I thought, you said we might chat today?' She bites her bottom lip.

Mira can see him trying to remember what he'd said and then it hits him.

'Mira, I'm so sorry, I completely – you know, there's something wrong with my phone, I put things in my calendar and they're just disappearing. I'm so sorry. Any chance we could do this another time? I'm afraid I have to run tonight but I promise we can—' He looks genuinely upset.

'God, yes, absolutely, no, of course, of course. It's no problem at all,' she says with a wave of her hand. She is mortified, wishes she could just disappear, can't believe how stupid she was to think he might have meant something.

Twelve

After her miscarriage, Hana discovered the world of online fertility message boards. She'd never come across them before, had no reason to, but once she found them, she was lost down a rabbit hole. She read posts with titles like 'Over-reaction to a chemical pregnancy?', 'It was only a chemical pregnancy but I'm so upset' and 'Terrified of chemical pregnancies'. She read them in the bathroom, the shower running, while waiting for the water to turn hot, and she read them on the bus or the tube on her way to work, but only when there was nobody sitting next to her. She very rarely read them when she was in the office, and if she did it was on her phone and not on her desktop, and she certainly never posted any of her own questions, but she took solace from the discussions that conveyed a little of how she was feeling. The comments from other women, telling the posters that they weren't over-reacting, that it was okay to be upset, that it was absolutely normal to feel terrified, made her feel less alone. They made her feel better.

Now that they've started trying to conceive, Hana's enticed by the message boards all over again. It's impossible not to be. At first, she only wants a little reassurance that there's no reason why she might have another early miscarriage. And then after that, she's curious to know if there's anything else she can do, other than making sure they have sex, to improve her chances of getting pregnant. In time she starts to check the forums before she checks her work emails, sometimes as soon as she wakes up, reaching for her phone while she's still in bed and Samir is asleep next to her, just in case there's something she doesn't know yet about the correlation between morning sex and chances of conception (one discussion points her to a study which suggests men might be more fertile in the daytime) or to double-check if it's too early to test even though it's only been a week or so since they had sex.

She grows familiar with all the acronyms: AF for Auntie Flo, meaning periods, BFP for a big fat positive pregnancy test, BFN for a negative. She reads threads about cervical mucus and trying to conceive in the first month. It's halfway through reading an evocative description of the difference between stiff, sticky mucus and slimy stretchy mucus that she begins to wonder what on earth she's doing. It's only their first month of trying. She's an intelligent, successful woman; she knows that it's far too early to be obsessing, and yet here she is, hooked on the advice of strangers on the internet. But these strangers, she feels connected to them. They're as obsessed as she is, and no one is apologetic for it.

She doesn't want to tell her friends that they are trying; it's something that's private, that belongs to her and Samir. Besides, many of them already have children, some more than one, and she worries they might think that she's brought her anguish on herself, for having delayed starting a family in exchange for her career. She remembers being perplexed by how desperate some of them were to have babies, even the ones who didn't have partners. And now, here she is, one of them.

The first two months, they follow the schedule exactly and have sex every other night for a week during Hana's fertile window. She marks the days on the calendar on her phone, on, off, on, off. Samir asks her to explain the science behind the alternate-day schedule and she's surprised and encouraged by how interested he seems. She'd read a post by a woman complaining that her husband had asked her not to tell him the ins and outs of her cycle, because he found it unsexy. But Samir is enthusiastic and it feels oddly reckless to have so much sex, unprotected at that, given that they'd fallen into a habit of only having sex maybe once or twice a month over the last year.

The first month, the sex is pleasurable; he takes his time, pays attention to her and she feels herself yielding to him. In the mornings, he's affectionate with her in an easy intimate way, planting kisses on her neck and her shoulder, telling her she's beautiful. They haven't been like this for a long time. Hana returns to the threads filled with success stories of women who conceived within weeks of trying – 'got pregnant on the first month of ttc!' – and tries not to get her hopes up. When her period comes one afternoon at work, she's disappointed. But all things considered, her disappointment's within reason. When she gets home she tells Samir the news matter of factly, and then she starts calculating with him when her next fertility window will be, filling in her calendar with little on, offs, on, offs.

The second month, there's a little less foreplay and the sex is a bit quicker. But Samir's not complaining about having to do it, and neither is she. Hana's moved by how patient he still is; they argue less and, when they do bicker, it's not as brutal and sarcastic as it was. It's been so long since they've made time for each other, always too busy in their own separate lives to even so much as go out for a walk. But now on weekends, they go for brunch or dinner or out to the cinema, just the two of them; and it almost feels like they're dating again. Something has changed between them, for the better. Every now and again Hana remembers the huge fight they had on the night Mira stayed over, the day before Samir changed his mind and said he was ready to try. She feels almost ashamed of how mean she's been to him in the past, given that he's now trying so hard.

One night, when they're in bed, Hana says, 'We'd have to be really unlucky for none of this to work.' Samir doesn't say anything, just smiles at her. Other nights, when they're not having sex, she stays up, supplementing her forum reading with scientific studies on women's fertility and quizzes on fertility advice websites.

'Don't you think,' Samir says, 'you ought to just take a break from all that? We've only just started. It can't be good for you, thinking about it all the time.'

Hana looks over wearily, zoning in on Samir for a moment, and then pressing her lips downwards, she carries on.

The third time her period comes, on a Saturday in early July, Hana's disappointment is far stronger.

'Samir, come here!' She summons him to the hallway and points at the wall-mounted coat rack that has been lying in the corner by the front door for at least four months. 'Can you put this up today?'

'Hmm. I need to check if I've got the right rawl plugs.' He's not even looking, scrolling through his phone.

She rolls her eyes. 'And those holes that need filling on the landing, where those frames were. Can you do that? I'm sick of looking at them every day.'

Now he does look at her; he says, pointedly, 'All right. But may I just remind you, it was you who took those pictures down. And will you be teaching our future child to say *please*?'

Hana grits her teeth. 'If you can't do it, then just tell me so I can book a handyman. I could have had it sorted out ages ago if I knew you were going to take this long—'

'Excuse me? What is wrong with you?' he says.

She doesn't reply.

'Hana? Seriously? Why are you being like this?'

She doesn't say anything for a while, aware she's overreacting. But finally, because he's staring at her, she gives in and puts her hands in the air and then drops them to her sides hopelessly. 'I just got my period, okay? It's pissed me off, all right?'

'Okay. But that's not altogether that surprising, is it?'

'I don't know, isn't it? We're doing everything right.'

'Yes, but we've literally just started trying.'

'You said that last month.'

Samir raises an eyebrow. 'So, what. Are you going to be like this every month?'

'Why would you say something like that? Why would you assume that we'll be in this position every month?'

He looks at the floor. 'Please don't read between the lines of every single thing I say, Hana. Just don't, okay.'

She stares into space, avoiding meeting his eye.

He scratches his head. 'Some people try for years, Han.'

She wants to tell him that when she sees blood, she's worried it might actually be another miscarriage, but she knows how irrational that sounds. She wants to tell him that she's only angry with him because it's her way of telling him she needs him. But these aren't things she can say so easily, so instead she snaps back, 'And that's awful for them, but it doesn't mean I can't be disappointed for just one day. We talked about this. You, not belittling how I feel.'

He turns away from her. 'That's not . . . I'm not going to be provoked into a fight with you, Han,' he says quietly. 'We said we wouldn't do that.' He looks at the coat rack. 'I'll put that up later.' He puts his trainers on.

'Where are you going?'

'For a run.'

'Well, for how long? When will you be back?'

But he's already pulled the door shut behind him.

Hana reads about something called the 'sperm meets egg plan', referred to on the message boards as SPEM. It's a conception plan that's supposed to help women get pregnant faster, by making sure intercourse is timed more precisely than merely cycle tracking. For this, she has to stock up on ovulation predictor kits. She spends a lunch break researching the best brands and then orders a huge box of multipacks. When they arrive, she stacks them up on Samir's side of the wardrobes, where there's more space than on hers. He sees them and says, 'Hana, is all this really necessary?' She explains to him that now they're in their fourth cycle of trying to conceive, adopting the terminology from the message boards she reads, they should concentrate their efforts. When he looks at her, she chooses to ignore his baffled expression.

According to SPEM, the best time to test is late morning or early afternoon. Hana has to take the ovulation kits with her to work; she decides 12.30pm is a good halfway point. Ordinarily, she keeps her home life and her work life separate, but now she keeps glancing at the clock on the wall during client meetings. She's distracted, desperate to test, anticipating the results. The first results keep coming back negative; she's not ovulating yet. But the SPEM plan says they're supposed to keep going every other day of the ovulation window regardless, either until her period arrives or two weeks after it's due. She calculates in her head; it's a lot of sex.

By the third alternate day of trying, Samir finds it hard to climax. She tries not to take it personally. She understands now, all those online threads warning about sex beginning to feel like a chore. She's working on a big, expensive divorce case that may potentially spark the interest of the press. There was a time she dreamt of working on cases like this, but now she can't remember why any of it mattered so much. On the same day she's asked to work late to prepare, her ovulation test finally comes back positive. She panics, not knowing what excuse she could come up with to leave the office early. In the bathroom stall, she takes a photo of the stick on her phone and sends it to Samir along with an exclamation mark. He replies:

I'm not sure if that's supposed to turn me on. But I don't think it does.

In the end, she manages to slip away at eight thirty, assigning several jobs to juniors; she's relieved, it could have been much later. By the time she comes home, it's past nine thirty. She hasn't eaten all day. On the way, she texted Samir to ask if he could make some dinner for her. She figured she'd eat first, then have sex, although she didn't spell this part out for him.

'Hey babe,' he calls out from the living room, the door partly closed. She can hear sports commentary coming from the television.

'Hi,' she calls back as she drops her bag on the floor. She holds on to the wall while she takes her heels off. She wanders into the kitchen for food, half expecting to see a plate prepared. She opens the fridge, looks in the oven, but there's nothing waiting for her. She wanders back out and into the living room where she sees that Samir is sitting on the green sofa, his feet up on the coffee table, next to empty boxes of takeaway.

'Long day, huh?' he asks, looking up at her.

'Didn't you get my text?'

'What text?' He looks at his phone and then raises his eyebrows as he reads her message. 'Oh, shit, that text. I swear I didn't see that until now.' He nods towards the brown boxes on the coffee table in front of him. 'If I'd known I'd have ordered you some.'

'You would have known, if you'd bothered to check your phone.'

'I'll just order you something now, it's not a problem. What do you fancy?'

'It's too late now. It won't come for at least half an hour and I'm starving. I didn't get a chance to leave my desk all day, and on top of that, we still have to do it, tonight . . .'

He looks at her blankly.

'Samir, the ovulation test result. I sent it to you this afternoon. How can you not remember? We have to have sex tonight.'

'But we did it last night, I thought you said alternating—'

'Yes, apart from when the ovulation test is positive, you have to do it regardless. It doesn't matter if it's two days in a row.' When she speaks, she's impatient.

He rests his head back on the sofa and looks up at the ceiling and then looks at her with a wincing expression on his face.

'Ah, you know what Han, I'm exhausted. If we did it last night, then surely that still counts—'

'No, no, we have to, you have to. I don't think you understand, Samir, I could get pregnant tonight. That's what the ovulation test is for, to predict when the best time is. It's not as simple as just taking one night off, it doesn't work like that.'

He looks at her strangely and passes his hand across his mouth. Eventually he says, 'Hana. Can't we take it easy tonight? Surely one night won't make a huge difference.'

She snatches the remote out of his hand and stares at him.

She says, 'No. I'm not exactly in the mood either, but that's not the point. You can "take it easy" afterwards. It's not like you don't anyway.'

He twists his lips. She waits for him to say something, but he doesn't. An absurd image comes to her out of nowhere, of her hanging over a cliff and him letting go of her hand.

Eventually he comes upstairs. They have sex. She can tell that he's finding it difficult to climax again. Samir doesn't look at her the whole time and doesn't say anything after. Immediately afterwards Hana feels terrible and ashamed for pressuring him into it. She knows, from everything she's read online, that it's the absolute worst thing she could have done. But in the shower, when Samir is asleep, it occurs to her that she shouldn't have to feel guilty. She shouldn't have to pressure him; he should be willing. It shouldn't be up to her to initiate everything. He should surely know how important this all is. It was simply too big of a risk not to try tonight when, for the first time, she had proof that their odds were high. Too big of a risk not to, the thought repeats in her mind. She falls asleep believing it.

Thirteen

Mira has been stuck on the opening scene for a week. The idea is that Natalia and Adam have just had friends over for dinner; the friends have a newborn baby. After they leave, Natalia grows miserable and starts crying. Adam doesn't know what to say. And Mira doesn't know what Adam should say. Mira thinks he knows why Natalia's sad, it's because she wants a child, but he can't commit to that and can't say what she needs to hear. The more she thinks about it, the more the idea of multiple actors feels ill-thought through and chaotic. Everything Adam says sounds wrong. Everything Mira writes is awful.

The following weekend, Mira decides to start again. She sets aside an hour to write on Sunday afternoon, bribing herself with the promise of something to look forward to later; an old friend of hers from school, Farah, has invited her over for an early dinner. Lili is in her room alone, her boyfriend in his own flat for a change, and she's talking on the phone loudly in French with the speaker on. Mira starts working and tries to ignore her, but it's impossible. She gets up and knocks gently on Lili's door and then pokes her head around it without waiting for Lili to answer, knowing she won't. 'Lili, would you mind just keeping it down please? I'm trying to work,' she says calmly. Lili makes a face at her and back in her room, Mira can still hear everything on her side of the wall.

She lets out a groan of frustration and puts on her headphones. She really needs to find somewhere else to live, but she can't think about that now. She tries to concentrate. She inches her way into the scene, first changing a word here and a word there, until she's ready to pick up the thread of dialogue where she left it trailing. She types slowly, unpicking, thinking as she goes, allowing the tension to slowly build until, suddenly, Natalia and Adam are arguing. Adam is trying to convince Natalia that they don't have to rush into things, that they have plenty of time, that there are so many other things they could do, like go away somewhere romantic. She writes quicker now, without thinking so much about what they're going to say. She is in the flow, the pace of her writing gliding like a needle, and she quickly fills up a page. The words keep coming. She is writing:

Natalia: Who said anything about Paris? I've been to Paris, I don't want to go to fucking Paris again.
Adam: Well, not Paris then, anywhere. We wouldn't have to plan, we'd be free. All our friends with kids – you see how regimented their lives are. They're always complaining, always so tired, hardly ever able to go anywhere or do anything . . . and have you seen the amount of stuff they have to cart around with them, it's just—

She keeps writing for another page until the argument ends with Adam walking out and Natalia crying, her head in her hands. Mira reads it back, once, twice. She looks at the pages in front of her and it feels like someone else has written them. Adam and Natalia are saying almost exactly what she remembers Hana and Samir said, that night they were arguing. It's possibly even word for word, though she can't be sure; it was a while ago. She highlights everything, ready to delete it. Because she should delete it. It's awful. She's awful. She's a terrible writer. She's a terrible person. She feels it like a blow to the head.

It's all wrong, she thinks, she's got it all wrong. The play isn't supposed to be about Hana and Samir, it's not supposed to be their exact words. Natalia and Adam aren't meant to be Hana and Samir, that was never her plan. Her plan was that they were supposed to be these fluid characters, who could almost be anyone in their situation. Mira had believed that when she'd start writing, her words would create something original, something that belonged to her, just like Dominic said, and she thought she was doing that, but now she just feels sick. She scrolls through everything else she has written before this scene, full of mistrust, unsure of whether there's anything else she's lifted from Hana's real life without noticing.

She shuts her laptop abruptly and throws her headphones on the bed as she gets up, and paces the small width of her room, her hands forming fists. She stops abruptly in front of her chest of drawers and glares at the piece of paper upon which she'd written the Hadley Prize deadline and 'You Can Do It!!!'. There's a low-level banging in her head; the sound of her stupidity, she thinks.

She snatches the paper off the wall, crumples it up, and as she does, her eyes fall to the frame with the old photo of her and Hana as girls. She hesitates, then she picks it up, stares at it with a kind of coolness. Hana's right, the picture is awful. She wonders why her mother even took it, and from there her mind leaps to all those other questions that sometimes, not often, but sometimes appear jumbled up in front of her. Like, why did she have to die in the first place? Would she have been proud of Mira? Enough time has passed that she can more or less think about these things without crying, but still, she feels her heart crack open again. Just a bit. She brings the frame closer to her face, closer and closer until it's almost touching her nose and the image turns blurry. In the background, she can hear Lili watching a reality show on television now, the volume so loud that Mira can hear every word the contestant is saying. She sets the frame back down, with more force than is needed. 'Lili! Turn it down!' she yells, but there's no response.

She looks at the time: Farah has invited her over at four and Mira will have to leave soon. But she doesn't want to go out. She doesn't want to have to get changed and sit on the tube for an hour and catch up with Farah and pretend like she's doing great and everything is wonderful with her life. She needs time to think, to fix what she's written, to write something else that will be better or today will have been a waste. She touches her face with the back of her hand. Her skin feels clammy and she can feel a pressure building at the sides of her forehead. She'll just have to cancel. There's nothing else she can do, she's not in the mood. She feels awful for cancelling, sending a message pretending she's ill, knowing that Farah would have already started cooking, thinking of all the waste, but she also knows she'd be terrible company; distracted, nothing of interest to say. She's aware of her phone buzzing, a reply already, but she doesn't bother to check.

Instead she sits back down on the bed and forces herself to look at the scene again, even though she knows it's the worst possible thing she could do when she's feeling like this. She starts to take out the sentences that feel too familiar and tries to think of something else. But without them, the argument falls flat, and she is right back at the beginning; stuck, all over again. And then, just when she thinks of a new approach, Lili puts some music on in her bedroom; bubble-gum teenage pop. Mira breathes deeply through her nose, presses her fingertips together in a triangle in front of her lips, rocks forwards and backwards a little. She jumps up, flings her door open, barges into Lili's room and goes straight to the corner, where the speakers are plugged in.

'*Mais qu'est-ce-que tu fais!*' Lili shrieks as Mira reaches over the desk and fiddles with the wires for the speakers, ripping them out. 'Those are not yours. You cannot just take—'

'I've had enough!' Mira says, her voice raised, shaking the wires in her fists. 'I'm trying to work. I ask you to keep it down but you never listen! I've had enough!'

Mira's expecting a fight, but Lili says nothing. She's been standing in the middle of the room during Mira's outburst; now, she takes a backwards step, even cowers a little.

Mira blinks hard, suddenly aware of what she's done, how she's coming across. 'I just, I was just trying to . . . sorry, here—' and she drops the wires on the floor, leaves her sentence hanging, runs out of Lili's room, grabs her bag and then slams the front door, not knowing where she's going.

In the end, she crosses the road, sits on a bench in the park for a while, hoping the fresh air might help her mood. She thinks of all the writing advice that says: 'Take a walk when you're feeling blocked!' But all she can smell is weed and it's giving her a headache. It's crappy advice anyway, never works for her. She reaches the park gates; she could either go left, up the hill to Hana's neighbourhood, or right into Crouch End. She hesitates. She feels an ache for Hana, wanting to know that she's all right. This play, it's making her think about Hana all the time, even though Mira's not seen her since the night she stayed over. But the hill looks so steep to walk up, and Hana's probably busy, so she turns left, catching a bus into Crouch End. On the way, she leans her head against the window and decides to go and see a film. In the dark she can at least be alone and miserable in peace.

The cinema in Crouch End is the sort where the seats are plush sofas. She asks what's on next. It's a Norwegian comedy drama she's not heard of. It's not exactly what she had in mind, but there are no other options. She buys a ticket and, at the last minute, orders a drink and a large box of sweet popcorn, fully intending to eat it all. There are only two or three other people in the auditorium and the curtains are still drawn across the screen. Mira dumps her bag on the sofa and slumps down next to it. She looks up a review for the film she's about to see; the first one she reads only gives it two stars out of five and calls it a 'hot mess'. She looks around and is taken back to when she used to work at a cinema like this, with Molly and Shay. She's about to message them when she senses someone approaching in her peripheral vision. It takes her a moment to realise who it is. Dominic.

He leans towards her, peering in the dark.

'Mira! I thought it was you, I wasn't sure. Bit difficult to see.' He puts his hands out in front of him, palms upturned as if he's asking a question and then, to her surprise, he stoops down and very quickly air kisses her right cheek. He lightly grips her right shoulder with his left hand, holding a drink in the other. He smells clean, like soap and limes.

'Oh,' Mira says. She sits up straighter. 'Dominic! What are you doing here?'

'Well, you see, I just ran out of sugar—'

'Of course, you're here to see the film,' she says, her tone self-deprecating.

'Indeed, I am.' He smiles at her, the light from the screen falling behind him. He's wearing glasses and looks handsome and geeky. She smooths her hair down with her hands, then starts fidgeting with the chain around her neck.

'I'm supposed to be working,' he says in a confiding tone. 'I'm writing this collaborative play for an arts festival and we've all got our own scenes to write, but I wasn't making much progress. When I saw this was on, it was the perfect excuse to stop. I love Östlund's work. Are you familiar with him?' he asks.

She gazes up at him. She opens her mouth to speak but she's already forgotten his question.

'Sorry,' she says, trying not to sound embarrassed. 'I missed that?' She motions to the screen, where the adverts are beginning, pretending she didn't hear.

Dominic suppresses a smile. He leans towards her and speaks a little louder. 'I was asking if you're familiar with his work, Östlund's work.'

'Oh, yeah. No. No, I'm not familiar with any of his work, actually—'

'I'm supposed to be in Row F.' Dominic takes his phone out of his pocket and checks his screen. He glances around at the almost empty cinema. 'Somehow, I don't think it's going to get busy. Do you mind if I join you or . . . are you waiting for someone?' He pushes his glasses up his nose.

'Oh, no, it's just me,' she says. 'Of course, please.' She means to sound cool, as if it's no big deal for her to be at the cinema by herself, but her voice comes out weirdly high-pitched. She rearranges her things, moving her bag and placing the box of popcorn next to the drink can on the circular side table attached to her seat. But as she turns back, she manages to knock the box over and its contents spill everywhere.

'Shit, sorry—'

'Oh, no. It's okay, don't worry about it, we'll just—' he squats down and starts scooping the popcorn up with his hands, shovelling it back into the box. She squats down to help him. He offers to buy her another box; she says there's no need. He insists, says it's his fault, for disturbing her.

'You're not disturbing me.' She stands up and takes a sip from her drink and to her horror, some of it spills on her sweatshirt. 'Oh God.' She wipes her lips with the back of her hand and then brushes the front of her top. 'I don't know what's wrong with me today.' She collapses back onto the sofa. He's practically kneeling in front of her. If she wanted to, she could reach out and touch the side of his face.

'Mira,' he grins. In the almost darkness, his eyes are bright. 'Am I making you nervous?'

'No!' she says, only a little too forcefully.

He laughs, not unkindly, as he gets up and dusts off his hands. He takes an anti-bacterial gel out of his pocket and squirts a drop into the centre of his palm, offers some to Mira. He sits next to her, both of them rubbing their hands, and the whole situation is so absurd, considering everything that has happened today, with her writing and with Lili, and the fact that she shouldn't be here at all, that she should be on her way to her friend's house, and she can't help but laugh too.

'I'm so sorry,' she says again. 'You really didn't have to clear this all up. We could have just sat somewhere else.'

'You're right. We could have been real idiots about it and just left it for somebody else to clean up.' He smiles at her and she laughs again.

Dominic moves forward and takes off his jacket. He folds it, placing it lightly over his side of the sofa, and then he pushes up the sleeves of his shirt. When he sits back, she catches his scent again, tangy like a salty margarita.

'By the way,' he says, turning to look at her. 'I'm so sorry I wasn't able to talk to you the other week like I said I would. My brother lives in New York, and we'd agreed to do a video call with his children, my nieces. I don't get to see them much and you know how it is, we have to diarise everything these days, even more so when there's a time difference. I felt awful for rushing off. But listen, we could chat after this, if you like, if you don't have somewhere you have to be?'

Mira's mouth parts a little and any frustration she might have felt towards him vanishes, along with whatever's left of her bad mood; she cannot be mad at a man who makes time to speak to his nieces. 'Yeah, no that sounds great. I'm not . . . I'm not doing anything after,' she manages to say.

There's movement in the row as someone from front-of-house appears to take last-minute orders. Dominic pays for another large popcorn for both of them to share. Mira wonders if they look like they're on a date, and it makes her giddy to think that they probably do. They lapse into easy silence when the trailers start, except occasionally Dominic tilts his head towards her and whispers, 'I want to see this one,' or, 'I've heard of this' or, 'This looks good.' Because the trailers are so loud, he has to turn his head and lean closer towards her to speak. When he does this, she can feel his breath on her ear.

The popcorn arrives. Dominic sets it between them. Inevitably, the backs of their hands brush when they dip into it. The sensation of his skin on hers sends a shiver of delight right through her. Mira feels like she's fourteen years old again, suddenly reminded of every boy she ever fancied in school. When the box is nearly empty, Dominic moves it to the floor and shifts in his seat, his legs apart, his knee almost touching hers. She moves just a fraction closer and then stays very still, measuring the forcefield between them, barely breathing. She's sure she's not just imagining it. His hand is so achingly close to hers, she could reach out and stroke it with her little finger. She doesn't, but about half an hour later he does, and after that, she can't really keep up with the movie at all.

Fourteen

At work, Hana is dealing with a new case that involves bullying and emotional abuse. Her client is in her late forties. She arrives at the office dressed tidily in jeans and a plain blouse, with flat brown shoes. But she greets Hana by apologising for her appearance.

'I wasn't sure how smart I should be.' She appraises Hana's tucked-in shirt, the pencil skirt, the full face of makeup.

'Oh no, don't,' Hana says with a wave of her hand. 'You look great. I wish I didn't need to wear these.' She points at her high heeled shoes. 'If it's all right with you, I might just take them off.' The woman laughs, visibly relaxing. Hana smiles as she takes off her shoes by her desk and then walks over in her tights, holding a slim file. She sits in the chair opposite the woman and puts the file down, asks if she'd like tea or coffee. She feels the woman warm to her. She can be good at this, putting people at ease and winning them over, earning their trust. She just doesn't know why she can't be like this with Samir. It's as though her work demands so much of her that by the time she gets home, there are only scraps of her left. She's not sure which Hana is more real: this one – confident and charming – or the one at home – petulant and argumentative.

Now Hana flicks through the case background in the file beside her. The woman's husband is five years older, a consultant in paediatrics. Hana introduces herself properly, with her usual spiel about the firm, and then looks across and asks the woman how she is. The woman's eyes well up.

'I'm sorry,' she says. 'It's just been such a long time since anyone's asked me that. You're very kind.'

'You can take your time,' Hana says, softly. Hana pours her tea, making casual conversation, before very gently steering the woman towards telling her about her situation. She clicks her pen, poised to take notes.

The woman nods, begins to recount how she and her partner first met, how he's controlling, how she's been unhappy in her marriage for years but had always made excuses. Hana notices the woman finds it hard to make eye contact and glances through the glass door every time anyone walks past. She sits pressed into one side of the chair, taking up barely any space on it. She says her husband's behaviour has affected her confidence to the point that there are times she can't leave the house. She explains to Hana that she'd studied art history and she has a friend, who runs a gallery, who has asked if she'd like a job, and she really wants to work there. But her husband tells her that no one in their right mind would ever hire her. She says it was this that finally led her to contact Hana's firm.

Now Hana tells the woman not to give up on the job, but just as she says this she unexpectedly thinks of her mother and she feels, not for the first time, a small knot of shame tighten inside her. Hana could have been so much more encouraging of her mother, instead of always criticising, constantly telling her that her art wasn't worth the time or trouble. It occurs to her that she's been doing exactly the same with Mira, and that she has to, *must,* do better by her. She suppresses the thought, wills herself to concentrate.

'—I feel so stupid,' the woman laughs nervously. 'I probably shouldn't even be here, there'll be other people who need your services far more than me. And if he were to hear any of this, he'd just say I've got no reason to complain, he's looked after me, he works hard, he pays for everything. Or, he'd say well, we're married, what do you expect, married couples argue. But the thing is, we don't actually argue anymore, you see. Because I don't say anything back to him. It's easier not to.'

Hana listens to every word. She passes tissues, nods, says she understands, commends the woman's bravery for making it to the office. She runs through her options, tells her what she tells all her clients in positions like this: to start by keeping a written record of her partner's bullying behaviour for a month, somewhere where he won't find it or see, like a note on her phone with the title 'Things To Do' or 'Shopping'. She tells her to note down dates, times, very brief descriptions of each situation and what he said and how it made her feel, and then come back to her. 'It's a long walk and these are small steps,' Hana says, 'but you've taken the first one and that's the hardest.' When the woman thanks her, her eyes have turned pale and watery once again.

For the rest of the day, Hana thinks about the woman. She replays what she said, about how she doesn't argue with her husband anymore because it's easier not to. It makes Hana uneasy. She thinks of Samir, of how she made him feel so guilty for not wanting to have sex, how he hasn't said a word back to her about it in the week since. They're not arguing either, but she knows there's only so long they can go on like this before one of them or both of them breaks, before everything they're holding in spills out. And she finds her own behaviour chilling; that the way she's been acting could, told a certain way, be interpreted as emotional bullying.

But what else is she supposed to do?

She wonders how many months she'll be able to keep on doing this, especially the way things are with Samir. It's not as if she *wants* them to be unhappy; they're trying for a baby, it's supposed to be amazing, life changing. In her lunch break, Hana searches the message discussion boards. There's a post titled, 'Am I being unreasonable for feeling annoyed with my husband's lack of enthusiasm for trying for a baby?' She's about to click on it when she catches herself and stops. She's been so wrapped up in it all, so obsessed with these message boards and ovulation kits and vitamins and making sure they only ever drink decaf, that it's only now she realises what it might be doing to them. Between work and scheduling sex, she can't remember the last time they had fun.

She just wants this part to be over. She's already had enough of this. She wants to be holding hands and going to scans and for him to call her 'babe' again (even though she pretends she hates it when he does this, she really doesn't) and to go out late at night to the corner shop because she's having some insane craving. She just wants to get to that part, and then the next part, and the next.

She knows she needs to lighten up, that stress is especially counterproductive when trying to conceive. They've stopped going out with each other at the weekends, haven't even sat down to have coffee together lately. She tries to picture them sitting in a restaurant, but the scene in her head is awkward; they wouldn't have anything to talk about, and that would feel even worse.

Another idea comes to her. A party. A party could be fun. They'd meant to have a housewarming party after the renovation, but they never got around to it. They'd had friends over, of course, couples round for dinner, but not a party. Maybe they could start during the day, in the afternoon, so that their friends with children could come, like a summer garden party. Samir would like that. He'd agree to that.

She looks through her calendar. It can't be too last minute, people will need enough notice, and she wants time to plan it, too. There's a Saturday towards the end of August, the day before her birthday. That could work. She makes a list of all the things she'd need to do. A menu, drinks, maybe flowers too. She'll ask Mira to help with the desserts, she can place a big order at Flora. A party, she thinks, relieved that there is something, now, to look forward to.

Fifteen

Outside the cinema, after the film is over, Mira and Dominic stand facing each other on the pavement. Mira smiles shyly, doesn't know where to look. Dominic held her hand for most of the film, and though Mira had hoped he might have made a more substantial move in the darkness, he hadn't. Now, he puts his hands in his pockets and raises his shoulders to his ears.

'So,' he says.

'So,' Mira says back. She can feel her cheeks turning warm, knows she's blushing.

Then he says, 'Do you maybe want to get something to eat?'

She has no idea how this is happening. She nods and makes a quiet noise in agreement. They walk away from the cinema side by side, his arm brushing hers, in the direction of the clock tower. He mentions a retro burger place; she says that sounds nice. Then, while they're waiting for the lights to change to red so they can cross to the other side, he gently pulls her towards him and kisses her.

While he is kissing her, very gently, very sweetly, his hands cupping the sides of her face, she opens her eyes, just to be sure she's not imagining it. She feels lightheaded, is overcome by the urge to burst into laughter or break into song mid-kiss. When he moves away, he says in a soft voice, 'I've been wanting to do that for ages.' Mira laughs, because what he's just said is so unbelievably cheesy but also so incredibly perfect.

'Do you mean that?'

'God, yes. Ever since you first walked into my writing group, fifteen minutes late, interrupting everything.'

She laughs again. This is true; she really was late to the very first session and has been late to many more since. Then he takes her hand and they keep walking.

'This was not what I was expecting when I woke up this morning,' Mira says. They've sat down next to each other in a booth in the burger place.

'No, I can't say it was what I was expecting either. But I wouldn't have it any other way.'

He looks at her intently and Mira holds his gaze, then rolls her eyes, smiling.

'My God,' she teases. 'Seriously?'

'What?' Dominic asks.

'Just . . . these lines. Where do they come from? Do you write them? Do you moonlight as a screenwriter for really bad romantic comedies?' She laughs. 'You can tell me, I won't tell anyone, I promise.'

'Hey,' he protests. 'What? I'm just saying how I feel. I'm very uncomplicated like that. I could tone it down, if you prefer.' They're sitting with their heads very close together. 'I could say no nice things about you at all. But that would be very difficult.'

She can't stop laughing. It goes on like this. He compliments her, she tries to accept them graciously, but can't without giggling because she's so unused to it; the men she meets on the dating apps don't tend to behave like this. Often, they don't want to talk at all, in too much of a rush for something else.

But Dominic does want to talk. And it's lovely, to sit with him like this, so close, their arms and their legs touching. He tells her about his cat; she tells him about Lili; they exchange stories of the craziest people they've ever lived with. He explains the premise of the play he's currently writing and had been working on that afternoon. It's a collaboration with three other writers, commissioned for an arts festival taking place in the summer. The play is about a family argument just before a wedding, and each of the writers will take a different character's perspective. Mira feels animated, her eyes gleaming. She is fascinated and asks him many questions about the process. She can't believe people even get commissioned, paid, to do these things. Dominic is so forthcoming about how the industry works, and she loves this, says how grateful she is to him for sharing. When he asks her about her writing, she makes a face. She doesn't want to go back to the despair she was feeling earlier in the day, not now when she's with him and all she wants is for him to kiss her again.

'Can we maybe, just . . . not talk about that right now?' She bites her bottom lip as she looks at him sideways. 'Can we maybe just–' and then she leans across and takes his face in her hands and kisses him instead.

'Shall we go?' he murmurs in her ear as he pulls away.

Mira nods and excuses herself to go to the bathroom while he gets the bill, trying to act composed as she walks away. But inside the cubicle she stomps her feet and mouths *'yes, yes, yes'* and pulls out her phone. She begins to compose a text to Molly: *YOU'LL NEVER GUESS WHAT HAPPENED TONIGHT!!!* But then she deletes it. It's too soon; she wants to keep this to herself a little longer.

Dominic is waiting for her outside. She can see him through the window, checking his phone. When she joins him, he makes a sorry-looking face.

'Mira, I'm so sorry. I didn't realise the time; I've got a hundred messages on my phone from the others on the collaboration. The organisers want to get together with us tomorrow, and see how far we've got, and we're supposed to have our first half ready, so I should really get back and carry on.' He gestures up the road behind him with his thumb.

'Oh!' Mira smiles up at him. 'Of course, I understand, you go, you have work to do!' She realises she's talking louder than she needs to, trying not to show her disappointment. Her phone is in her hand, and she glances at the time. In her normal speaking voice, says, 'I have to be up really early for work, too.'

'But I'll see you very soon. Writing group?' He points at her, while walking backwards away from her, as if to hold her to it.

'Of course,' she says, mentally calculating how long it is until then. When she realises it's eleven days away, she feels deflated. She stands there for a moment, touching her lips.

The next day, she hums to herself while working, even doing the jobs that she usually hates, like emptying the bins and cleaning up after young children. A tired mother comes in with her toddler, ordering a coffee for herself and an almond croissant and milk for him. He spills the milk within seconds and smears the insides of the croissant all over the table, but Mira skips straight over to them, smiling at the toddler and kneeling to talk to him at his eye level. Afterwards, Angela looks at her funny and says, 'What the hell is wrong with you?'

Dominic emails her later the same day.

> *Hi Mira,*
> *I just wanted to say I had the most unexpected and lovely day yesterday.*

I hope you did too.
D x
*ps it was very hard to concentrate on getting any work
done last night.*

She writes back spontaneously, without overthinking it:

*I did. I didn't tell you, but I was having a really rubbish
day when you turned up at the cinema. And suddenly . . .
well, let's just say you turned it around.*
    *ps sorry about the distraction . . . hope you got what
you needed done for your meeting today.*

They switch from email to text.

*Dominic: btw, if it's okay to ask, what was your bad day
about? Sorry I didn't realise x*
*Mira: don't be sorry, you weren't to know. Just . . . frus-
trating writer's block I guess. But then you came along so
it's all good!*

She reads her message over and cringes. She writes another
immediately.

*Mira: although actually you're a proper playwright so
maybe you don't suffer from any of this*

After that she doesn't hear from him for two days. She checks
her phone constantly, wonders if she was too enthusiastic in
her first email. When she's not agonising over why he's not
messaged her back yet, she fills the time bringing Molly and

Shay up to speed in their group chat. She tells them all about the cinema, the kiss, the restaurant, his messages.

Molly: WHAT
Shay: WAIT WHAT
Molly: ????
Shay: This happened FOUR days ago and you're only telling us NOW??

She complains she hasn't heard from him since her last text and wonders what that means. They complain she's being too cryptic, demand to know the details of their first kiss. Their response is exactly the right kind of distraction she needs from her disappointment. And then, the following evening, when she's at home eating pasta and watching television and feeling sorry for herself, her phone buzzes.

Dominic: Sorry I didn't reply sooner! I've been snowed under. I'm in Crouch End . . . do you want to meet up? I could come to you? I could help with your writer's block?

Her mouth falls open, her fork hovering in the air. But then another message comes straight through.

Dominic: Goodness, just realised how that sounds, that was not a euphemism btw and a genuine offer to talk it through. I'm very embarrassed now.

She laughs. She looks down at the T-shirt and the jogging bottoms she's wearing and then around at the flat. Lili is out. It takes her all of ten seconds to decide.

Mira: God yes.

She deletes it and starts again.

Mira: Haha. Of course, come round.

She rushes around the flat, quickly washing dirty dishes and picking up items of clothing left on her bedroom floor. She splashes cold water on her face, dabs some concealer under her eyes and blusher on her cheeks and changes into a loose denim dress. The bell rings; she buzzes him up. They are kissing before he's even through the door.

Later, they are lying next to each other on her bed, fully dressed on top of the sheets, when he rolls over onto his side to face her and says, 'So, about that writer's block?'
Mira laughs. 'Yes, about that.'
She sits up and ties her hair back with a band that was wrapped around her wrist.
'Do you want to tell me about it?'
'Ah. Not really.'
He reaches out and plays with the end of her ponytail. 'Sure? I could help. There's always a way out of these things.'
He looks at her with pleading eyes. She smiles; it is impossible to resist. 'So, remember how in writing group one time, the time I was supposed to read–'
'Yes, I do remember, because you forgot to bring anything.'
'*Anyway*, I asked you about the ethics of, say, borrowing from someone's life to write about–'
'I remember. And we all agreed that writers do it all the time.'

'Yeah, but . . . that someone is my sister.'

He nods. 'Okay. Am I allowed to know the details?'

She hesitates, unsure if she should tell him. 'I don't – I don't know.'

'Well have you written much?'

'A little.'

'Okay, so you've started writing – that's good. But you're being too hard on yourself because it's your sister. I don't think there's anything wrong with being inspired by a real-life situation, that's what all writing is. And you're not writing about her, specifically, as a person, just writing about whatever the subject is.'

'Yeah, but that's the thing. I wrote this whole scene but it . . . it sounds like her. My character actually sounds like her. She says the exact kind of things my sister would say. She says things my sister may possibly have even said in real life.'

'Did she say these things in real life?'

'Would it matter if she did?' She asks the question while screwing up her face, as if she doesn't want to hear the answer. She knows that the first thing she did when she left Hana's house was try to remember exactly what she said.

Dominic leans on his elbow, props his head on his hand. 'Listen, even if you have accidentally used something she once said, it'll change organically, the more you write, the more your character develops and turns into someone else. The fact you're even deliberating to this extent shows you care about her but also about your work.'

'Maybe.' She brings her knees up to her chest and wraps her arms around them and for a while, neither of them says anything. He reaches out and strokes her shin. Mira says, 'You know, my mother was an artist, well she was a teacher at a college, but she was also an artist, and whenever she used to get stuck, she would just draw and paint my sister and me, again and again. She used to say it was better to draw something than nothing, and that it was easier to draw what was right in front of her rather than create something out of her imagination.'

He considers this, nodding. 'That makes sense. I suppose you could say it's the same with writing. Does she still paint?'

'No. She . . . she died.'

He sits up and moves his hand from her leg to her arm. 'Mira, I'm so sorry.'

She looks at him and smiles, touches his hand with hers. 'Don't be, you weren't to know. It was a long time ago. It's been eleven years. I was . . . twenty. Sometimes it's hard to remember, everything from back then gets blurry.'

He shifts so he is closer to her and leans his head against her shoulder. For a while they sit there like this, not saying anything. Then, playing lightly with her fingers, he asks, 'What were her paintings like?'

She pauses. 'Simple. But beautiful. She'd paint flowers, people, tabletops, living rooms. Us. My sister and me. Observations of everyday life, I guess. Big colourful canvases. I wish I had one to show you but they're all in my sister's house, she's got more space than me. My mother, she always dreamt of having a show somewhere, or illustrating a book or something, but the most that ever happened for her was selling a few pieces at a craft market. But she didn't mind. She never gave up. She just kept on painting because it made her happy, fulfilled. . . And then there's me, dropping out of university straight after she died. Always giving up on things before I've finished. Too scared of trusting my instincts.'

Mira tries to laugh self-effacingly.

'Don't say that. It's not true.'

'Well, it kind of is–' she begins but then Dominic pulls her close to him and kisses her mouth to stop her from talking.

Then, he tucks her hair behind her ear and says quietly, his eyes slowly passing over Mira's face, 'You were so young—'

'*She* was young. She was only fifty. Heart attack. Sounds bad to say it, but I'm glad it wasn't some long drawn-out illness. I think that would have been even more unbearable. But anyway, I'm okay. We're okay now.' She smiles at him, as if to demonstrate how perfectly okay she is.

He nods, rests his head against her shoulder again and begins tracing his fingertips lightly along the inside of her arm. Mira lets out a small breath. Talking like this, being touched like this: she feels cared for. After a while, he lets his hand fall to her lap and says, 'You must get it from her.'

'Get what?'

'Your creativity.' He sits up fully now. 'And what she said, about painting you because you were there, in front of her, I really do think that applies to writing too.'

'What do you mean?'

'Just, looking around you, at what's in front of you. Seeing the beauty in it. Being observant, noticing details, being able to capture them. That's what she did, and it's what you're doing too. Whether or not you've written about your sister, or used her words, you're paying attention. That matters. You just have to keep writing.' He taps her forehead lightly. 'You can't lose focus; you have to be disciplined.'

She laughs as she swings her legs off the bed so that she's sitting with her back to him. 'Disciplined? Is that so?—'

'Yes. So next time it's your turn to read a scene you'd better be prepared.'

'So, like, no distractions?' She's standing up by the side of the bed.

'None at all. Especially if you want to enter the Hadley.'

'Well, then you'd better go.' She gestures at the door, but he grabs her by the wrists and pulls her back down and starts kissing her all over again.

Sixteen

It's Friday morning. Hana is leaning on the kitchen counter, waiting for the kettle to boil. She's dressed for work, her handbag on the counter next to her. Samir is sitting at the dining table, his laptop in front of him. Hana flicks through a note on her phone – it's the list of all the people she's inviting to the party. She's made it clear that though it's the night before her birthday, which falls on a Sunday this year, it is not in fact a birthday party, just an excuse to get together with friends. She's excited; it's been ages since they've done something like this and, by luck, everyone she's asked so far happens to be free that weekend. The idea also seems to be working, in that Samir seems relaxed and they're talking to each other normally. Having something to chat about, to look forward to, to work towards together has made a subtle difference in the mood between them at home. Hana's sure that if she can just make this party a success, everything else will also work out.

She's invited friends from work, friends from university, friends without children, friends with. She thinks she'll put on a kids' movie night in the TV room, fill a tray with little stripy bags of popcorn and little cups of milk, so that they have something to occupy them while the grown-ups are outside socialising. It matters to her that she gets this part right. She doesn't normally invite her friends with children, as they can't always find babysitters and sometimes their schedules just don't match up, but this time she's told them to bring the kids, has insisted, describing it as a summer party, for everyone. She'll have to take the rug up, of course, and cover the sofa; or maybe have them sit on the floor so that they don't stain the upholstery. And she'll need to make sure that there's nothing left in the room that could get broken. She realises there's an awful lot that could get broken. She clicks her pen several times. It might be safer to ask Samir to set something up outside, instead. She looks at her list again and next to *movie night* adds a string of question marks.

Now she reads the list out loud, in between bites of toast, counting off her guests on her fingers.

'So we've got Allegra and Will, Tasneem and Simon, Amber and Tom, Danyaal and Layla, Sadie from work and her brood, Jackson and his brood; Alicia and her husband—'

'Alicia has a husband?'

'Second husband. Yes. How do you not know that? She's *your* friend. We've just never met him. Tom or Jon or something.' She goes back to reading out her list. 'Neighbours on the left side, neighbours on the right side, neighbours directly opposite . . . who else can we invite?'

'What do you mean?'

'It just doesn't seem like enough.'

'God, Han, you've practically invited your entire office and the whole street. How many more people are you aiming for?'

'Entire office,' she repeats, laughing. 'Hardly. I just want there to be enough people here to make it feel like a party.'

'What kind of party do you have in mind?'

'A party, Samir, needs people. I want people milling.' She makes a stirring motion with her hand. 'I want it to feel full. Lively.' She looks out the window. 'I just want everyone to have a good time. I want us to have a good time. It's been so long since we've done anything nice. I just want it to be fun.' She feels a little shy, saying this.

'Babe,' he says. 'It will be fun. Just don't get all stressed about it, okay?'

She looks down at her list again; he hasn't called her 'babe' in weeks. She clears her throat. 'And don't forget, I need you to put those festoon lights up outside. And please remember to call that boy—'

'What boy?'

She looks at him with an impatient expression, as if he ought to know who she means by that description.

He laughs. 'I'm sorry, Han. How am I supposed to know who you're talking about? You know, for someone who's so detail-oriented, whose job demands it, sometimes your lack of clarity is astonishing.'

'The boy who does everyone's gardens,' she says.

'The who?' Samir laughs again, and this time it makes her laugh too. She doesn't even mind him making fun of her. She's so relieved at this moment of lightness between them. She tries not to think about how she's a day late: it is only one day. It is taking all her willpower not to think about it. She knows there's no point testing just yet. Talking about the party is just a distraction.

'You know, the boy!' she persists. 'The teenager who lives up the road, tidies everyone's gardens for pocket money. Sweeps up leaves and mows lawns. His number's on the group chat for our street. Leon or Leo. Something like that. I asked him to come for a quick tidy-up outside, it's a mess. Could you please just follow up with him? I'll text you his number.'

Samir nods, chewing, and gives her a thumbs up, his mouth full. 'Want me to invite him too?'

She throws a tea towel at his head. 'So, you'll sort the garden out. Then I need to sort out food and drink. I'm going to order desserts from Flora, I just need to check that with Mira, I might do that today, and then I'll see if I can find a caterer—'

'Wait, caterers? How much is this party going to cost?'

'Well, are you going to cook for everyone?'

He looks at her blankly.

'Exactly.'

He raises his eyebrows. 'No, but we don't need lots of food. Why can't we just add a bunch of nibbles to the online shop? It won't be that difficult to open some boxes and put things on plates.'

She pauses, considering. 'I don't know. Party food from the supermarket, it just doesn't feel very special. And I want it to feel special. I don't mean like big fancy caterers, I just mean someone to put together a few fresh platters, not things out of a packet. Big bowls of nice fresh salads, that kind of thing. I won't spend too much. It'll be nice. We haven't done anything like this in ages.'

'Right. A special party. Definitely *not* a birthday party?'

She looks at him pointedly and then back at her list. 'So, I still have a bunch more people from work to chase, and a few friends from uni. And you can invite your American friends, but you have to tell me which ones first, I'm not having you turn this into one of your reunion frat parties.'

Samir salutes her by way of reply while still eating his cereal, and then drains his coffee in one go. He wipes his mouth with his hand.

'What about Mira? I assume she's coming?'

'Well, no, I haven't seen her, I haven't asked her yet.' Hana feels caught out. She really should invite Mira. But instead, she says, 'And, anyway, she won't know anyone.'

'Nonsense! She knows Tasneem, you all went to school together. And she's met Allegra and your group from university loads of times. They're always asking about her; they love her. Everyone does.'

'Yes, but she'll be bored,' Hana insists. 'She won't want to socialise with lawyers and tech people and their children, that's not her thing.'

'It's her birthday too—'

'It's not a birthday party! She hates birthday parties as much as I do.'

'You keep saying that, but – shit!' Samir glances at the clock on the wall. 'I've got a call. I've got to run. Just ask her. If you don't, I will. Be *nice*, Hana.' He dashes into the hallway.

'I am being nice,' she calls out behind him.

Hana begins typing a text to Mira on her way to the bus stop when, at the last minute, she takes a detour and decides to walk via Flora. She needs to order the desserts anyway. It's the end of the week and Hana's not in such a rush to get to work. She glances at her watch; the café won't be open yet, but she remembers Mira saying she's there early to set up.

Hana raises her hand to the window, cups it like a sailor looking out to sea, and sure enough, there's Mira right in the back, behind the counter and in front of the small open kitchen, carrying cartons of milk and white cardboard boxes stacked on top of each other. She stops to fiddle with something on the coffee machine and then she opens a box and starts placing pastries into the little display unit with a pair of tongs.

Mira is wearing a striped top and dungarees, a navy-blue apron around her waist and her hair in a ponytail. She looks at least ten years younger than she really is. It's galling, really, how wholesome and pretty she looks, so much like their mother. It suits her, Hana thinks. She studies her own reflection in the glass critically, rubs the corner of her mouth with her thumb. She's aged at least five years in the past six months. She remembers a party she'd once gone to with Mira. She can't remember whose, or why they would have gone together, but she can recall Mira was wearing a red velvet vintage dress that flared out at the waist. Hana had told Mira she was overdressed, but really Mira looked beautiful, like a 1950s' film star. She moved around the room like the sun, everyone turning their faces towards her. Maybe this is why she's held off inviting Mira to the party, because she fears the inevitable comparisons.

She knocks on the window again. Mira still hasn't noticed her. Hana assumes she must have her headphones in. Now, watching her work, it surprises Hana, how Mira seems so at ease, how she moves seamlessly around the kitchen, her actions quick and efficient. Then again, it's not as if the work is exactly challenging. As soon as she thinks it, her hand flies up to cover her mouth, as if she'd said it out loud.

This time she rattles the door, and now Mira looks up. When she sees it's Hana, she waves and smiles, pulling her earphones out one by one and dropping them in the front pocket of her apron. She comes to the door and unlocks it.

'Hana! What's up? How are you? Everything okay?' Mira reaches towards her for a hug.

'Oh!' The embrace takes Hana by surprise. 'Someone's in a good mood.'

'Yes, I suppose I am.' Mira walks behind the counter and puts her hands on top of it and smiles.

Hana narrows her eyes at Mira suspiciously. 'Okay,' she says slowly. 'Good to know.' But she's smiling as she says it.

She looks around her. Flora is tiny, with eight little bistro tables placed in front of two banquettes that line the wall. 'I can't believe places like this actually survive and make money. She does pay you properly, doesn't she, the owner?' She just can't help herself saying this.

'So, how come you're here? Aren't you normally at work by now?' Mira says, ignoring Hana's question. She glances at the clock on the wall as she reties her apron around her waist.

'I don't need to go in so early on Fridays.'

'Nice.' Mira leans towards Hana, across the counter. 'Some of us start work early, you know,' she says in a loud whisper, and when Hana realises she is mimicking her, she swats her arm, telling her to stop it. Mira stops laughing and Hana says, 'What's different about you? Something's different.'

Mira shrugs innocently. 'Nothing!'

'No, there is.' Hana points at Mira and widens her eyes. 'I know this,' she twirls her finger at Mira, like she's painting a circle. There's a certain look in Mira's face, a brightness. 'Wait a second. It's a man, isn't it?'

Mira bursts out laughing. 'It's not!'

'It is.'

'Okay, so it might be.'

'Ah.' Hana's interested now. 'I knew it! So, details.' She raps the counter with her knuckles. 'Who? When? What does he do for work?'

Mira laughs. 'Calm down. It's early days yet. Anyway, what can I get you?'

Hana surveys the counter with its piles of freshly unboxed blondies and brownies, momentarily distracted, her eyes lingering on the walnut cookies. 'Nothing. I came in because we're having a party in a few weeks, just a few friends. Do you still do orders for collection?'

'Party, nice!'

'Well, do you?'

'Do I what?'

'Take orders, Mira. I just asked you.'

'Always happy to take orders from you, Han!'

Hana raises an eyebrow. Mira opens a drawer under the till and rummages for an order form. 'Here. Just fill it in, drop it back or text me and tell me what you want and when and I'll sort it out.'

'Fine.' Hana takes the order form out of Mira's hands. 'You know, you should tell your boss to put all this online, it will save people from having to come in.' Then she looks up and catches Mira's eye. 'But thank you.'

'How's Samir? I haven't seen him for ages. He hasn't been in for a while. I should text him; we need to catch up.'

'"Catch up",' Hana looks at the time on her phone. 'Anyone would think you two were best friends.'

Mira ignores her again. 'So, a party, that sounds nice. What's the occasion?'

'No occasion. Just. A get-together. With friends. Why are you being so nosey?'

'I'm not being nosey! I'm just asking.'

Hana takes a quick breath in and closes and then opens her eyes and tucks her hair behind her ear. 'Right, sorry. Just–'

'Are you okay? You seem a little more on edge than usual.'

'I am not. I'm just. Tired.'

'Hmm,' Mira crosses her arms, studying her critically. 'Yeah, you do look a little tired.'

Suddenly, Hana is overcome by an urge to stay and tell Mira everything; about Samir, about trying, about last year's chemical pregnancy, about being a day late. Instead, she pulls her shoulders back, looks at her phone for the second time. 'Thanks for that compliment, Mira. Right, I'd better get a move on. I'll text you my order.' And without saying goodbye, she opens the door and steps outside. It's only then that she realises she didn't invite Mira to the party.

Seventeen

Mira watches Hana leave the café. 'Bye then,' she calls out, but Hana's already gone. Mira can't put her finger on it, but something about Hana is different. She turns away, thinking about this, when the door opens again and Hana is back, looking shamefaced.

Mira laughs softly. Without speaking, she tears off a brown paper bag from where they're hanging by the counter and slides two walnut cookies inside. Hana begins to refuse but Mira raises her hand insistently.

'You *do* look tired. You work too hard.' She holds the bag out towards Hana and pushes her phone away. 'Just take it. It's on me. It's just cookies.'

Hana presses her lips together and it's obvious to Mira she's trying to suppress a smile.

'Hana,' Mira says, laughing. 'Would you just—'

'Thank you,' Hana says, and this time she says it like she really means it. 'About the party—'

The phone rings and Mira puts up one finger, asking Hana to give her one second. Hana waits for a few minutes but then gestures to the clock and waves, rushing out the door again. While Mira is on the phone, she watches Hana walk up the road, pause at the zebra crossing for the traffic to still, then disappear around the corner. She smiles as she answers the caller's questions about opening times, bemused. It never fails to surprise her that, out of all the people in the world, it's Hana, and all her peculiar, particular ways, she's related to. She tries to ignore the little twinge of guilt she feels.

Since her conversation with Dominic about writing, Mira feels like she's regained her footing. She knows her spirals of worrying are slowing her down. Dominic keeps telling her he'll read whatever she's written so far, whenever she wants, and this too is motivating; but she doesn't want to send him something incomplete; she wants to be able to show him something finished, something good. He jokingly sets her challenges, messaging her to remind her to write five hundred words that day, telling her he won't come over to see her if she hasn't and, though it's not serious, it helps her to stay on track.

She begins to write again, properly, after work and on the weekends. She draws up a timetable, outlining how many scenes she needs to write by when in order to finish a first draft sixty days before the Hadley Prize deadline, so that she's got time then to edit it. When Dominic tells her he's proud of her, Mira pretends like it's no big deal, but it is. She's more determined than ever to write this play and not give it up, not like *Pavements*, not like all the other plays she's abandoned before getting even halfway. For the first time, she believes she might actually do it.

She grows strict with her schedule. When her friends message to ask her to come out, she says no, she can't, or she limits it to coffees, suggesting they come to Flora if it's during the week and she's working. When Hana calls on weekends with backwards invitations for her to come over for dinner, Mira says she can't stay long. And when Dominic tells her that he might not be able to see her quite as much between playwriting groups, because things are getting busier for him with the festival, she doesn't take it personally. It feels good to tell him that she's busy too, feels special to know that they are both writing, that this is what it's like, being in a creative relationship (though she keeps this thought to herself, not really knowing if she can call it a relationship yet).

But it's still difficult to write in the flat. It's been awkward with Lili ever since that incident with the music and the speakers. Mira's said sorry, has tried to make it up to her by being helpful around the flat, but Lili just ignores her. And she still plays her music too loud anyway. Plus, Mira finds it annoying that she has no space for a proper desk in her bedroom. Her back aches from sitting on her bed or her floor. She tries to write in different places, but she can't seem to settle anywhere. The local library isn't open early enough, and when she does go in one Saturday, she ends up opposite one man intent on cleaning his ear with his little finger and flicking the contents away, and another who chews gum with his mouth open. Another time, she goes to the British Library, feeling excited at the prospect, like this means she is a real writer, but she's disheartened to find there's no space and it's full of students and that she has to pay to be a member to sit in the nicer, quieter bit.

On the weekends, Mira tries to work in different cafés, the way people come and work in Flora, but she feels guilty for staying too long and not spending nearly enough. None of her friends have rooms she can borrow, and she wouldn't want to ask anyway, knowing it will lead to questions about how the play is going that she doesn't want to answer until it's finished. Every now and again, she thinks of asking Dominic if she might write in his flat, but she's worried it might sound like she's using it as some sort of ruse to spend more time with him. They never go to his anyway; he always comes over to hers after playwriting group, because it's closer than going back to Highgate. He doesn't stay over, though. He's travelling into central London every day to work with the other writers and the festival organisers and his place is walking distance to the tube, he's told her, whereas Mira's is a long bus ride away. Mira feels a pang of disappointment when he doesn't stay, but she can see now how it's easier that way. Plus, with Lili's boyfriend around, there'd never be enough hot water for everyone, and besides, she has to be up so early anyway, to open Flora.

And that's when it occurs to Mira that there's a solution staring right at her. She has the keys to Flora. She's the one who opens up at seven. Why not wake up earlier, come in even earlier, and write in Flora, before setting up for the day? She mentions it to Dominic; he says it's a great idea, that he always gets his best writing done first thing. She thinks about asking the owner for permission, but she's barely involved in the day-to-day running of the café; she owns lots of different businesses and hardly ever comes in, certainly not that early, leaving pretty much everything to Mira, at least during the week. And so, one morning, Mira decides to simply let herself in.

It takes her a while to get used to it; her brutal new alarm, creeping out of the flat before 5.30am. Sometimes Dominic texts her to check that she's awake, to encourage her to keep going. It's almost impossible to get enough sleep as it is, what with Lili and her boyfriend always making noises that Mira doesn't want to have to think about. But her body adjusts to this new rhythm, and it's perfect, being in the café before anyone else is in, while it's still and the light outside is soft and the traffic sleepy. The café is always spotless in the morning, because it's Angela's job to tidy up before she finishes her last shift. Mira loves how neat it is, the chairs still set upside down on the tables, the floors mopped, the faint smell of geraniums and lavender from the cleaning products. Her thoughts feel less chaotic, less impossible than they do in the mess of her bedroom and the flat in general. If only she could be tidy like this all the time, she thinks.

One day, just before seven, she is finishing up a passage of dialogue when she hears a knock at the window. It's Samir, in his running gear. He waves at her. She waves back. He points at the door.

'Hey,' he says, as she unlocks it, looking behind her as if he is expecting to see someone else there. 'I didn't know you were open this early.'

'We're not technically open yet but I can make an exception.' She leans against the doorframe and smiles at him. 'Do you want to come in? Coffee? Your usual?'

He nods, following her inside. 'So, what are you doing here so early? Putting in some overtime?' He looks in the direction of the table she's using as her desk.

'You could say that. My own overtime. I've been writing.'

She's not entirely sure if she wanted him to know this, but she's said it now.

'Early morning writing, that's committed,' Samir says, clearly impressed. He grins at her, like a proud father.

'Samir. Stop it. Stop looking at me like that,' she says, as she sets to work, weighing out the coffee and tamping it.

'Sorry! I'm just really pleased to hear that. I'm so glad that you're doing it – you're doing something that really

139

matters to you. You know, I really believe you can do this. I admire you, following your dreams like this. Not many of us do.'

'Thanks.' Mira is touched. She turns and reaches behind her for a mug, and places it in position on the coffee machine. 'I don't know if my dreams will ever come true,' she laughs self-consciously as she says this, 'but that really means a lot, you saying that.'

'Honestly, though. I find it super inspiring that you haven't given up. Takes a lot of courage. I can live my creative life and all my dreams vicariously through you.'

Mira snorts. 'My life doesn't feel very creative. Let's just say my living arrangements are hardly conducive to inspiring creativity.'

'Ah yes, Lili and Le Boyfriend. I take it that's why you come and work here?'

'Yeah, it's just so hard to do anything with them always there. They take up so much space.' She passes him his black Americano and he takes it from her, thanking her, complimenting her as he always does on her coffee-making skills.

After a moment Samir says, as if he's been thinking about it a while, 'You know, I might have an idea how to fix that. Your living arrangements, I mean.'

'Not again, Samir.'

Every now and then Samir tries to convince Hana to let Mira live with them, pointing out that his sister, Natasha, lived with him before she could afford a decent place of her own. But Hana and Mira have been there before: they've tried that and it didn't work.

'No, I know,' he puts up his hands placatingly. 'I know you guys say you could never live together again but I'm not talking about that. There's someone I used to work with at the bank; he's got a place in Highbury, I think.' He takes a sip of coffee. 'I'm pretty sure he said he was being seconded to one of the overseas offices for, like, six months, and these things always end up being longer. He didn't want the hassle of renting it out through an agency, and he's kind of loaded – comes from a rich Middle Eastern family I think – so he was hoping to find someone to housesit. You've done that kind of thing before, right?'

Mira is stunned. This sounds perfect. 'Well, yes. Absolutely, I've done that. I would love that.'

'No promises,' Samir says. 'I don't know if he's still up for it, but I'll look into it. I'll let you know, for sure.'

'Thank you.' She grins at him.

He laughs. 'Don't thank me yet, I haven't done anything.'

'How's Hana? Everything good? She came in the other day.'

He shrugs. 'Yeah, she's good, same as always.'

He looks at his phone uncomfortably and Mira watches him, curious now. She finds the way he does this, the way he swallows and angles his body slightly away from her at the mention of Hana's name, interesting. She makes a mental note to herself to find a way to think of how to describe a reaction like Samir's in a stage direction or a piece of dialogue, later.

He looks up. 'By the way, when she came in, did she mention the party we're having?'

'Yeah, she placed an order for it, macarons and mini cheesecakes, I think. Do you need to change something?'

'No, I mean – didn't she ask you to come?'

Mira laughs. 'No. Not unless her ordering macarons and cheesecakes was her way of asking me.'

141

'Well, in that case, I'm asking you. We're having a party. Save the date, two weeks on Saturday. The day before your birthdays.'

Mira squirms. 'Ah, you know, I'm not really into the whole birthday—'

It's true, she really isn't. It's one of the few things she has in common with Hana; neither of them enjoys their birthday. Their mother loved to make a fuss over the day, throwing them elaborate shared parties which they never asked for. Only, instead of inviting their school friends, she'd invite her artist friends. Before the girls got to blow their candles out, she'd raise a toast to herself, to celebrate what she called her 'double birthing day'. Much as they loved their mother, both Mira and Hana found this excruciating.

'What is it about you two and birthdays?' Samir asks. 'It's not technically a birthday party. But put it this way, there may or may not be birthday cake too. If there is, Hana won't know about it. And you won't either.'

Mira raises a brow. 'Good luck with that.'

'Honestly, come along. It will be good to have you. You can hang out with my friends and not Hana's snobby ones. And, hey! Maybe I'll ask Raef, the guy with the flat, if he's around, and if he is, you guys can talk about it. What do you say?'

Mira narrows her eyes and tilts her head from side to side as if to say, maybe.

Later, it occurs to Mira that if Hana and Samir are throwing a party then things must be okay between them. Whatever has happened, she is relieved that they've sorted it out. But she's also relieved for herself, because it makes her feel a little less guilty about the play.

Because they are both so busy with their writing, it's hard for Mira and Dominic to find time to see each other, but she still feels connected to him. He asks her how she is, how the writing is going, sends her interesting links to articles and songs from his playlists. He offers to walk over when she's working and see her in action in Flora. She says she'd love him to but she might end up distracted and spill coffee over her customers. *Ah yes*, he texts, *I wouldn't want you to lose your job.* He sends her the popcorn emoji in a reference to her previous clumsiness. The play for the festival is taking up more and more of his time, but Mira loves the fact that they both value what the other does, that he takes her writing seriously, too.

One week, he's so busy with the festival that he has to cancel playwriting group; Mira finds out in an email he sends to everyone. She wonders why he didn't text her and tell her about it first, but it's not a big deal. They'd agreed that they wouldn't make it obvious to anyone at playwriting group that they're dating, so she guesses it might be that. Or he was just too busy to mention it. She understands, she really does. She texts him:

Mira: Hey! What a shame about Thursday. Hope it's all going okay. Listen, I was thinking we haven't spent much time together lately. Let's do something at the weekend.
Dominic: I'd love that x

Mira, a few days later: Hey, so still up for this weekend? I'm going to make sure I meet my goal of finishing one more scene, and then you can be my reward ;)
Mira: Hey, everything okay?
Mira, on Friday: ?
Mira, after the weekend has been and gone: What's going on?

Eighteen

It's nearly 9am and the café door is locked, though it should have been open half an hour ago. It is Friday, the day before the party, and Hana has taken the day off to run errands and prepare. She's waiting outside the café, impatient. Several potential customers have been and gone, confused as to why they can't get their coffee this morning. It's only when Hana rings Mira for the fifth time that she picks up.

'Hana, sorry, I can't talk I'm late for work—'

'Where are you?'

'I'm late for work—'

'I know you're late for work, so does half the neighbourhood. Where are you?'

'What do you mean? Wait, where are you?'

'I'm outside your place of employment. At least six people have come and gone and asked why you're closed. As if I should know. If your boss finds out—'

'Shit! Shit! I'm literally two minutes away, I'm right round the corner. If anyone's waiting tell them I'm on my way—'

'Well hurry up then!'

Hana looks at her phone, but Mira has already hung up.

Ten minutes later, Mira comes running round the corner, her backpack flying off one shoulder, an oversized shirt unbuttoned over a vest, keys in hand.

'Shit! I'm sorry! I'm sorry!'

Mira tries and fails to unlock the door, her hands fumbling with the keys. When the door does open, she practically falls in. Hana follows her. Mira rushes straight to the back to hang her bag up and wash her hands as fast as she can. She ties an apron around her waist while flicking on the switches for the coffee machine and the oven.

'Hana, have you got a minute. Would you mind, please, giving me a hand? Please? Angela isn't coming in today, it's just me. You know I wouldn't ask but I'm so behind on setting up and—'

For a second Hana looks appalled, but then she says, 'Fine. But I'm not wearing an—'

Mira throws an apron at her.

'I'm really only here to check on my order, by the way,' Hana says.

'What order?' Mira's busy opening and closing cupboard doors, seemingly at random. She motions to Hana to help set down the chairs, but Hana doesn't move from her spot.

'Mira, my order. The macarons and the mini cheesecakes! For the party tomorrow. I texted you my order!'

'Oh, *that* order. It's all fine. I placed extra with our bakery suppliers and they'll be in the morning delivery so yes, I told you already, I'll pick them up and bring them tomorrow.'

'Fine,' Hana says. 'Good.'

'Satisfied?'

'Yes. Thank you,' she adds.

'So are you going to just stand there or can you help me with these chairs?'

Hana helps Mira set up, turning the chairs over while Mira puts out the pastries. By way of thanks, Mira makes her a flat white and gives her an almond croissant on the house. Hana protests, asking Mira if she even knows how many calories are in those things, until Mira waves her impatiently away in the direction of the tables.

Hana nibbles at the croissant while she drinks her coffee. She glances at her phone but she can see Mira in her peripheral vision, still trying to do ten things at once, and it's distracting. The café starts to fill up. Hana overhears someone placing their order and when Mira repeats it back to them, reading off her notepad, she says orange juice instead of apple juice and a plain croissant instead of a chocolate one, and they have to correct her and start all over again, and when she passes someone else the card machine, she's forgotten to put the price in and laughs nervously, saying how silly she is, that she must have been away with the fairies. When a young mother comes in with her toddler, she asks Mira twice for the children's menu but Mira doesn't bring it. The mother looks impatient, like she has to be somewhere soon, and so Hana smiles at the toddler, wiggles her fingers in a wave and then reaches behind her and passes her the menu herself. It's almost painful to watch Mira's mistakes. When the morning rush is over and the woman and her baby have left and there's no one else but Hana and Mira there, Mira throws her head back, arching her back, sighing loudly.

'What's going on with you?' Hana says.

'Sorry?'

'You turn up two hours late for work—'

'I was not that late—'

'You got at least two orders wrong. You almost forgot to charge someone. You're obviously distracted. And you look exhausted.'

She reaches out for Mira's chin so that she can scrutinise her face, but Mira pulls away.

'I didn't realise you were making notes. What are you, a café critic?'

'So go on then, what's wrong?'

'Nothing. I'm fine.'

'You don't look fine. You're acting all weird. I thought you liked this job.'

'I do!'

'Then you'll have to try harder to keep it, Mira.'

At this, Mira looks for a moment as if she might cry and Hana, realising she might have gone too far, tries to change the subject.

'How's your writing going?' She tries to sound enthusiastic.

Mira doesn't say anything.

'Did you manage to enter that prize yet, or—'

'No.'

Mira rubs her forehead. In front of her is a tray of upturned glasses. She begins drying them slowly with a tea towel, setting each one down firmly.

'Well, hadn't you better get a move on—'

'No, Hana,' Mira repeats, louder now. 'No, I haven't finished the play. Just like you knew I wouldn't finish the play. Just like I always don't finish things. Just like I always "fail to accomplish".'

She mimics Hana's voice, does the speech marks. She picks up another glass, dries it, puts it down hard on the counter. She keeps going, setting them down harder and harder, until one of them slips off the counter and falls on the floor, smashing into little pieces.

'All right,' Hana says, getting up. 'All right, now. Let's just calm—'

Mira covers her face as she begins to cry, sobbing into her hand. Slowly, she slides down the cabinet so that she's sitting on the floor, pressing her knees together like a child.

'Oh,' Hana says.

She looks at the little bits of broken glass on the floor and deliberates, unsure whether to sweep them up first or go to her sister. But Mira makes another shuddering, sobbing sound, so Hana picks her way reluctantly over the shards, hesitantly, joining Mira on the floor. At first she doesn't say anything, not knowing how to begin. But Mira is crying even more now.

'Oh,' Hana says again. 'Mira. What's going on with you?'

She puts her arm around her sister and rubs her hand briskly up and down Mira's forearm as if to warm her up. Then she stops, abruptly.

'Why . . .?' she asks. 'Why don't you ever tell me when something's wrong?'

Mira lets out a little teary laugh at the earnest expression on Hana's face. 'Why do you think, Han?'

'I know you don't think I care, Mira, but I do. I'm not that heartless. I do care. I have to.' She hopes it hasn't come out as begrudging as it sounds to her own ears.

Mira says nothing.

'So, do you want to talk about why you're smashing glasses on purpose?' She gestures with her hand at the mess. Mira looks as if she's about to say something, but then she hesitates, reaches up to touch the back of her neck.

'No. Only, all men are dicks.'

'Ah,' Hana nods as if now everything makes sense. 'Yes. Yes, that they are—'

'No offence to your husband.'

'He has his moments.'

There is a pause and then Hana says, 'We're trying for a baby.' She leans her head back against the unit.

Mira turns to look at her sister, her mouth gaping in surprise. She wipes her eyes, blinks lots. 'That's amazing, Han.'

Hana smiles, turning her rings around on her fingers.

'Is it, like, IVF or are you—?'

'What? No, we're trying, as in trying-trying. What makes you think we'd need IVF?'

Mira shrugs, abandoning the memory of overhearing Hana and Samir's argument. 'No reason. Will you tell me, as soon as you . . .?'

Hana shoves Mira sideways with her shoulder. They sit quietly for a minute.

'So,' Hana asks slowly. 'Who is he?'

'His name's Dominic. We met at my playwriting group.' Mira doesn't say anything else.

'Do you want to tell me anything about him?'

'No.' Mira sighs. 'But I really liked him.'

Hana nods, understanding.

Then Mira says, 'We were dating for, like, five weeks. That's not nothing, is it?'

'It's not nothing, no.'

'And then he just disappeared. He ghosted me.'

'What? No explanation at all? Nothing?'

'Not a thing. And I thought everything was going fine, it was going great. But now, nothing. Doesn't reply to my texts. Doesn't answer his phone.'

'Do we think he might have lost his phone?'

'No! He could have emailed!'

'Well, then, you're right. He's an idiot. He's a total dick.' Hana's face is serious, her eyebrows raised high for emphasis. Mira laughs, she's never heard Hana use that word

149

before. It's funny, hearing her say it. 'God, it makes me so angry that there are men who think they can get away with behaving like this. I see this sort of thing, this entitlement, all the time at work. Bunch of pricks.'

Mira touches Hana's arm.

'Han. Are *you* okay?'

Hana ignores her. 'But if you could just let me say this one thing, Mira—'

'Hana.' Mira covers her face with her hands. 'I really don't want one of your lectures right now.'

Hana pulls her hands away. 'Look at me, for God's sake. I'm not going to lecture you. I was only going to say, Samir told me how you've been working really hard on your play. He said you've been coming here early to write. And I . . . I haven't seen you be so dedicated to something in a long time. I was only going to say, I think that's brilliant. Honestly, I think it's amazing. I think writing . . . it's good for you.'

Mira looks at her sister, wipes her nose with the heel of her hand.

'Do you mean that?' she asks.

'I do. And I don't think you should let your momentum drop just because of this. It's the worst thing you could for productivity. Keeping your momentum going is everything.' Hana shrugs, matter of fact. 'There's always going to be men like him, like this Dominic, who act like idiots. Don't let them – don't let *him* – distract you. Focus on your writing. Focus on moving forwards with your work, instead of standing still. That's all I mean. Don't just give up.'

Nineteen

Mira hasn't given up, not really. It's just that she's not been able to write anything since Dominic ghosted her. She's shocked by everything Hana's said. Hana sounds as if she actually might be proud of her. She's told her to keep on writing. She's never heard Hana say anything like this before. Mira laughs softly, not because anything Hana's said is remotely amusing but because she's sad and moved at the same time and there seems to be no other way to express this.

'What?' Hana asks. 'What's so funny?'

Mira moves her head closer to Hana's, so that their foreheads are almost touching. She takes Hana's chin in her fingers, holding it lightly. Hana looks at her suspiciously as Mira studies her features, touching the angles of Hana's face like it is the petal of a flower. She thinks of that childhood refrain, *loves me, loves me not*. In a way, she's spent her whole life wondering just that, if she's loved, if she's not. She shudders involuntarily, as she takes her next breath. In that moment, she realises that she is loved, by Hana, the one person she has in the world, and the thought of that catches in her throat.

'What are you doing?' Hana bats Mira's hand away. 'You're being weird! Why are you being weird? Why are you touching my face? Don't touch my face!' Hana jerks her head back, out of the way.

'I'm glad you're here,' Mira says in a gentle tone. She shifts so that she's sitting up straight.

They sit next to each other, their arms folded over their knees, not saying anything. It's enough. Enough to speak for all the years buried between them, behind them, before them; all the years they've spent hating each other, loving each other, like this.

When they hear a customer come in, Hana shouts from the floor, 'We're closed, there's been an accident.'

There's a shuffle and the customer calls out, 'Sorry!'

Hana gets up and quickly walks to the front of the café and flips the sign on the door around to 'Closed'.

She comes back into the kitchen and looks at Mira with a comical yet annoyed expression. 'If you heard someone say there'd been an accident, would you honestly just leave? Would you not check that everything's okay? I mean, we could have lost limbs back here with all this broken glass—'

She slides back down to sit next to Mira and carries on talking, arguing with the imaginary customer, righteous, indignant. Mira puts her head on Hana's shoulder and closes her eyes and lets her speak, listens to her going on and on, until she feels okay, until she feels steadied again.

Later, when Mira has washed her face and Hana has swept up the broken bits of glass, and it's time for Hana to go because she has a couple of beauty appointments booked ahead of the party, Hana looks at Mira and squeezes her arm hard. She says, 'Just come to the party tomorrow, won't you? I promise, no one knows it's our birthday.' Then, when she's by the door, she calls out, 'And anyway, you have to come! You have to bring my order!' without looking back. But Mira knows that what Hana's really trying to say is, she wants her there.

After Hana leaves, the rest of the day passes in a blur. Mira makes herself some toast and then takes her phone out of her pocket and quickly, before she can change her mind, deletes all of Dominic's text messages. There. That makes her feel better. She looks around defiantly, half expecting an audience to applaud her.

She flips the sign on the door back round to 'Open'. It's a busy Friday afternoon; a steady stream of orders for coffee and cake to take away, freelancers wanting to sit at the bigger tables with their laptops, the before and after school-run rush. Without Angela there, Mira has to handle it all on her own. And she does. She keeps hearing Hana's advice to keep moving. And so that's what she does.

As soon as she gets home though, the day catches up with her. She feels ready to crawl into bed, exhaustion tapping on her shoulder. At least she doesn't have to work tomorrow. She takes in her room. It is a total state; half-filled glasses of stale water left on every surface; a crumpled pile of yesterday's clothes turned inside out on the floor. She flops onto the mattress, face down, and pulls a pillow over her head. Tomorrow, she thinks, she'll deal with it tomorrow.

She's still lying in this position when Lili walks into the room without knocking. Mira lifts a corner of the pillow. She can see Lili's feet.

'Lili, what? Why are you here?' Mira's voice is muffled. She's still embarrassed about the scene with the speaker wires. She takes the pillow off her face and looks at Lili sideways. Her eyelashes feel crusty, mascara flaking off. 'I'm sorry. I'm very tired. I mean, what's up?'

'Eric and I have decided. We are moving in together.'

Lili wiggles her hip to the side and taps her foot on the floor three times.

Mira lies very still for a moment and then, summoning the last of her energy, rolls over and sits up. It takes her a moment to understand what Lili is telling her.

'Wow. Congratulations,' she says. 'Where are you moving to?'

Lili laughs. 'We are not moving. You are! He is moving here!'

Mira looks at her, confused. 'Excuse me?'

'He is in. You are out.' Lili is impatient now. 'You can't stay. You are not a nice flatmate. You have gone crazy, you throw your stuff around, you shout at me—'

'Wait, *I'm* not a nice flatmate?' Mira starts, but then she feels bad again. When she next opens her mouth to speak, the tone of her voice is more conciliatory. 'Lili, I'm so sorry about what happened with the speakers. You know that. And I've apologised countless times. It was just a really, really bad day.'

'Every day is a bad day with you—'

'What! That's not fair, that's not even true,' Mira protests.

'You are a nightmare these days. You have to leave. We want you gone as soon as possible. Two weeks, maximum.'

'What?' Mira stands up and pushes the hair that is stuck to the sides of her face out of the way. 'You have to be joking Lili. That's not . . . you can't just . . . I need to find somewhere else to live. Don't you have to give me notice? I'm sure you have to give me notice—'

Lili laughs. 'This is my parents' apartment. I can do what I want.'

She leaves the room and Mira rushes out behind her, following her into the kitchen. Lili starts clattering dried pasta into a pan.

'Lili,' Mira says. 'Lili, we can sort this out! Do you know what? It doesn't make a difference if Eric moves in. He's here all the time anyway and we're managing, aren't we, the three of us? I'm up and out way before you in the mornings, so we don't ever have to fight to use the bathroom. And we can draw up a rota to take care of the tidying. You know, we should have done that ages ago—'

'No, no. You're not understanding. We want this flat to be for just the two of us. Me and him, not me and him and you—'

'Lili, please.'

'You're sad because your man left.'

'What? No, I'm not. Even if I was, it was just a little bit. And anyway, how do you know? And what's that got to do with all of this?'

'He left you because you make such a mess.'

'What? I don't think that's fair. I'm a lot neater than you are.'

'No, your life, you make such a mess of your life! You say, "Lili, put the volume down, I'm writing." All the time, you are writing – writing, but nothing comes of it.'

Mira stares at Lili, openmouthed.

'That's not a very nice thing to say, Lili.'

Lili points at herself, jabbing her chest. 'I have plans. I want to start my own marketing agency as soon as I've handed in my dissertation. So I need your room to be my office.'

'But, two weeks, Lili,' Mira repeats. 'That's just not enough time.' She races through the options in her mind. She has to live somewhere nearby, for Flora, and the only person who lives that close is Hana.

'I don't know why you live here anyway,' Lili says. 'When your fancy sister, she lives in Muswell Hill. Why don't you save your money, stay with her?'

Mira looks at her, incredulous that she has read her mind. 'It's not . . . it's just not as simple as that, okay? Some things are complicated. Do you know what, why am I even explaining myself to you? It's none of your business!'

'Fine. But it has to be two weeks, wherever you go. I don't care, because Eric has to move out of his old place and he will need somewhere to store his stuff before we rearrange things and make my study so—'

'God! I can't believe you! I can't believe you'd do this to me! After everything I've put up with from you!' Mira stomps back to her bedroom. She slams the door.

Twenty

Hana's on her way home from the hairdressers when it starts to rain. At first it's only a very light summer drizzle, so light Hana isn't even sure if it's raining at all. She stands on the pavement, an open palm turned upwards, before deciding that it is nothing. She's still a few minutes' walk away from home when the sky suddenly darkens, as if a child had knocked over a pot of grey paint across the heavens, and in an instant the rain is falling thicker and faster. Hana looks about her in a panic, she hadn't thought to carry an umbrella in the middle of an unseasonably hot August. By the time she's through the front door, the rain is falling in sheets, as loud as a standing ovation. She stands in the hallway, water dripping off her, astonished. Her newly perfect hair is ruined, stuck like pieces of string to her face. She shivers.

'Samir. Samir, are you there?' she calls up the stairs. 'Samir!'

She looks in the mirror and touches her disastrous hair with her hand. She begins twisting pieces around her fingers, squeezing the water out of the ends. She is doing this when Samir jogs down the stairs.

'My hair!' She turns to him, her expression helpless. 'The rain.'

'Ah.' He makes a what-can-you-do-about-it face. 'Unlucky.'

'Unlucky?' she repeats. It is only rain, she knows her hair is not the end of the world, but still, she's disappointed.

She's upset. It matters to her that everything be perfect for tomorrow's party. She's taken the day off, which she hardly ever does, so that she might for once feel good about herself. She doesn't know why he needs her to explain all of that, to spell out everything about how she feels. She doesn't know why he can't just tell, why he can't just know instinctively what she needs from him, and when. She wonders what it would take for him to console her, to join in and commiserate.

'Sorry,' he laughs. He bites his bottom lip. 'Sorry. You're right. It's not funny. It's . . . unfortunate.' He turns overly serious and steps towards her, puts his hand on her shoulder and squeezes. 'Hana. I'm truly sorry for the loss of your blow-dry.'

More and more, mocking her seems to have become Samir's default reaction to anything Hana does or says. And though, once, a very long time ago, she might have found it funny, now she finds it cruel, as if it's a game to him, belittling her. She knows, though, that he wouldn't believe her if she told him that this is how she feels; he would find something else to make her feel small. He whistles as he walks off in the direction of the kitchen.

'Tea?' he calls out.

She straightens her shoulders. 'Later,' she calls back. 'I'll make one myself, later.'

Upstairs, she changes out of her wet clothes and in the process, she realises she's started her period. She stares at her underwear, at first not feeling any particular emotion. This surprises her. Maybe she's simply getting used to the inevitable disappointment. They'll try again. What else is there to do?, she thinks grimly. She lets out a long breath, decides she won't mention it just yet to Samir. It's only when she starts to sort herself out with a sanitary towel that she realises her fingers are shaking.

By morning it's warm again but it's still raining thickly, the leaves on the trees and the lawn slick and shiny, the paving stones stained two shades darker, little puddles gathering in the corners. Hana looks out of the kitchen doors in despair. Samir is on his laptop, the screen angled away from her.

'Shouldn't Leo be here by now? Didn't you say he was coming at ten?'

'Who?'

'Samir. Leo. To do the garden.'

'Oh. Yeah, so no.'

'No what?'

'He's not coming.'

'What do you mean, he's not coming? Why?'

Samir points to the window without looking away from his screen.

'He's not coming because of the rain?'

He shrugs.

'Why did you leave him to the very last minute? He could have come yesterday.'

'It was raining yesterday, too.'

Hana spends the morning unpacking the online drinks order, texting Bridget, her cleaner, and double-checking what time the caterers will be delivering the grazing boards. She calls Mira several times to check on the dessert order and also to see that she's okay after yesterday – and make sure she is still definitely coming – but Mira doesn't answer. By midday, she's done everything on her to-do list. Her guests won't arrive until three o'clock. Hana can't help but feel a little restless, as if she needs to do something with her hands to feel productive. Though it's still relatively early to get ready, she goes upstairs and decides she will blow-dry her hair herself after yesterday's fiasco. After a long shower, she's standing in the bedroom with her head upside down, the hairdryer on max, when Samir comes in and touches her between the shoulder blades. She startles at his touch through her robe, whips her head back in a panic.

'God, Samir. You scared me.'

'I got you this.'

He holds out a large square cardboard box, grinning inanely, like a child giving someone a present. Her hands full with the hairdryer and brush, Hana looks at him, the exasperated expression on her face making it clear she doesn't know what he expects her to do with it. She tosses the hairdryer and the brush onto the bed and takes the box from Samir. With nowhere else to put it, she sets it down on the carpet.

'Just open it,' he says.

'What is it?'

'Just open it. Look.'

'I don't like surprises.'

'Hana!'

Hana crouches down and scrapes at the pieces of Sellotape on the edges with her little fingernail, looking up at him warily. Samir's still beaming at her, encouraging her with his hopeful expression to open the box. She peels away the tape and then lifts up the lid. Inside, there is a large cake, the fancy, old-fashioned type from the traditional bakery in Muswell Hill, covered in white fondant icing with hard rose-coloured swirls on the edges. The words *Happy Birthday! Hana & Mira* are spelt out in dark chocolate writing with an *x* for a kiss under each of their names. It is not the sort of cake Hana would have chosen for herself.

'What is this?'

'It's for you. And Mira. For the party.'

'But, why? It's not a birthday party.'

'I thought it would be nice. I was going to keep it a surprise, but I wanted you to see it first. I thought it might cheer you up after this morning, make up for the rain spoiling your hair yesterday and Leo not coming for the garden. I know you were disappointed—'

'But it's not a birthday party.'

Hana stands up and takes a step back and looks at him. 'Samir, you didn't tell people, did you? That it's a surprise party for our birthday? Please tell me you didn't do that—'

He opens his mouth a little.

'Samir!'

'All our friends will be here! I just thought it would be nice,' he says. 'It's literally your birthday tomorrow, what's the big deal? You're the one who's been saying we haven't done anything fun for a while. Wouldn't you like to have your friends sing you "happy birthday" and blow out candles with Mira? It's a reason to celebrate—'

She raises her hands in the air. 'Samir, I'm not five years old. And we've both told you how much we really, really don't like birthday parties. Mira's not going to care.'

He looks at her pleadingly.

'Fine,' she says. 'Fine. I'm sure it'll be lovely. We'll put it on the table. With the other desserts I've already ordered.'

'Hana. It's just a cake—'

'Of course. And like I said, we'll put it out with everything else. Everything else I've already planned.' She emphasises the word 'already' making her general disappointment felt.

Samir looks at the floor, turns to leave, and then he stops at the doorway and turns around. 'You know, you could at least say thank you.'

She stands with her hands by her sides, astonished. 'I did.'

'You didn't.'

For a moment neither of them says anything. They just keep looking at each other. And then Samir drops her gaze.

'My God,' he murmurs. 'Do you have any idea how hard it is to live with someone like you? Do you know how hard it is to know that whatever you do, no matter how simple or well-intentioned, it will always be the wrong thing? To know that you can never do anything right, that you will always be a disappointment?'

Hana stands, hands by her side, not knowing what to say. Samir touches his fingers together, the tips brushing his lips. He stares intently at the floor.

'You know, I wasn't going to say anything. I wasn't going to spoil this day for you, this day that you have for some reason so desperately . . . wanted, to show everyone that, I don't know, things are going so well for us. For you.'

He gestures in her direction, still not looking at her. 'But I have to say, Han, I have to say this. Has it ever occurred to you,' and now he looks straight at her with a coolness in his eyes, 'that your child, the one that you want so much – with me, apparently, in case you've forgotten – may make mistakes and let you down one day, too?

'And then what? What happens to your love then? Will they just not be good enough for you either? Will you hold their mistakes against them, the way you do everyone else? Is that the kind of parent you are going to be?' he carries on. 'Because that's cruel. That's horrible. I don't know if

I can stand by and watch that, Han. I just don't know if I can do that. I don't know if I can do any of this anymore. I don't know if I really wanted any of it in the first place.' He leaves the room without looking at her.

Hana stands frozen. She feels the floor tilting, the walls and the ceiling crowding in, the space growing smaller and smaller, tighter and tighter, until she can no longer stand. She crumples to the floor, her body numb. What can't Samir do anymore? What doesn't he want, exactly? There are too many questions crowding her mind; she can't think. She presses the heels of her hands hard into her eyes, and gently rocks back and forth. She's afraid that if she starts crying, she might not stop.

The rain stops in time for the party, and the sky is clear and full of light. Sunshine falls through the shutters in stripes on the oak floorboards. Hana has bought a new summer dress to wear, a crinkled cotton in the colour of strawberries, with ribbons to tie at the shoulders in little bows. She'd laid it out on the bed earlier, all ready like a ballgown. She looks at it now from her position on the floor. She can't imagine ever having been the person who bought it; it feels too bright, too pretty, too young, the ribbon straps fiddly and girly. It is too late, she thinks. Their guests will be here soon. And there's nothing she can do about it but blindly feel her way through the fog of desolation shrouding her. Her legs feel heavy like stone, whether it's from the period pains or everything else that's now happened, she can't say.

She gathers what's left of her strength and pulls herself up to standing. She ties up her still damp hair into a ponytail with the band around her wrist, never mind about blow-drying it now, and opens her wardrobe door. She picks out a simple heavy black linen dress with a square neckline and buttons down the front that she's had for ages, the black faded from years of washing, one of the buttons chipped, the fabric soft and creased. She wonders if she's being melodramatic, wearing black, but this will have to do now. People are arriving. She hears the doorbell ring downstairs; from outside the faint sound of bird song, the clatter of garden chairs being dragged outside. She hears the door open, Samir laughing as he greets old friends. She hears someone ask, 'Where's the birthday girl? I thought this was a surprise!' Then she hears Samir laugh again and say, 'It's not a surprise, man, she invited everyone!'

The bell rings again; more people, talking all over each other in the hallway, Samir saying, it's okay, she knows, come in, come in; then children's footsteps running about the place. There is only so long she can stay up here. She wonders whether, if she stays in their bedroom, Samir will come and fetch her. If maybe then he can explain what he meant, maybe she can say sorry. The cake box is still on the floor. She thinks of picking it up over her head, dropping it. But that wouldn't do, it would only make a mess. It wouldn't fix anything. She stares at her reflection in the mirror, thinking how ugly she is without makeup on. Mechanically, she dabs concealer under her eyes and blusher on her cheeks, douses herself in perfume, and then collects the cake box and goes downstairs, pretending to smile.

Somehow, she endures the party. And it is a fine party, all things considered. Her guests are having a good time; that's important. No one would know, to look at her, that she's been told the thing she most feared about herself. Although, underneath her dress, her legs tremble, she manages to greet everyone warmly. They've brought small gifts and birthday cards, so many bouquets of flowers, she doesn't have enough vases. She laughs, kisses her friends on their cheeks, thanks them all, makes sure everyone has a drink and something to eat. The grazing boards look amazing, people take it in turns to stand over them and take pictures on their phones. Everyone tells her how great the party is. People are milling and the house feels full and lively, which was exactly what she wanted, wasn't it? Her friends compliment her, fawning over the house renovation and how she's decorated. The ones who've brought their children along say how thoughtful she is, to have planned something for them. Samir is the life and soul, talking loudly with his friends, his laugh like a boom. She watches him move around the room as if nothing has even happened, which is exactly what she is doing, too.

From the corner of her eye, while talking to her old school friends, she watches him with one of his single female friends from college. He kisses her cheek, tells her how fabulous she looks, makes a big show of telling her she smells good, all the while his hand pressed to the small of her back. His over-exuberance makes Hana feel sick. She feels like grabbing someone, any one of her guests, holding onto their wrists and blurting out that it's all fake, the whole party is just for show, that she's not okay, no. But, of course, she doesn't. She wouldn't ever do that. Instead, she smiles and makes conversation with her friends and talks about work with her colleagues, all the while feeling like she is somewhere else. She's in an audience, observing herself impassively in a scene from a film. Her mind plays tricks on her, showing her glasses she could break or plates of food she could throw, little things she could do that could add some drama, shatter this perfect set-up.

Mira still hasn't arrived. Hana calls her several times, smiling at people as she walks through the house, her phone pressed to her ear. Upstairs, alone on the landing, she hisses into Mira's voicemail, 'What's wrong with you? Why aren't you here? Where are you? Look, I'll need those desserts soon, so you'd better be on your way. Samir's gone and bought this birthday cake, and it's got your name on it as well as mine. It's just awful. So if you're not here, it's going to look even more stupid. So, just, please. Hurry up and get here. It's all . . . it's all awful. It's the worst possible thing. Mira, I need—' but then the signal cuts off and she stares at her phone. You, she was going to say. I need you here.

From somewhere behind her she hears a commotion, a flurry of giggles and shushes, senses small sets of eyes watching her. When she turns around, there are two children, an older girl and a smaller boy, pressed together. Sadie's children – Annabel and Oscar. Annabel stares at her unsmiling, unfriendly, holding onto her little brother by his clothes. But Oscar smiles at her, his nose crinkled, his round face shining with delight. He crosses and uncrosses his legs and looks at her through his choppy fringe, making an O shape with his mouth. He is wearing denim shorts that fall past his knees and a little white button-down; his cheeks have caught the sun, like over-ripe peaches, and his eyes are big, wondrous. He is so beautiful, Hana thinks, marvelling at him. He is so beautiful that her heart might actually break. He looks at her expectantly, as if he thinks she's a nice kind lady who might hand him an ice cream or give him a toy. The girl, whose face is long and thin and looks alarmingly like a stern, tiny version of Sadie, says to Hana, 'You said stupid.'

Hana is thrown off guard. 'So what if I did,' she says quickly. She has no time for this. 'I'm allowed to say what I like. It's my house. But you're not allowed to be up here. Off you go. Go on, downstairs. Don't come up here again.' She points her finger, speaks more sharply than necessary.

Annabel looks at her crossly. Oscar looks as if he might cry. Hana feels stung, watching his little body go, the way he lands, a little clumsily, on each step, reaching up for the banister rail. But she's said it now, and there's nothing she can do to take it back.

Twenty-one

When Mira finally arrives at the party, she has to ring the bell twice, balancing the three boxes of macarons Hana had ordered from Flora between her thighs and the brick wall, until someone she doesn't know lets her in. They disappear before she has a chance to thank them. From the hallway, she can see people standing around the open-plan kitchen holding glasses and laughing loudly. She can't believe how many people Hana has invited. She tries to shut the front door with her leg, still holding the boxes, and for a split second she can see herself dropping them. It's exactly the kind of thing Hana would expect her to do. Finally, she manages to close the door and then she looks about her. She doesn't recognise anyone. Everyone is still wearing their shoes. The men are wearing shirts with the sleeves rolled up to their elbows, pastel-coloured chino shorts and deck shoes; the women are all in gingham or floral summer dresses and Saltwater sandals. Instantly, she regrets coming. Mira is wearing the same outfit she was wearing yesterday, pale jeans and a striped shirt unbuttoned over a vest.

She notices two young people carrying platters of cheeses and artfully arranged fruit and vegetables through to the open-plan kitchen, where they're putting together the finishing touches. Mira resists the urge to ask if they need any help, which seems like a better option than having to socialise. She can't quite believe, either, that Hana hired caterers for tonight, but, then again, she can. With Hana, everything has to be formal, arranged. It surprises Mira how clean and tidy the house still is, even though there are so many people in it. Then she notices Hana's cleaner, Bridget, in the living room, handing out bags of popcorn to the children, talking to them in an animated way. Mira is surprised to see her and also relieved, because she likes Bridget; here is someone she can talk to. Mira has met her a few times, at Hana's house, and Bridget, an older woman in her late fifties, has always been so friendly. But then she understands that Bridget is only here because Hana must have asked her to help out, to watch the children and tidy up behind people. And Mira feels embarrassed that Hana would ask such a thing.

In the kitchen she sets down the boxes of macarons on the counter and, because she can't think of anything else to do, helps herself to a drink. Samir sees her and comes over to where she's standing. He puts his arm around her forcefully and says 'Here she is!' so loudly that people look over in their direction and she spills some of her drink.

He's wearing an Arsenal football shirt and a pair of navy shorts in jogging-bottom fabric, as if he forgot people were coming over.

'Nice outfit.'

He puts his thumbs up, then kisses her on both cheeks. He holds her shoulders tightly and shakes her from side to side. 'Birth-day-girl!' he says, in time to the swaying. 'It's yo birthday!' he sings, his hand beating through the air to an imaginary bass line.

'I thought this wasn't a birthday party,' she says, looking around her hesitantly, wishing he'd stop.

Samir laughs as though she has said the most hilarious thing, so loudly that people look over again. She's come to deliver the macarons, and also, more importantly, because she's hoping Samir might introduce her to the friend he mentioned, the one who's looking for someone to housesit, seeing as in a fortnight she'll be homeless.

'Is your friend here? The one with the flat?'

'Lots of my friends are here.'

Mira knows from the drunkenness that something must have happened between him and Hana who hates it when he drinks. The football shirt makes sense now, too, another clue that they must have argued, otherwise there's no way Hana would have let him wear that with people coming over.

'But the guy with the flat,' she says again, 'is he here?'

'He'll be here, don't worry, I'll talk to him, it's all in hand. But first, let me introduce you to some people. There's tons of folk I want you to meet.'

Mira puts a hand on his arm to tell him there's no need, but Samir has already jumped away from her and, out of nowhere, he grabs a woman by the shoulders and steers her away from the little group she's standing in over towards Mira. The woman is tall and thin, with a bob haircut that is longer at the front than at the back, and she's wearing long earrings that look like ancient gold coins. He introduces them, tells Mira her name is Alicia and that they've known each other for years, both of them having moved from the States at the same time, and then says that she simply has to meet Alicia's husband.

'He does the sort of stuff you do,' he says.

Mira doesn't know what he means by this so she just smiles at Alicia stupidly. When Alicia asks what Mira does, she says she works in a café.

'Is that what your husband does too?' She immediately feels stupid, because Alicia looks so rich, it's obvious he doesn't. Alicia takes a long sip of her drink, shaking her head. Her earrings hit the side of her face. Mira stands there, glad she at least had the foresight to pour herself a drink so that she's got something to hold in her hands. She doesn't, at first, notice Samir bringing the husband over, dancing behind him as if he's doing the conga. She's startled when Samir says in his loud, booming voice, 'Here he is. Found him!'

As Mira turns towards him, she takes in a small involuntary breath. Her eyes fall on Alicia's husband's face and Samir says, 'So, Dom, Mira; Mira, Dom!'

Mira momentarily glances at Dominic but she's so unsettled she can't bear to look at him and quickly lowers her eyes. She can hear Samir and Alicia talking but can't follow whatever it is they are saying, painfully aware of Dominic in her peripheral vision. She catches a flash of his hands by his side, his dark jeans, the cuff of his shirt folded back. He's wearing a wedding ring. Mira's never seen him wear a wedding ring before. She can smell limes, the scent of his tangy aftershave. It's too confusing; she feels disorientated, feels her heart banging. She brings her fingers to her forehead, acutely aware of the light falling sharply through the open doors, and shapes of people standing in little clusters. Everything sounds louder, the sound of people talking and laughing, the scrape of cutlery on plates, glasses clinking. She swallows hard and then somehow manages to interrupt whatever Samir is saying with, 'Excuse me, I'm sorry, just one moment,' and then she sets her glass down on the counter and runs out of the kitchen. On her way out, she brushes past Hana who says, 'There you are! Well? Did you bring them?' and when Mira ignores her, Hana calls out, 'Where are you going?'

A small child she doesn't know calls, 'You're not allowed upstairs,' but Mira mumbles about it being an emergency and goes upstairs anyway. She locks herself in the guest room ensuite and stands with her head hanging over the bathroom sink. She splashes water on her cheeks and presses the backs of her hands to them. She looks into the mirror now and presses her fingers hard into her skin, as if pushing something that has fallen out back in. Then she lies down on the bathroom tiles, pressing her back into their flat coldness, and stays there.

Eventually, there is a knock on the bathroom door and Hana calls out her name and asks what's wrong and what on earth she's been doing in there for so long.

'Nothing. Nothing's wrong.' Her voice comes out flinty. 'I just felt a little dizzy. I think it's the heat. I think the heat got to me.'

'Do you need anything?'

'No.' Mira thinks she might cry.

'By the way, where are the macarons?'

Mira sighs in exasperation and turns her head in the direction of the door. From the tiny gap between the door and the floor, she can see the shadow of Hana's feet. She slowly gets up and unlocks the door.

'They're obviously not in here, if that's what you mean. They're in the kitchen, on the counter. Where else do you think they would be?'

'Well, what did you leave them there for? Anyone could knock them over. You should have given them to the caterers to put somewhere safe.'

'Hana, please. Could you just not—'

'What?'

'Just stop. Stop with the constant—'

'Constant what?' Hana makes little fists with her hands next to her side and turns her voice low, speaking through her teeth. 'Constant trying so hard to keep things together because my marriage is bloody falling apart?'

Mira frowns. 'Wait, what are you talking about? Hana, what's going on?'

She reaches out for Hana, but Hana flinches, then she's gone.

Mira lies on the guest room bed on her front with a pillow over her head, unsure of what she's feeling, whether it's sadness or anger or humiliation or all three. She would like, very much, to leave, but she can't bring herself to move and doesn't know where she would go anyway, now that she's being thrown out of her flat. She can't bring herself to text her friends, to tell them what's happened; she needs a little more time to work it out for herself. She wants to remember what Dominic's wife looks like, but when she thinks of her all she can remember is the glint of her earrings and the sharpness of her collarbone; the rest of her face has blurred like wet paint on an artist's palette. Mira remembers she still has his number, though she really should have deleted it when she erased their text history. Now she starts to write and rewrite messages to Dominic to tell him she is upstairs, but it feels too risky, and besides she doesn't know what she would say or what she's even expecting. In the end she just sends him a question: *Your wife?* and then hides her phone under the duvet so that she's not tempted to stare at it and wait for his reply.

Eventually Mira opens the door and goes out onto the landing and crouches down beside the banisters, both hoping and not hoping that she might see him. The same little girl from before notices her and Mira puts her finger to her lips, like it's a secret. Finally, because there's nothing else to do, and she's hungry and thirsty, Mira goes downstairs. All the adults have moved further into the back, spilling out through the bifold doors into the garden. It's possible that Dominic might have already left, but the thought that he might not have, that he's somewhere in the same house as her this very instant, is almost too much to bear. She pauses at the kitchen threshold, not knowing what she would do if she sees him. She scans the men on the patio. When she doesn't see him, she feels disappointment rather than relief.

She wanders into the living room, feeling as if her feet are not quite touching the ground. The children are watching a film on television, sat cross-legged on the floor, each with little red-and-white striped cardboard bags filled with popcorn. She notices Bridget sitting on one of the armchairs, supervising. The shutters are closed and there is a tall white fan on. Both the cool air and the dark room seem inviting; she goes in. The animated film is about a girl who has bad luck and releases all the other bad luck that exists in the entire universe into the world. The irony is not lost on Mira. The plot is unnecessarily complicated, though, the colours in the scenes far too glaring and the girl's eyes too big. The storyline is outrageous, the girl has many unbelievable challenges, and Mira struggles to keep up, whereas the children seem to know exactly what is happening. In the end she goes back upstairs, locks herself in the bathroom and lies down on the floor again.

Twenty-two

To Hana's despair some of her friends, the ones with children, all start looking at their watches at around 8pm, saying it's about time they started to make a move. She didn't think anyone would leave this early and she's struck by quick panic. She doesn't want people to leave so early, that wasn't the plan. The house was supposed to feel full, it has to. She can't consider the alternative; she needs to prolong the moment before everyone leaves and the house falls empty, nobody left but Samir and her.

She cajoles them to stay.

'We haven't opened the macarons yet! Or would anyone like a hot drink, before you go? I can bring some blankets down if the children are feeling sleepy.'

'Oh God, no,' Allegra says, with a wave of her hand. 'We're already past bedtime. If we stay any longer, all hell will break loose tomorrow.' She winks conspiratorially at the other mothers. Between them, they summon their husbands to fetch bags and change children into pyjamas so that they can fall asleep on the way home. Hana can only smile weakly, offering the bathroom upstairs for the children to get changed in, but inside she feels the reverberation of the misstep she's made. Bedtime, of course. How stupid of her not to have realised. She imagines Allegra's conversation with her husband Will in the car heading home, criticising people like her, people without children, who just don't understand the importance of sticking to routines.

There begins a circus of protesting children being carried upstairs, limbs flailing, to get changed and brush their teeth, an overtired and out-of-tune chorus of 'But I don't want to!' and 'Well that's what we're doing, so—' playing out. Hana tries to make herself useful, turning on the lights upstairs in the family bathroom, which becomes a communal changing room, but there's not a lot she can do. Sadie realises she's forgotten toothpaste and Hana's about to offer some, when Allegra passes her a bright little tube with cartoon characters on it. Of course, Hana remembers, children don't use adult toothpaste; another mistake but at least she's saved from making it. Sadie's little boy is sleepy and he leans against his mother, trying to crawl into her lap. But Sadie puts her hand out – 'Not now, Oscar!' – because Annabel is on the edge of a meltdown, refusing to get changed in the bathroom with everyone else. Hana points down the hall.

'You can use our room, it's just on the left.'

'Thank you,' Sadie says. 'She's such a little madam, honestly. I bet you're glad you don't have to put up with any of this! Would you mind just keeping an eye on Oscar?'

Sadie gently pushes him in Hana's direction. To no one in particular, Sadie says, 'Honestly, three-year-olds are so much easier than eight-year-old girls. She's like a teenager already.'

Allegra and Amber laugh, still busy with their own children. Oscar is already in his pyjamas, a pair of yellow sleep shorts and a T-shirt with pale blue ice creams dotted all over it. Hana crouches down as he stumbles towards her. He is warm and smells like vanilla and mint. 'Do you like ice cream?' she says, gently touching his T-shirt with her fingertip. He looks down to where she is pointing, as if he's not seen the pattern before, and then nods, slowly. 'What flavour's your favourite? My favourite is . . . strawberry.' She makes her eyes big, and he smiles at her and says, 'Chocolate!' She feels the whisper of longing.

'Goodness,' she tells him quietly. 'You're gorgeous, aren't you?'

Amber raises her eyebrows. 'Could it be that our high-flier career girl is finally getting broody? Hey, Han?'

Hana just smiles, tired, and holds Oscar, resting her chin against his hair.

'Oh, I don't know.'

'See, you're a natural,' Allegra says.

Hana smiles through pressed lips, it is hard not to interpret this as anything but patronising. Now that her daughter is changed, Allegra puts her hand in the curve of her back and stretches, resting the other hand on her stomach. The conversation inevitably turns then back to Allegra's second trimester and her scan dates, both of which they've talked about in detail already. Amber's two sons are playing with the toilet paper and when she notices the trail they are making, she tells them off, orders them down the stairs. Allegra calls her husband to carry their daughter and then Sadie appears, with Annabel changed. Oscar reaches out for her, yawning like a lion cub. Hana passes him to Sadie and he looks up at her shyly through his fringe, his eyes drooping under the weight of his thick lashes. This is all she wants. This wonder.

Hana follows them all down the stairs. Now everyone is back in the hallway, clustered by the door. Sadie passes Oscar to her husband who tips him over his shoulder like a small sack of potatoes. Again, the parents say they really must go, can't believe how late it is already, what a wonderful afternoon it's been. Hana thanks them all, the perfect hostess. Out of the corner of her eye, she senses Samir coming towards her. He hasn't looked at her all night. But he's here now. She considers whether she ought to be encouraged by this. They're saying goodbye together, standing beside each other, being a couple.

Samir reaches out and ruffles Oscar's hair playfully, even though he's falling asleep. But when Hana instinctively puts her hand out to try to stop him disturbing him, Samir moves away. He spends what feels like a long time shaking hands with the dads, cracking jokes about how the party is only just getting started. Hana stands to the side and begins to feel impatience bothering her like an itch; saying goodbye is taking forever. She no longer wants them to stay. She wishes they would all just hurry up and go.

And then, finally, they do. Hana watches them leave, waiting at the door and waving as, one by one, they strap their children into their car seats and drive away. Now that it's only the adults left, someone turns the music up. Hana recognises it as the old-school nineties' hip hop that she knows Samir and his friends like. She stands on the front step. She wonders if anyone would notice if she just slipped out into the night, walked away. But she's being ridiculous. As if she would do something like that.

Back in the house, she opens the macarons and passes the boxes around, topping up drinks for the stragglers who are left. She spends a little while discussing office politics with her friends from work, and then she finds her friends from school and they sit around talking about where they've been on their summer holidays and mutual friends they've seen recently. But it's less than an hour later when the others start to look at their watches and say they should go, too. The pendulum of Hana's emotions swings back again; once more, she's not ready for them to leave, even though she's exhausted. She says, 'So soon?' in a way that is both optimistic but also a little desperate. But they insist. They say it's been lovely but they really should go; they've got early morning yoga, or work they've got to catch up on, or friends coming round for brunch or family for Sunday lunch. Another round of goodbyes on the doorstep and they are gone. They leave so quickly, it's hard for Hana not to take it personally. The only guests left now are Samir's friends, all outside in the garden.

Hana wanders through the ground floor collecting plates and glasses. As she moves through the rooms, she finds herself looking at the pictures and photographs on the walls and the decorative objects on the shelves, wondering where they all came from. None of them feel like they belong to her or like she even chose them. What did Samir mean? What can't he do anymore? What doesn't he want, exactly? The questions gather at the front of her mind again, but she can't think straight, has no answers. Wearily, she lies down on the sofa in the living room, which is where Bridget finds her.

'I went upstairs for you and I tidied the bathroom the children were all in,' she says. 'They left it in a mess.' She laughs lightly.

'Oh, Bridget, you didn't have to do that as well—'

'No, I want to make it less hard work for you tomorrow.'

Hana smiles. She is overcome by gratitude. Bridget has worked for them for five years; she's always telling Hana off, saying she works too hard. She's lovely like that. Hana worries sometimes that it's too much, asking her to clean the house though Bridget's getting older, but she says she doesn't mind. She only cleans two or three houses a week now and jokes that she's cheating because she likes to clean houses that are already tidy. She has a daughter in her twenties who is studying for a Spanish degree. Bridget is so proud of her, showing Hana photos of her on her phone at any opportunity.

Now Hana says, 'Bridget, sometimes I think you're the only person in the world who wants to make things less hard for me.'

Bridget laughs. 'Nonsense. You have that lovely husband of yours. So, tell me, did you enjoy your party, Hana?'

'Honestly? Not really, Bridget.'

'Are you sad?'

'A little bit, yes.'

Bridget pats her legs.

'You need some rest. You work too much at that job of yours.'

Hana smiles sadly. She orders a taxi to take Bridget home. As Bridget's at the front door, getting ready to leave, Hana calls for her to wait. She runs into the kitchen and picks up the birthday cake, still in its box, which in the end they didn't cut, didn't even speak about, and carries it into the hallway. She passes it to Bridget.

'We had too much,' she says.

'But this is your birthday cake!'

'No, no. It was just a joke. Samir was being silly, funny. It's a long story. Please, take it home and enjoy it.'

She presses the box into Bridget's hands. Bridget puts her hand to Hana's cheek and says, 'Happy birthday.' A thought comes to Hana then: she could ask Bridget to stay. Bridget would look after her, tell her what to do, show her how to make things right again. But then the door opens and shuts, and the taxi is gone, and there it is again, the feeling of something being over too soon.

It occurs to Hana that she hasn't seen Mira all evening. She must have left. She was acting so weird upstairs, probably still upset about that man ghosting her. Hana remembers telling Mira something about her marriage falling apart; it just came out, it's all such a blur. She feels a flash of annoyance. Of course, Mira would just disappear without telling her. Still, she makes a note in her head to message her in the morning and check that she's okay.

All she wants now is to go to bed. She walks into the kitchen, desperate for a glass of water. The bifold doors are wide open and she can see Samir and his friends outside. Someone has taken the speakers outside. Samir is sitting on top of the garden table, his back to the house, his feet planted on a chair. His friends are gathered around him and he is gesturing with his hands as he talks. He looks like a king holding court, the others all looking up to him. She doesn't want to join them. It's not like they'd expect her to, she rarely socialises with his friends unless she absolutely has to. They have very little in common, and she's certain none of them like her anyway. This doesn't bother her; she doesn't especially like them. It astonishes her that while, on paper, Samir's friends are all wildly successful, all highly intelligent, in reality they lack charisma. She's told him this before. He told her she was being judgemental and harsh.

The air is much cooler now and Hana hugs herself, warming her arms with her hands. She goes over to the doors and begins to heave them shut. It takes some effort and the doors creak, which causes everyone to turn around and look at her.

'Don't mind me,' she calls out. 'It's getting cold. Are you all okay out there? Can I bring you anything?'

Samir looks at her over his shoulder and she looks back. A cigarette dangles between his fingers. He brings it up to his lips, takes a drag, looking at her. She can't stand it when he smokes. He hasn't spoken to her the whole evening, not properly, not beyond asking if there was any food for the vegans or if they had more glasses, but it seems to her that the look he gives her now holds an entire conversation, maybe even their whole marriage.

'No,' he says. 'We're good thanks. We're okay.'

Someone says something then and someone else laughs and, slowly, Samir turns back around. Hana wipes down the counters. She leaves the lights on when she goes up to bed.

Twenty-three

Mira didn't leave. She's still exactly where Hana left her, in the bathroom attached to the guest room. When Mira wakes up, she's face down on the tiles, half of her body numb. She has no memory of falling asleep here, doesn't even know how it's possible to fall asleep on a hard tiled floor. She winces, slowly gets up to her knees and then stands shakily. Mira opens the door, practically falls down on the bed. The lights are off. She doesn't know what time it is. She reaches instinctively for her phone in her back pocket, but it isn't there. She feels on top of the bedside table and then props herself up on an elbow and flings the pillows aside one by one until she finds it. She looks at the time: it's nearly 4am. It's only when she's about to turn the screen off again that she notices two messages unread, the first sent eight hours ago, just after Mira had left the kitchen.

Dominic: been looking for you everywhere can we talk?

Dominic: don't know if you've gone, we're leaving now. i'd like to be able to explain in person, if you could allow me to. X

He had sent the second message an hour after the first. After reading them it is impossible to sleep and all she can focus on is the 'we' in 'we're leaving'. She feels a sharp pain in her stomach and realises she hasn't eaten since the morning. She

183

goes down to the kitchen and opens the fridge. A voice from behind her says, 'Can't sleep either?'

'God, Samir. You scared me.'

He's sitting in the half-dark at the table, turning a glass round and round in front of him with his fingers.

'Nightcap?'

'Something like that.'

After a while, Samir asks, 'Where'd you disappear to, anyway? You ran off.'

'Yeah, I know. Sorry about that. Nowhere. Had a head-ache.'

She opens a cupboard, takes out a plate, asks if he wants anything; he says no. She's serving herself cold pasta salad when he says quietly, almost to himself, 'I don't know if we're going to last.'

Mira says nothing. After a while, she comes to the table and puts her plate down. 'Okay.'

'We had a fight tonight. Big one, before the party. A lot of . . . cold truths spoken. Mostly by me. She acts like everything's all my fault. There's nothing I can do right. And she wants to bring a baby into this mess. Everything, everything is about this baby that doesn't even fucking exist. That I don't even know if I want.'

Mira raises an eyebrow.

'Sorry.' He exhales loudly. 'It's just a lot. There's a lot going on in my head.'

Groaning, he drops his head into his hands. They sit in silence, Mira eating; she's still so hungry. Samir sits up and pours himself another glass of something from a heavy bottle. He fidgets with the top, rolling it between his fingers before spinning it on the tabletop. Mira watches him. It's the exact sort of thing Hana would find annoying. She can see why. Then she thinks about characterisation, of how she might describe all these little gestures of panic and uncertainty, but she files the thought away; she's not going to keep writing the play, knows that it's over too.

Suddenly, Samir looks around furtively, as if he's making sure there's no one else in the room with them. He clears his throat and when he next speaks his voice is low. 'Can I be honest with you?'

Mira half-nods.

'You must know she wants kids, right?'

Mira nods again. 'She told me you're trying.'

'She told you that?' Samir looks puzzled. 'I didn't think she told anyone anything.'

Mira shrugs.

'See, I always thought I'd want kids too.' Samir shifts about uncomfortably. 'But now the more I think about it, I think I'd be fine if we didn't. Like, I wouldn't be sad about it. I'd be okay. I wouldn't feel like I'd missed out on anything. Did you see them tonight, all those parents?

'I just don't know if that's what I really want, if that's who I see myself becoming. And aside from that, the way things are with Hana and me, the constant arguing. You know, I thought it would make things better between us if I just went along with it and agreed to try for this baby to make her happy.' He fidgets with the bottle top again, this time rolling it back and forth against the table top with the palm of his hand. 'But it doesn't feel good to me, at all, to be bringing a child into this. There's no way Hana would understand. This is literally everything to her, literally, like . . . it's just so complicated. Ever since last year—'

'What happened last year?'

Samir pauses. 'So, she didn't tell you everything then?'

'Tell me what?'

'She miscarried.'

Mira's mouth falls open. 'Oh, my God, I had no idea. *Hana*. Why didn't she—'

'It happened very early. And she didn't even know she was pregnant. We weren't even trying. So I didn't think she'd be that upset about it—'

'Samir, you can't say that—'

'I know—hear me out. She was only five or five-and-a-half weeks pregnant,' he reasons. 'Technically, I don't think they even call it a miscarriage when it's that early. And it all happened pretty quickly. She was away for work when it started and by the time she got home—'

'You mean, she was all by herself?' Mira tries to imagine the reality of this, feels utterly helpless for Hana.

'Hey, I didn't even know about it until she got back from the doctors,' Samir says, a touch defensively. 'But what I'm trying to say is, to me it felt like something . . . medical, rather than a baby we'd lost, you know? I assumed, because she's so matter of fact about everything, that she'd have seen it the same way.'

Mira studies Samir, shaking her head in indignation. 'I'd say that's a pretty shitty assumption to have made.'

'So you're saying it's my fault? That things are so bad between us?—'

'I'm not saying anything is anyone's fault. But for Christ's sake, she *miscarried*—'

'Look, I'm trying here, Mir, I'm really trying to make things better. But I don't know what more I can do.' He sounds so sad. 'I don't know what to do. She wants a baby so desperately, and we're just so . . . broken. I don't know. What should I do? What would you do?' he pleads.

186

She lets out a long breath. Mira really doesn't want to get involved. She can't believe Samir might seriously think Hana wouldn't be upset about the miscarriage, no matter how early it was. But then he rubs his hand over his head, looks so miserable, she feels she has to say something, if only for Hana's sake. She tilts her head, holds out her hands like she's tipping a scale, balancing the predicament in her palms.

Choosing her words carefully, she says, 'I don't know if I'm the best person to ask. I'm obviously not an expert on marriage. But I guess you need to ask yourself what you want. Only you know the answer to that.'

He nods.

'But,' she adds quickly, 'I mean, you guys are married. That has to mean something. And how do you really know if you want a child until you've got one anyway?'

Samir turns his glass round with his fingers like he's twisting a screw. 'Can't miss what you don't have.'

'Don't know until you try,' Mira replies without missing a beat.

Samir dips his head in acknowledgement.

'You know, she was on at me to get married like a year after we met, always with the pointed remarks, "Everyone else is getting married so why can't we?" And this place,' he gestures to the ceiling with his eyes, 'this house was all her idea. Now it's the same thing with children. There's no room for manoeuvre, you know?—'

'Well, I guess not with children, no,' Mira says, abruptly. She doesn't like the way he's talking about Hana, it feels like he's going too far. Suddenly, Mira feels exhausted. All she wants is to go back upstairs, to be alone and not have to think. But Samir continues, as if she hasn't spoken.

'—And there's no room to mess up either. I don't know if she has any idea how hard I try for her, to make her happy. But she's not happy and I'm not happy. It's just not working. She looks at me every day like I'm a failure, like I'm not up to her high standards.' He pauses, passes a hand over his face. 'I love her, yeah. But I also really hate that about her. The constant criticism – it's like she doesn't know any other way to be, you know?'

'"Hate" is a strong word,' Mira says. 'And she's like that with everyone. It's her defence mechanism.'

'You two,' he's watching Mira, 'you're just so different. It's so easy to sit here and talk to you—' Then, he's reaching across the table and kissing her.

It takes Mira's brain half a second to compute what's happening, that his mouth is on hers. She shoves him backwards, hard, with both hands, then gets up and jumps away from the table, putting space between them.

'Samir, what the actual fuck?' Mira's face is screwed up. She reaches behind her for the light switch and they squint at each other in the brightness. He puts his head in his hands.

'Oh, God,' he shakes his head. 'Oh, God, no. Shit. *Shit.*' He looks up, runs his hand over his mouth. 'Shit, Mira. I'm so sorry. I'm fucked up.'

'Too right,' she agrees, outraged. 'What the *fuck* was that?'

'Shh, shh, please,' he sits up, holding out a hand. 'I don't want Hana to wake up.'

'*Now* you care about Hana?' Mira laughs bitterly. Samir gets up from behind the table and comes towards her and she shoots him a warning look as if to say, *don't even think about it.*

'I'm sorry,' he pleads, his hands clasped together in front of him. 'I'm so fucked. I don't know what just – please. Please. Don't tell Hana.'

Mira stares at him, furious. 'Whatever you're playing at, sort it out. You're an adult. Don't pull this shit on me. She's my sister . . . Unbelievable.' She glares at him, aware of how much she sounds like Hana right now. She turns, walks away, feeling not the slightest bit sorry for him.

Upstairs, she hesitates outside Hana and Samir's bedroom door, and then, almost without thinking, she opens it. Hana is asleep, breathing steadily, and Mira feels her whole body empty with relief that she's not heard anything. She has an urge to touch Hana's hair or to crawl into bed with her, lie down next to her, like they did sometimes when they were little. They did that when their mother died, too, falling asleep in the same bed, too exhausted to move. They'd come home from the hospital and, at some point, made their way upstairs, ending up in Hana's room, on her double bed, just lying there exhausted, staring at the ceiling. When Mira got up to go to her own room, Hana asked her where she thought she was going, then told her not to be stupid and gripped her arm, pulling her back down again. That memory comes back to Mira now, so close she feels it right in front of her, like a speck of dust turning in the air. But she knows that if she did this now, Hana would wake up and would want to know why Mira is acting so strange. So, she closes the door softly behind her, goes back to the guest room.

She has a compulsion to brush her teeth, and as she's doing this, furiously brushing, she thinks about Samir and what an idiot he is. Although she's mad at him, the reality of it is that the kiss, if she can even call it that, lasted barely longer than a second or so. There were no tongues, her mouth was closed: there was nothing remotely sensual about any of it. She shudders at the memory of Samir's mouth on hers, his lips cold and dry. She stares at her reflection in the mirror, closes her eyes. She thinks of Dominic and his angular wife, with her earrings and jutting-out collarbone, of all her other crappy relationships and attachments that weren't really long enough to be considered relationships in the first place, and wonders why this sort of thing always happens to her.

Undressing, she drops her clothes on the floor and finally gets under the sheets. Her body aches. She is exhausted, the corners of her feel rubbed away. It is a relief when the tears finally come. She cries just a little bit, though she's not sure for what or who exactly, before, at last, she falls asleep.

The light is thin and pale when Mira wakes up in the morning, the faint sound of Sunday morning coming in from somewhere outside. She looks at the time, it's ten o'clock. She panics; she doesn't want to see Hana or Samir this morning, and Hana never sleeps in past seven, no matter how late she went to bed the night before. She throws on her clothes, grabs her phone. But when she opens the door, the house is entirely silent in the thick, blanketed way that means everyone in it is still asleep. Before she leaves, she gently opens Hana's door and, through the crack, she sees her hair spilled out on the pillow, and she feels a spot of tenderness, a patch of warmth under her chest. Mira has no idea where Samir is; she doesn't care.

On her walk home, Mira Googles 'My brother-in-law kissed me' and concludes, after reading other people's horror stories, that nothing of significance happened. As far as the actual details of physical contact went, it was almost incidental. But at the same time, thinking about what happened makes her feel vaguely nauseous. He crossed a line, and she doubts she'll forgive him. She should tell Hana. Hana should know. But then she remembers everything else Samir said last night, about having children or not having them, and what Hana said about her marriage falling apart. That's when Mira decides it would do no good to tell Hana about it. No matter what happens now, Hana'll have all of this to deal with anyway. She doesn't need to know this on top of that. By the time she reaches her flat and unlocks the door, Mira decides to put the whole sorry incident down to a stupid lapse of judgement by Samir. Quite frankly, she doesn't want to have to think about it again.

Later, Samir messages her:

I'm so sorry.
I don't know what happened.
I have no idea why I did it. I must have drunk too much.
I have no idea what came over me.
It's the stupidest thing I've ever done.
A total moment of idiocy. So stupid. Big mistake.
Please don't tell Hana. She's perfect, I'm the one who's such a dick.

She doesn't reply. She hasn't even had a chance to process what happened with Dominic and now Samir keeps on messaging her, his messages all saying more or less the same thing, how stupid he's been, what a mistake he's made, how he didn't mean any of what he said, promising her he's going to pull himself together and be an adult like she'd said. Eventually, Mira writes back: *Jesus, I get it, enough.*

She's relieved that Lili and her boyfriend aren't home, and she takes advantage of it, taking a longer than usual shower. While she's washing her hair, she remembers it's her birthday, Hana's too. Out of the shower, she studies herself in the mirror impassively. She pulls on a long T-shirt over her underwear, wraps a towel around her head and walks to the kitchen, puts the kettle on. All she can think about is Hana and Samir and what a mess everything is for them. While she waits for the kettle to boil, she taps on her phone, sends a birthday message to Hana. Then, she starts typing another message to ask Hana if she wants to go somewhere, see a film or do something. When Hana doesn't reply to the first message, Mira suddenly feels her face turn hot and she momentarily panics, wondering whether Samir did tell her about the kiss after all. But then she thinks of all his incessant messages; no, he wouldn't dare. Still, no reply from Hana comes, and so Mira deletes the one she was composing.

She makes herself tea and toast, which she eats standing up in the kitchen, and she notices what a state the flat is in. She feels an impulse to tidy, decides it might be a good thing to do for herself on her birthday – symbolic somehow. She pulls on some leggings and runs a comb through the tangles in her hair. Then she spends three hours scrubbing, dusting, hoovering. She sorts through her laundry, changes her bed-sheets, collects old glasses of stale water from around the flat and washes them up. She empties the bins, washes down the shower door until it's sparkling. All the while, one little question just sitting there in the back of her mind: *what if?*

In her room, she sets piles of books and clothes straight and finds the old photo of her and Hana on their birth-day when they were small. She thinks of their mother, *her* mother. She reaches out and lightly touches her younger self's face. What would that little girl think, if she could see Mira now?

Mira feels restless. She wants to do something. She wants to write.

Her phone keeps buzzing with birthday messages from her friends. There are friends who every year insist they go out for her birthday, but her closest ones have come to understand that she doesn't want to and they don't think it's weird. Still, Molly texts to see how she is and check she's having a good day and to say that she's around later, if Mira changes her mind. Mira deliberates. It's tempting. She could talk to her about Dominic and the party last night. But she hasn't worked out how much she wants to share yet, needs to go over it in her head. Plus, there's that urge to write. So she thanks Molly, tells her that she's okay, that she's feeling inspired and plans to catch up with some writing, but that she'll let her know if things change. Then, to stop any further interruptions, she turns off her phone.

She sits in the living room, at the small table positioned by the window overlooking the street. She's never sat here to work before. It's always covered with piles of post. But now it's clean and clear, and it's a space where she can think. She opens her laptop, goes to her play. At first the world before her feels so distant: Natalia and Adam seem like strangers. But as she reads it, they begin to feel familiar again. It takes her a while to catch up on the life that she's written for them. She feels her away into the document, cutting and pasting, deleting commas or em-dashes, moving a line of dialogue here or there, then putting it back again. She fiddles with the stage directions.

At the time she'd abandoned the play, Mira was finding it hard to convey Natalia's sense of growing frustration with Adam. She remembers abandoning a whole section because she didn't know how to write it. Now, she realises her mistake; she was trying too hard to do too many things. It only needs to be simple – one gesture, one telling look, a few words, that could help carry the weight of it. She deletes a chunk of dialogue, starts again.

She finds the right note and it's like she's slipped inside a song. The words begin to flow. Writing quickly, the words keeps on flowing. She loves writing dialogue, conversations going back and forth like a ball in a tennis match, the occasional gasps, the excruciating slips. It feels like playing with figures in a dolls' house, moving them around, giving them voice. It feels like swimming under water, everything else around her muffled, and she's deep, deep inside of it.

When Lili opens the front door, Mira finally comes up for air. And now she hears everything – the clatter of Lili's keys dropped on the table, the crinkle of her shopping bags – with so much clarity. Lili looks around the spotless flat, asks Mira suspiciously what she's been up to and Mira has to blink a few times to remember. She stands, stretches, picks up her things up from the table and holds them to her chest. She smiles at Lili and says, 'You're welcome', even though Lili hasn't thanked her for anything, then walks into her room and climbs onto the bed, sitting cross-legged in the middle, her laptop in front of her. The words are there. Not even the noise of the television coming from the living room can distract her.

It is only when she stops, at about five o'clock, that she realises she hasn't thought about Dominic, or Lili, or Hana or Samir, the people who take up so much space in her head. Yesterday was a complete disaster but now Mira feels lighter, quieter. Somehow, when she's writing, she feels put back together again. The voice in her head that tells her she's a failure is harder to hear when her mind is busy, when her hand is moving across a page or her fingers are typing.

When she turns on her phone, there are two texts from Dominic and three missed calls from Hana.

I need to see you.
Please, I can explain

She feels the rush of anger course through her body and starts typing back, furiously:

*Funny how **now** that I've met your wife, you want to explain. Why, what happened, did you lose your phone before, when I kept asking where you were?*

Her thumb hovers over 'send'. But what's the point in even having this conversation? She doesn't want any explanations. What was it Hana said? Men, a bunch of pricks? She laughs quietly and then deletes her message, followed by the entire message thread and then finally, this time really, Dominic's number. She lets out a long breath, aware that her hands are trembling. She knows she won't hear from him again.

Mira calls Molly, asks if it's not too late to do something after all. Molly squeals and tells her to come around, they'll order takeout and watch a film, whatever Mira fancies. She doesn't tell Molly about Dominic, doesn't want to waste her birthday thinking of him more than she has done already.

Mira leaves straight away, and at Molly's they order Korean food and Mira suggests they watch *Marriage Story*.

'No! That's far too sad!' Molly says.

'But I love it,' Mira protests. 'I'm in the mood for it. *Please?*' She doesn't say that she thinks it could also kind of be research for her play.

Molly gives in. The couple at the heart of the story are in the theatre world; those scenes, especially, remind her how much she wants this for herself, and watching those parts leave her uplifted, excited. Molly pauses and rewinds the scene when Adam Driver sings 'Being Alive' and they watch it five times, singing along like they're in a musical, making up the words until Molly remembers they can put on the subtitles. Mira's moved when she reads the lyrics; she's never considered how beautiful they are. At the line '*Someone to know you too well*', she feels wretched. Though she feels silly, she begins to well up, but it's not Dominic or herself she's thinking about. The song makes her think of Hana. She feels an ache in her chest. It's not a feeling she expected.

For the rest of the evening, she keeps checking her phone, feeling guilty that she's not called Hana back. But after the kiss with Samir last night, she doesn't know if she can trust herself to sound normal on the phone: Hana will know instantly that there's something wrong. But even so, Mira can't stop thinking about her, wondering how she is and what she's done today – and, most of all, if she's okay.

Twenty-four

It's Sunday morning, the day after the party. Hana's lying curled up on her right side in bed, her back to the door. Her eyes are crusted with last night's mascara and there are black smudges on her pillowcase. She's been awake for hours, heard Mira leave the house. There's a soft knock on the bedroom door, but Hana doesn't turn over or answer. The door opens and Samir comes in. She hears him set something down carefully on his bedside table. She glances over her shoulder, though not directly at him, and catches sight of a tray.

'Hey,' he says, 'I brought you breakfast.'

She sits up in bed, drawing the sheet around her. She looks at him expressionless. He looks awful, the circles under his eyes as dark as bruises and his lips dry. He's still wearing his Arsenal top and the shorts he had on yesterday. He must have slept downstairs or on the futon in his office. She wonders if any of his friends are still here, grown men lying on a floor somewhere like they're college kids. She desperately hopes not.

'I thought you might . . .' He lifts his hand towards the tray, the look on his face chastened. 'I know it doesn't make up for anything, but—'

She looks at the tray. On it, there's a glass of orange juice, a mug of tea and a croissant on a plate. There's an envelope propped up between the glass and the mug.

'I got you a card.'

Now she looks directly at him again.

'I'm sorry about the cake and the party.'

'You're sorry about the cake and the party,' she repeats flatly, staring into space.

He looks at her like he's about to say something, but instead he just lowers his eyes. She brings up her legs towards her, clasping them to her, and rests her head on her knees. She closes her eyes, afraid of the things he might say, or she might say, and all the ways in which they could go on hurting each other.

He lets out a long shaky breath. 'I know this is a shit start to your birthday—'

She lifts her head, opens her eyes. 'Samir, I really don't care about my birthday.'

'I'm sorry, I – I know it's probably the last thing you want to do, but I booked the spa at The Grove for you, ages ago. You know, that fancy hotel you always wanted to go to, the one in Hertfordshire. I guess you probably don't want to go, but if you do, it won't take longer than an hour to drive there. I could take you if you don't want to drive, or you can take the car, whatever you like.' His voice trails off.

She stares at her hands. 'I don't think I'm in the mood.'

'No, of course. But just in case, you know. Like if things, if you, feel better later. It's all there for you. I printed off the confirmation, it's in the card.' He points at the envelope. She still doesn't look at him.

'Okay. I guess I'll go now. Give you some space.' He steps away from the bed.

As soon as he closes the door, she curls up on her side again and starts crying. She doesn't normally ever cry like this, so uncontrolled and exposed. Even when their mother died, her grief was composed, self-possessed, at least when compared to Mira's messy and rather public displays of falling apart. Hana was mournful in a quiet way that belied how overwhelming the situation really was. But someone had to carry on and make practical decisions, and that someone was her, even though she was only twenty-two years old. It was not as if she could rely on Mira to help.

Now she cries, about everything that's happened over the years: about Samir, about herself, about her relationship with Mira that's always up and down, the baby she wants, the pregnancy she lost, the mother she no longer has. She doesn't know what's happening, what any of it means. If she'd just accepted that stupid cake and said thank you, would things have been different? Or is Samir to blame for this mess, because he ordered the damn cake in the first place? But the cake, the stupid cake, is insignificant, Hana knows, of course she does. And all those things Samir said yesterday, about Hana, about not knowing if he wanted any of it, the baby, in the first place, all of that would have come out eventually. She can't blame a cake.

She wipes the tears from her eyes now, takes in long, deep breaths. The questions crowding her mind fall away until just a handful is left. What did Samir mean when he said he didn't know if he could do any of this? What is 'this'? She's terrified what the answer might be, doesn't want to think about the possibilities. She just can't face it, not now, not today, not on her birthday.

Today she turns thirty-four. And Mira thirty-two. What a pair, she thinks; what a mess their lives are both in. Mira, in that godawful flat, with her dead-end job and her hopeless playwriting dreams and that man who's disappeared on her. And Hana herself – with the job and the husband and the house, and still so unhappy. She and Mira are as lost as each other, both wanting things that are out of reach.

She checks her phone. Mira's already sent her a text, saying happy birthday. Hana should call her back. She should check that she's okay. God only knows what yesterday was about, Mira locking herself in the bathroom like that. She sits up in bed, her finger on Mira's name, but the thought of calling her sister feels draining. Hana will also have to explain her comments to Mira, that her marriage was only just hanging on by a thread. She doesn't know if she even wants to talk about it. No, she'll call Mira later. She sets her phone aside. She'll get up first. Have a shower, get dressed. One thing at a time.

She can hear Samir moving about the house, his heavy steps downstairs and then upstairs and downstairs again. Finally, she hears the click of the front door closing, and it's only when he's gone that she swings her legs around and gets out of bed. The tea on the tray has grown cold and is scummy on top, the juice and croissant equally unappetising. She carries the tray downstairs and pours the tea and juice down the sink, then throws the croissant in the bin, along with the card in its envelope. She's sure there won't be a declaration of any kind in it – Samir only ever signs his name, sometimes doesn't even write 'happy birthday'. As if to prove something to herself, she retrieves the card and opens it. Maybe he's written something in it, something meaningful, something that will make it easier for her to call him, tell him to come back home. A folded square of paper falls out of the card, the email printout confirming her appointment at the spa. But that's all there is. Sure enough, all he's done is sign his name. The satisfaction of being right doesn't feel as good as it should do.

That's when Hana decides she will go to the spa. It's better than staying at home feeling sorry for herself, and besides, it'd be a waste not to: Samir has paid for everything. Yes, she wants to be lying in a dimly lit room, her phone off, no one able to reach her. She unfolds the booking confirmation and is surprised when she sees it's a package for two. The date on the booking confirmation is from a month earlier. She finds this reassuring, hopeful even; a sign that when he made the booking, which wasn't that long ago, he'd intended for them to go together. So, surely, whatever he said last night was just in the heat of the moment. He didn't mean it. Couldn't have meant it. But the relief quickly gives way to sadness. Is she supposed to go alone now? It's not as if she can go with Samir. She doesn't even know where he is.

It occurs to Hana that she could call Mira, see if she wants to come with her. She's pretty sure Mira will be free; like Hana, she stopped making a big deal out of her birthday years ago. She's surprised that the idea isn't as unappealing as she might ordinarily find it. It's been so long since she's done anything alone with Mira, just the two of them. Hana calls Mira, three times, but Mira doesn't pick up, the phone going to voicemail. After that, Hana gives up; she'll be late if she doesn't leave now.

On the drive out of London she is calm; she listens to a podcast about failure, and hearing about someone else's failures and how they got through it makes her feel better about her own. The distraction is what she needs. For a while, she forgets about Samir, about what he may or may not have meant. The roads are clear out and it is cooler, more bearable than the unthinkable heat of earlier days. The journey isn't unpleasant and, in the end, Hana's relieved that Mira didn't pick up, relieved for the time alone.

When Hana emerges from the treatment room, she's led in her robe to a fig-scented lounge full of low recliners and blankets made out of the remnants of sari silks. Her skin feels flushed, like she's been in a hot bath for slightly too long. She feels different, softer, as if she'd give herself over to anyone right now, do exactly what they wanted. Her mouth feels dry like she's woken up from a long sleep, and she's hazy, as though everything that happened yesterday and the conversation she had with Samir this morning were just a dream. Here, with the candles and the low lighting and the delicate music, it's easy to believe that.

When Hana steps outside, into the car park, she finds she has to blink hard, little white shapes dancing on the insides of her eyelids. She's incredibly sleepy. Her limbs feel floppy. She'd like someone to position her, tell her where to sit and how, mould her hands to the steering wheel, place her feet on the pedals, keep her head balanced on her neck. She wonders if Samir will be in when she gets home. She wonders what might happen if she were to make a gesture towards him. If there's a way to be normal for one night. But she can't imagine him touching her, or her touching him.

She wonders if it's a service you can buy – someone to teach you how to hug. She imagines someone else putting her arms around Samir's neck for her, showing her how to hold him – 'like this,' they'd say – and a memory comes to her of Mira as a stagehand for a school show, dressed in black so she couldn't be seen when she was positioning and repositioning the set. She thinks how easy it could all be if every couple had someone beside them to move them, put them where they needed to be, piece them back together when they fell out of sync. Perhaps that's how people stay together in the end; because other people tell them what to do, how to be.

On the drive home, she tries to imagine what a reconciliation between them might look like. But she can't. They don't ever make up like that; the only time it's happened was when they agreed they'd start a family. Normally, they brush whatever argument they have had into the corners of their relationship, where they don't have to look at it. Until the next one comes along. They go round and round in circles. It's just how they are. It's the way they've always been.

Twenty-five

Samir comes into the café and Mira deliberately takes her time to serve other customers before him, even ones who came in after him. It's the first week of September, schools are open again, and Flora is packed, full of parents catching up over coffees after the school run. When, finally, there is no one else in the queue, she turns to him and says, 'What?'

'Do you talk to all your customers like that?' He laughs nervously but the joke falls flat.

'What do you want, Samir?'

'I wanted to say sorry.'

'You've said sorry.'

He looks around, lowers his voice, 'I know I've been an idiot.'

'Samir. We've had this conversation already. It's Hana you need to apologise to, not me. I'm out of this. Is there anything else? Do you want a coffee? Because if not, I'm busy here.'

Mira turns away from him and he says quietly, 'I want to make it up to you.' She pulls her shoulders back and turns around, about to launch into him again, when he says quickly, 'The housesitting thing. I've sorted it.'

'Sorry, what?'

It's not as if she'd forgotten, but she'd given up on it materialising. Lili has started leaving Post-it notes on Mira's books and cups and plates and anything she might have left in their communal living areas with 'THIS MUST

GO' written on them. Mira has decided her only option is to pander to Lili, keep cleaning the flat and beg her to let her stay a little longer until she finds somewhere else.

'I've spoken to Raef,' Samir explains. 'I've sorted it out for you. Told him all about you. Told him you're a playwright who needs somewhere quiet to live and to write and that you'd be perfect to look after his place while he's away.'

Mira raises her eyebrows in surprise. Even though she doesn't want to give Samir the impression that she forgives him, she finds herself smiling at his description of her.

'He just wants to meet with you, have a chat, take you through whatever he needs to, and then it's yours.' He takes out his phone and fiddles with it. 'There, you've got his number now. He's expecting to hear from you so just drop him a message when you've got a minute.'

'Wow,' she says, taken aback. 'Okay. Are you sure he said it's okay?'

'I'm sure,' Samir replies with a sorry smile.

Mira softens, just a little. 'Thanks. That's actually – that's really good of you. I appreciate it.'

He nods. Neither of them looks at each other.

'It doesn't change anything, though,' Mira adds. She lowers her voice. 'I mean, what you did was still shit. You're still an idiot.'

He nods again, still looking at the floor. 'Have you spoken to Hana?'

'I'm not going to tell her, if that's what you mean. I don't think that would achieve anything—'

'No, that's not why I'm asking,' he says quickly, 'that's not what I meant. I just meant, if she'd said anything, about how she's feeling. But thank you. I appreciate that, you not saying anything. A lot, actually.'

'To be clear,' Mira says, 'I'm not not telling her as a favour to you. And I'm not not telling her just because you've found me a place to stay. One thing doesn't cancel out the other.'

'No, of course. Understood,' Samir nods.

'So, what now?'

'I guess I'm going to try and think about things and put things right. I'm going to give her some space, you know? I think that's what she probably wants.' He looks at Mira, nods and shrugs at the same time, looking for reassurance.

Despite herself, Mira feels sorry for him. 'Okay. Yeah, I think giving Hana some space would be good. And Samir,' she touches his forearm, looks about to see that no one is listening, 'the stuff you were saying, the baby stuff, it's not my business, but whatever you decide, please be honest with her, and kind. Don't hurt her.'

Twenty-six

For a week after the party, Hana only sees Samir in passing. She's preparing several cases at work and doing long hours in the office, not home until late in the evenings. They circle around each other like distant planets through the kitchen, the bathroom, the bedroom. When she thinks about this analogy, she's comforted by the knowledge that planets within a solar system still gravitate towards each other, no matter how far apart. It means there's still a force between them, holding them in place.

At night, they fall back into the habit of going to bed at different times. Hana goes upstairs first. It's surprising how easily she succumbs to sleep, her mind and her body exhausted, giving in the moment she lies down in bed. Most of the time she doesn't even notice when Samir comes in. But if she wakes in the middle of the night, she's reassured that he's there, next to her, fast asleep. Soon it'll be her next cycle. She wants to be able to try again, and when she sees him asleep beside her, it doesn't seem so impossible that they will.

Years earlier, when Hana was still a trainee, she'd been introduced to a long-term client of the firm, an exuberant woman in her sixties who had famously divorced three husbands. Hana remembers the woman leaning across the desk, a cloud of heavy perfume hovering around her, and saying to her, as if she was letting her in on a secret, 'Darling, remember, the moment he moves out of your bed is the moment you know it's all over.' It was an absurd thing to have said, she was a particularly over-the-top client, but when Hana sees Samir asleep next to her, she can't help but think of it. It's not over. Whatever it is that's happening between them, it's just a bump in the road, a hitch, a blip. It does, admittedly, feel bigger than any of their other past arguments, but they'll be okay, because they always are; they always get over these things. Samir couldn't have meant what he said, she thinks, because he booked that spa day for them both. It's not as if he's planning an exit strategy. What he said the day of the party, he said in anger. It was just what happened, in the moment.

They haven't spoken about it, though. She can remember the gist of what he said the day of the party, in the bedroom, with the cake, but she can't remember every single word or the order in which he said it. Then again, they're not the kind of couple to sit around and dissect their own behaviour. It's also not as if they're ignoring each other, either. They're talking to each other like everything is okay, mostly. Hana lets him know she's working late; Samir tells her he's going to the gym. He texts her to ask if she's seen his keys or a delivery that was supposed to have come for him; she tells him where to find them. There's a familiar pattern to this; it's how they work things out. They'll move on. She knows it.

A fortnight after the party, Samir announces he has to make a work trip to New York to meet with clients.

'Okay,' she says.

'It's only three days.'

'Okay. Which client?'

He tells her and she listens and tells him she hopes it goes okay.

A day later he says, 'So I'm supposed to fly back on Friday, but I'm thinking I might as well extend it and take the weekend, come back Sunday night. Means I won't get back until really late, but it also means I can spend some time with my parents and Natasha. I haven't seen them for so long.'

Hana agrees. 'Makes sense. I assumed you'd go to see them. I'd do the same if it were me.'

She buys gifts for his parents, a jumper each for autumn, and for Natasha she chooses a scented candle and a pretty soap dish in the shape of a lemon.

'You didn't need to get them presents,' he says, when she passes them to him while he's packing.

'I know, but I wanted to. We haven't seen them for ages. You should tell them to come and visit soon.'

She's aware she's trying too hard. The last time her in-laws visited was the summer before her miscarriage. She had counted down the days until they left and complained about them often to Samir.

'Sure.' Samir puts the gifts in his suitcase. He looks up at her. 'That's really nice of you to say.' Hana smiles at him. She feels hopeful, better, more certain that the past is behind them. By the time he's back, she'll be approaching her next ovulation window. And surely by then, after some time apart, they'll slip back into normality.

Samir's flight to New York is early on Tuesday morning. He'll need to leave home at 3am to make it to the airport.

'It makes sense if I just sleep in the guest room,' he says, the night before. 'I have to get up so early and I don't want to disturb you.'

'No, of course. Of course. But wake me up before you leave, will you?'

In the middle of the night, she stirs in her sleep, but when she wakes, it's already morning and he's long gone. She texts him, furious.

Why didn't you wake me up???

When his reply arrives, it says:

I came in but you were fast asleep, it felt wrong to disturb you. You've been working so hard lately. X

Hana feels stupid for panicking. While Samir's away, he texts her small updates to tell her that he's landed, that the meeting went well, that Natasha and his parents send their love. She takes all of this as a good sign. They're being unusually polite with each other. There's no bickering, none of the usual bullet fire of snarky comments. It still doesn't feel entirely normal. But maybe this is how they put things right this time. Maybe this is where they've gone wrong before.

At home, alone, she scrolls through the fertility message boards. She's not looking for any specific advice, it's just something she does on default now. She reads a thread about the strain that trying to conceive puts on relationships. There are twenty pages of chat. '*My husband says it feels too forced*', '*I can't do it anymore*', '*I hate that every month I still get my period*'. She puts her phone down. She's put way too much pressure on him, let herself get so carried away. They just need to relax, that's all. It's so obvious, so simple. They just need to relax, not worry about timings and ovulation kits. Samir was right all along; they should have taken a holiday, been spontaneous, gone to Paris, had a lot more pleasurable sex when they wanted to, instead of it being strictly scheduled.

Later, when she's putting the laundry away, she opens Samir's wardrobe and sees all the remaining ovulation kits stacked up in their white boxes. She considers them for a moment, then gathers them up and dumps them in a rubbish bag. That night, she browses holiday destinations and luxury hotels.

On Sunday, he texts her from the airport to tell her that he's checked in but there's a delay and he probably won't be back until after midnight. *No need to stay up*, he writes. But she does stay up, she wants to see him. She's desperate to. She wants to tell him that she knows she got it all wrong, went about it all the wrong way, show him the hotel in Rome she'd like to book. She showers, goes to bed in her prettiest camisole and shorts set. She's lying in bed, half-reading a book, trying to stay awake, when she hears a car pull up outside. There's movement in front of the house, a car door opening and closing, the boot next, the swing of the front gate and a key in the lock. He is home. She feels a jolt run through her, nervous and excited. She'll wait here, she thinks, rather than take him by surprise downstairs. She can hear him moving about, turning lights on and off. There's the bump of his suitcase against the wall as he carries it upstairs. She brushes through her hair with her fingers. She waits. But instead of turning at the top of the landing to come towards their room, she hears him open the door to the guest room. The door shuts. She sits up, baffled. She sits like this for two minutes, then throws back the covers, barges into the guest room, flinging the door wide open.

'Hana,' Samir says, surprised. His case is open in front of him on the bed. 'You're awake. I thought you were asleep.'

'No, I'm not asleep, I've been waiting for you to come home.'

'Why? I told you not to—'

'Why didn't you come to me?' she snaps at him.

'Excuse me?'

'Why are you sleeping in here? Why aren't you in our room? Why didn't you come to me?'

He laughs lightly. 'Because I thought you were asleep. I didn't want to wake you.'

'Like you didn't want to wake me when you left?' She feels her eyes prickle with the sting of angry tears.

He avoids making eye contact with her. 'Hana, I've literally just got off an eight-hour flight. I'm shattered. Can we do this in the morning? Please?' He returns to emptying his suitcase, unzipping his toiletries bag and taking items out one by one.

She watches him and then, unable to help herself, she says, 'Did you really go to New York for a client meeting?'

He laughs again, but this time like she's being stupid. 'Yes, Hana. I really went to New York for a client meeting.'

'So you're telling me that you suddenly going away on this trip – this has nothing to do with us, with the things you said to me before the party?'

He scratches the back of his neck.

Then he says, quietly, 'What do you want me to say, Han? There was a client, I went to see the client. But yeah, I also felt like I needed to get away. I needed . . . need space.' He looks at her and there's something in his expression, the way it is so calm and yet also distant, that unsettles her.

'From me? Space from me? Get away from me? Is that what you're saying?' She wishes that she didn't sound as if she needed so much from him.

'From . . . whatever it is that's going on, Han.' He lets out a long breath, holds out his toothbrush and points with it. 'Every time we argue, afterwards you pretend like nothing's happened. I can't keep doing that, this, anymore. This . . . whatever it is that's happening, it's too big to ignore.' He lets out a long breath. 'I want to talk about it, I do, but not like this. Not right now. You can't just lay into me as soon as I've got home after a long flight—'

She feels herself float above her body, the panic rising. She raises her voice, her hands spread by the side of her head.

'No, no. Fine. You want to talk about it, then let's talk, now, why wait? You're not the only one who's tired of this. Why don't you start by telling me what the hell you meant that day, when you said you weren't sure if you wanted any of it in the first place? When you accused me of being such a "cruel" and "unloving" person, unfit to be a parent? What is it that you don't want anymore, Samir? What were you talking about? Because you can't just not tell me and then disappear to New York, not when we said, not when you agreed, that we'd start a family and—'

'Hana!' he shouts. 'Please! Can you hear yourself? Just. Enough. I can't. I can't . . .'

He sits on the edge of the bed and holds his head in his hands. He sits very still like this. Hana senses her devastation before she can name the feeling.

'This is too much,' he whispers, 'I can't keep doing this. It's just too much.'

'No.' She rushes towards him, stands between his legs, puts her finger on his lips, her other hand gripping his shoulder. 'No, no, no. You don't mean that. Don't say that.' She wants to shake him, shake all of his doubts out of him. He doesn't touch her.

He opens his mouth to speak but she interrupts again. 'No, listen, Samir, I understand. I do. I understand why you felt like you had to get some space. I've been doing some thinking too, while you were away, and I know, I know I went about all this in completely the wrong way. I was acting crazy. I know that now. It was wrong of me to have insisted on timing everything—'

'Yeah, but it's not just that—'

'No, but I understand. I really do. I took things too far, too soon. We didn't need to start that conception plan straight away. It was stupid of me. We should have just taken it easy. And I know that now. I just got carried away, and impatient, and I've seen what it's done to us, to you. It's too much pressure, I understand. I've even thrown all those ovulation kits away.' She shrugs her shoulders, tries to laugh.

'Please,' she says, softer now, desperate but also consoling; she falls to her knees before him. 'Please, just don't give up on the idea of having a baby entirely. I promise we can work it out. Please. You said you were ready, remember?'

He looks at her for a long time. Hana holds his gaze intently, pleading with him silently, but his expression is sad, faraway. Then, eventually, he drops his forehead to her shoulder. She puts her arms around him and holds him. And then, ever so quietly, he says into her, 'I don't know Han, I just don't know anymore.'

Twenty-seven

Monday morning, and Mira has the day off work. Today she's finally meeting Samir's friend, Raef, about housesitting. They've been messaging for a while, but Raef was waiting for confirmation from his job as to when he'd be leaving. Mira had to grovel to Lili, ask if it was possible to stay until she had found a new place. Because Mira has been keeping the flat clean, Lili said okay, but the situation has been getting more and more terrible. Lili and her boyfriend continue to hog the living room and eat her food in the fridge.

Then Raef got back in touch, apologising for having taken so long. He's leaving at the end of the week. Everything needs to happen quickly. So, today, Mira is going around to his flat, to meet him and see the place, see if the housesitting might work out for them. She dresses with care, choosing a floral tea dress instead of her usual jeans and whatever clothes are on the floor, and spends more time than usual putting her makeup on. She's desperate to make a good impression; this flat is her only option and she doesn't know what she'll do without it, other than beg Hana to stay with her, which she doesn't want to do.

The flat is in a small square with a gated garden in the centre. Mira feels like she's entered the pages of a children's book, the kind set in an old, beautiful London of curved cream-coloured townhouses with wrought iron gates and nannies flying among chimneys. She stands for a moment at the garden, leaning through the railings. There's a pergola in the middle of it, draped with honeysuckle and jasmine, benches placed next to rosebushes, huge mounds of lavender. She checks the address twice; she's in the right place. She looks for the building with the door painted pillar-box red, as Raef instructed, then presses the buzzer and waits for him, looking about her, in disbelief, at the possibility that she could live in a place like this.

Raef comes down to open the door, presses his hand into hers warmly. He's wearing a bright white T-shirt and faded jeans, no shoes and a pair of rust-coloured socks. 'Hello.' He grins at her and Mira's nerves disappear. Samir had told her that Raef works in finance, but, standing there in front of her in his socks, he looks about twelve years old and is the least intimidating landlord that she's ever met. She compliments the square, says she's been to the area before but never knew this existed. As she follows Raef up to the first floor, he says over his shoulder, 'Samir says you're a playwright, that you're working on something? That's exciting!'

She's taken aback by his enthusiasm. She's about to offer some sort of disclaimer on her limited achievements thus far, but, instead, she says, 'Yeah, that's right. I've got a deadline for a play I'm writing.' It feels good to say it, it feels real. It feels thrilling, actually.

Raef warns her, as he goes to open the front door, that the flat is very small. He's apologetic about this, jokes that it'll only take about thirty seconds to see the whole place. And it is small, smaller even than the flat she's living in now, but she wouldn't have to share this with anyone and it's beautiful. Mira gasps as soon as she steps in. The floors are dark wood, the walls pale grey. From where she is standing in the hallway, she can see large patches of light falling through the sash windows in the living room. 'I'll take it,' she says, looking about her, and it's only when Raef laughs that she realises she's said it out loud. She follows him into the living room. The walls are filled with pictures in thin oak frames, quiet studies of landscapes and the sea, and there are slim bookcases in every available space, neat rows of books and magazines in box files.

When he notices her looking at the magazines, back copies of *The World of Interiors* and *Elle Decoration*, Raef explains, embarrassed, that they belong to his older sister; that she lived here first, before she got married, and that the decor is largely her doing. Mira realises that the flat must belong to his family, and she feels self-conscious, because he must know that all of this is beyond her reach. The bedroom is simple, but charming; a double bed, a small row of wardrobes, a yellow-striped blanket draped over the back of a wicker chair. In the corner there are two suitcases standing ready for Raef's departure. She wonders briefly if he's single. He's so organised, Hana would love him.

Raef has set up the narrow second bedroom as a study, a simple desk made out of a plank of wood running along the length of the wall under the window. He runs his hand across the desk and tells her it was reclaimed from an old bakery, an absolute bargain, and she wonders how much, exactly, a bargain is to him. When Mira leans forward to look out of the window, she can see a neighbour's cherry tree. It's perfect.

In the kitchen, he puts the kettle on and explains that he'd tried having tenants and it had ended up being stressful, so he didn't want to go through an agency again. Mira nods, leaning on what she thinks are marble-topped counters, cupping her chin in her palm, as if she understands the difficulties of renting out one's property. He also says he doesn't want to have to put things in storage, which is why someone housesitting the flat suits him. Mira agrees again, sympathising, wondering how much he must earn not to need rent for six months. She thinks of her things, and it dawns on her that the only thing of worth that she owns, really, is her laptop, and even that's an old one of Samir's. She's accumulated lots of stuff over the years, books and clothes and shoes and piles and piles of notebooks, but none of the sorts of things that make a home. Even the bed she sleeps on is not her own. But she's not above borrowing, and right now she would be perfectly happy, more than happy, to borrow Raef's home and pretend it's her home instead.

Years ago, she'd followed a series in a weekend newspaper supplement about writers' homes. She loved this series, loved poring over the photos of messy rooms full of books and piles of paper on desks and objects everywhere. Hana was decorating her house at the time, looking at identical pale neat rooms for inspiration. Mira held up the spread and said, 'How about an eclectic creative mess?' Hana replied that Mira was already such a mess and calling it creative was cheating. Raef's flat is simple and sparse and very, very neat – and she can already see herself here, making coffee like Raef is doing right now, sitting at this small white kitchen table for breakfast, hazy light falling through the thin cotton blind.

A space like this, somewhere all of her own, somewhere peaceful and calming – just like the café before she opens up – is just what she needs. In the time it takes for the kettle to boil, she imagines streamlining her life, minimising her wardrobe, living tidily, emotionally and otherwise. She pictures taking up yoga, meditation, waking up early and writing efficiently at the desk overlooking the cherry tree, her notes organised. She'd finish her play, even start something new. Yes, she'd be able to do it because there'd be no other complications in her life: no married playwrights, no annoying flatmates, no brother-in-law to accidentally kiss her.

She bites the skin at the sides of her thumb as she waits for Raef to finish making the coffee. She wants to live here so badly that she doesn't think she can bring herself to leave. She asks Raef how many more people he's interviewing, and he laughs kindly, setting down a small wooden tray with a coffee pot and a plate of pastries in front of her.

'Oh, it's not an interview. The flat's only going to be empty otherwise, which seems like such a shame if there's someone like you who could make good use of it. I don't want my plants to die and I'm too lazy to redirect my post, so really, you're doing me a favour.' He says he likes the idea of a writer living in the flat. 'It's amazing. You're doing something creative with your life.'

It takes Mira a minute to understand what Raef's saying – that it's okay, it's fine, it's hers, she can move in.

The first person Mira calls to tell about the flat is Hana.

'I'm at work,' Hana says when she picks up the phone. 'I've not got long. Go.'

'I'm moving,' Mira says quickly.

'What?'

'I'm moving!'

'Yes, you said that, where?'

'You should see this place! Honestly, it's beautiful, it's so beautiful—'

'Can you afford it?'

'It won't cost me much. Just bills. It's a housesit. He's going overseas for six months, maybe even longer. I won't even have to share.' Mira laughs. 'My God, it's like a dream.'

'Are you sure it's all above board?' Hana says. 'You're going to live in a beautiful flat, basically for free, while this person's not there?'

'Yes,' Mira says impatiently. She's walking quickly and Hana can hear the wind down the phone.

'No sexual favours involved?'

'Hana! No. It's not sketchy. Samir helped me find it; it's a friend of his. Raef. Do you know him? I'm going to call him to say thanks in a bit.' She sounds breathless on the phone.

'Fine,' Hana ignores the question. 'So where is this place, anyway?'

'Highbury.'

'But that's going to take you ages to get to work every morning.'

'It won't. There's a bus that goes straight to the Broadway from Highbury Corner. It's quick. I did it this morning. I'll still be in time for work. So it's fine, really. Or I'll just start a little later and leave the opening up to someone else. Either way, it's worth it.'

'Okay.' Hana sounds bored. 'Well, congratulations. Was there anything else?'

'Well, I was wondering—'

'Of course you were.'

'—if you wouldn't mind giving me a lift there with my stuff on Saturday morning? Lili wants me out as soon as possible and, to be honest, I don't want to stay there any longer than I have to. And the flat's free from Friday.' She screws her face up in hope, the equivalent of crossing her fingers. 'Please?'

Mira waits for the inevitable sigh, some little comment about how inconvenient it all is, can she not just book a taxi, but to her surprise, it doesn't come. There's just a pause and then Hana says, 'Yes, sure.'

'*Really?*'

'Yes, it's fine. I'm free Saturday.'

'Thank you, Han,' Mira says. 'You'll love it, you'll see on Saturday—'

'Great.' Hana's voice sounds far away and Mira takes her phone away from her ear to check the reception.

'Hana? Hana, are you there? I can't hear you.'

But Hana's already ended the call.

Twenty-eight

Hana's nights are restless. She lies awake for hours, staring at the ceiling, turning this way and that, the words haunting her: *the moment he moves out of your bed is the moment you know it's all over.*

But is it over? Is it really over? At times, in the dark loneliness of the night, lying in bed without Samir, it feels like it might be. The possibility frightens her, a whirlwind of worst-case scenarios blowing through her mind. But at other times, when it's morning again and autumn is beginning to stir outside, a scrappy wind nudging yellowed leaves off the trees, a skittish energy comes over her, an adrenaline. And when she feels like this, she refuses to believe that it can be over, vows when she looks in the mirror that it's not. That stupid woman, that stupid client was wrong; she married the wrong man three times. What would she know? This, she thinks, this is how a couple works things through. Hana should know; she's led so many round-table negotiations. It's just that she's never had to do it for herself before.

That night in the guest room, when she'd knelt on the floor in front of Samir, he'd told her that he didn't know what he wanted anymore. He said he needed time to think about the future, about fatherhood and babies, all of it. He said he needed to think about it on his own terms, in his own way. And she'd agreed to it, helpless, because there was nothing else she could do. She felt ashamed, on her knees, wished desperately she didn't have to want so much from him; but conceiving a baby is not something she can do without him.

'How much time do you need?' she'd asked.

'I don't know, Han. I can't answer that,' he'd said. 'I can't put a timeframe on everything that's going on in my head.'

At first, she tries hard to be patient, not to snap, not to make demands of him. It takes everything she has to be this kind of person, which is to say, to be someone else. She offers to cook more, so it's not all left to him, in case that is also something he begrudges, and she stops working late, leaves the office at a reasonable hour. When she's home, she tries not to spend all her time checking her work emails or browsing her phone. She optimistically suggests outings on the weekends, normal things, couple things, like a trip to the cinema, a walk through the park, a visit to see friends, things they used to do. When she mentions going out for their anniversary, he says, 'Sure, might be nice.' She is heartened when one evening he also says yes to going out to watch a film; but then when the time comes, he forgets and tells her he's going to a gig. Another time, one Sunday afternoon, she suggests they head into Crouch End for a coffee and take a walk through the park on the way. She's surprised when he says yes. The October air is brisk but still and dry and the sky a hazy swirl of deep pink and grey-blue. It's not yet dark, and the park is surprisingly busy, dog walkers and parents and children playing, stealing the last moments of the day. Up ahead, Hana can see sagging balloons, red and blue, tied to a black railing, the flagging remnants of a children's birthday party that must have taken place in the pavilion. There are children running everywhere, climbing trees, jumping in heaps of golden leaves.

A little girl scoops up a pile of dead leaves and throws them above her head, a small cloud of orange, yellow and red. 'Watch me, Mama!' she cries, her delight obvious. 'Watch me, I've made it rain colours!' But her mother isn't watching. She's staring at the screen in her hand, and just says, 'Hmm, that's nice.' This bothers Hana. She wouldn't do that, she thinks. No, she wouldn't take her child to the park only to spend all that time looking at her phone. She would watch. She would be alert, she would catch them before they fall, stop them from stepping in dog shit. She would pay attention. She knows she's being judgemental and unfair, but it upsets her. *Look*, she wants to grab the woman and say to her, shaking her, *look how lucky you are*. The detour through the park darkens her mood; every footstep feels foreboding. Samir hardly speaks. Hana tries not to imagine what he's thinking as they walk through the park full of families. She tries not to obsess about whether this is what he wants, whether he can think of nothing worse.

Late one night, when she can't sleep, and she's downstairs in the kitchen with the lights off, Hana types *'my husband no longer wants a baby'* into the search engine of the message boards she reads. She hasn't been on the message boards for a while, not since she threw the ovulation kits away. She's emotionless as she types and hits 'search'. She's neither upset nor angry. She feels efficient, like she's conducting research. She scrolls through the results coolly.

On one thread, women commiserate with the situation.

Have you tried the pill trick? one commentator suggests. *'Accidentally' on purpose get pregnant? Easy!*

I don't think I could do that to him, the original poster replies.

Hana clicks out of the thread and chooses another.

A woman says her husband of six years doesn't want children, but she does. Her husband said he always thought he would but he knows now he doesn't. People tell her to leave, that he's a bastard, that's he's strung her along, that he's deceived her by marrying her knowing full well that's what she wanted. But she says she loves him. She says:

It's not babies per se I want. It's to be a family, with him. I think he'd make a great dad but I appreciate it's better for him to be honest than bring a child into the world he doesn't want. I feel like I lose out whatever I decide, whether I stay with him or not.

Hana finds this response breathtaking, heartbreaking, infuriating. She is almost moved to write a reply, though she doesn't (she never does). All these women, she thinks, all of us. She wishes she could tell the woman that people leave each other for a lot less than this. She bookmarks the post to come back to, which she does, again and again, sometimes opening it up in an incognito window at work. Her perspective on whether the woman should leave or stay changes every time, depending on how she's feeling that day.

Later, when Hana is adding a reminder in her calendar to go round to Mira's to help her move to Highbury on Saturday morning, she notices there's already one reminder saved in red. *Anniversary.* Their seven-year anniversary. She runs her index finger across her bottom lip and then she quickly picks up her desk phone and calls one of the trainees.

'Name me somewhere good for dinner,' she says. 'Anywhere. Quick.'

The trainee fumbles and then gives her the name of a French brasserie near Bank. Hana puts down the phone and looks it up. It only takes a second to book it online. There, it's done. She doesn't know if Samir will want to go, but it feels worse to let the date slip by forgotten. She adds it to their shared calendar, hopes he'll see it.

He does. Samir texts Hana on Friday, the day before they're supposed to go out for their anniversary dinner.

hey so just so I know, we're not doing gifts tomorrow right?

She stares at her phone before she types back:

I don't mind either way. I won't be offended if you don't.

She wills him to reply, to say something, to insist otherwise. But no other message comes.

During her lunch break she decides on a whim to take a taxi to Carnaby Street, where there's a men's clothing store she knows Samir likes, one that sells expensive T-shirts with characters from Marvel comics and odd food references embroidered on the chest pockets. Hana's pretty sure he's older than their preferred demographic, but since he's started working for himself and no longer needs to wear formal shirts, he's become a fan of the brand. Mira and Hana used to tease him about this, joking that this was his mid-life crisis. When she's in the shop she feels distinctly out of place in her pencil skirt and high heels, hip hop playing on wireless speakers unnecessarily loud. Now she feels the joke's on her. Everything – the T-shirts, the music, her reflection in the mirror – depresses her. In the end she walks out empty-handed, and it is a wasted trip.

It's when she's putting on her coat at the end of the day that the realisation that her marriage is beyond saving hits her like a slap in the face.

Around her, her colleagues turn off their computers and talk idly about their weekend plans. 'Oh, God,' she says, so quietly that no one else hears. She stumbles a little. Nobody notices. Someone says something funny; she doesn't know what. The conversation around her continues. She smiles at no one in particular, pretends for a minute to be checking something on her phone. She knows better than to make a scene. Instead, she loops her scarf around her neck, buttons up her coat, picks up her bag and, silently, pleading with her body to move and do what she needs it to do, she leaves.

Though she can't feel her legs, she manages to walk to the station, but she walks slowly. She ignores the people muttering and pushing past her because she's in their way. She thinks of the line everyone says when they fall in love; how when you know, you know. Perhaps it's the same at the very end. She just knows. Perhaps it's as simple as that and the rest of it – the disputes, the negotiations, the messy divorces – are just desperate complications people make for themselves.

How long has she known? Longer than she cares to admit. Maybe she knew when Samir went to New York. Maybe she knew the other night, when she passed him on the stairs and he breathed in and pressed his back to the wall so that he wouldn't have to touch her. Maybe she knew from the way he'd got in the habit of leaving a room the moment she came in, apologising, as if the idea of being in the same space as her was unbearable. Maybe she's always known, from the very beginning, that they would eventually wear each other out.

On the overground train home, the driver announces that he has to stop in order to let another train go past and regulate the timetable. It's at that precise moment, when the other train rushes past in a furious blur and the windows rattle hard and her head feels as if it might burst from the screeching, that all her emotions rise to the surface. She could scream now and nobody would hear above the ghastly squeals of the wheels on the track. But the train passes, the moment gone.

Twenty-nine

On Saturday morning, Hana turns up at Mira's flat an hour early. Mira is still in bed when the doorbell rings. When she gets downstairs, Hana turns around holding two coffees.

'You're early.' Mira's voice is croaky.

'Couldn't sleep,' Hana replies breezily. 'Besides, I thought you said you couldn't wait to get out of here.' She hands Mira a coffee as she brushes past her. 'Your breath stinks, by the way,' she calls out from the stairs.

Inside, Hana stands in the middle of Mira's room, surveying the mess. She looks at Mira. 'Honestly, you've not even started?'

'I haven't had a chance yet.' Mira looks shamefaced. Hana raises a brow. 'What? I've been busy.'

'You do know,' Hana says flatly, 'that my life is like a thousand times busier and more complicated than yours. And yet. Here I am.'

'It won't take long,' Mira cajoles. 'I promise. I hardly have anything to pack.'

'You *say* that.' Hana looks doubtfully about the room.

Mira goes to the bathroom to brush her teeth and splash water on her face and when she comes back, she hesitates in the doorway. Hana is leaning forward over the chest of drawers, peering at Mira's playwriting notes stuck to the wall on lurid sticky squares. Hana's hand flits up and she plucks a Post-it off the wall and squints at it, trying to make sense of Mira's handwriting. She reads it out loud.

'We'll *figure it out. We want the same things,*' she says. 'N *meets A's eye. He hesitates.*'

Mira rushes over and snatches the Post-it out of her sister's hand.

'It's nothing,' she says. 'Nothing. Just old notes. Need to throw them away.'

She quickly grabs a handful of Post-its off the wall and holds them in her hands like confetti. She doesn't know what to do with them. 'There. That's at least a little bit of packing done.'

'You're being weird,' Hana says, still studying the wall, although it's obvious none of it makes any sense to her. She moves her gaze from the wall down to the top of the chest of drawers and her eyes fall on the childhood photo of the two of them. She picks it up.

'Wow,' she says. 'Hideous.'

'I know,' Mira agrees.

Hana tells her to hurry up and get a move on, she's going out this evening, she wants to get home in the afternoon so she's got time to get changed. Mira asks where she's going.

'Nowhere,' Hana says, moving things about. 'Just dinner. Our "anniversary".' She makes speech marks with her fingers.

'Sorry, I forgot. I wouldn't have asked if I'd remembered.'

'Don't be sorry. It's not your anniversary, no reason you'd remember it. I almost didn't. He certainly wouldn't have if I'd not reminded him.'

'Han,' Mira says hesitantly. 'Are you okay?' She's hardly seen Samir lately. Even though he helped her out with the housesitting, things are still awkward between them since that awful kiss. He's not come into the café like he often does for breakfast on Fridays. He didn't answer the phone when she called to thank him about the flat – only replied to her text to say she was welcome, he was happy it worked out.

'I'm fine.' Hana wipes her hands on the top of her jeans. 'Let's get started then, else I'll be here all day.'

Mira drops the conversation. At least they're going out for dinner, and the last time she spoke to Samir he had said he'd work things out.

Hana insists Mira sort through her wardrobe and throw away old tops with holes in them. Mira puts together cardboard boxes to carry the piles of what Hana refers to as junk. Every now and again Hana comes across something that belongs to her, a bottle of perfume or a pot of lip balm or a top, and she looks at Mira outraged while Mira laughs and says 'What!' or else shrugs apologetically.

As Hana's sorting through Mira's books, she comes across a hardback on the art of playwriting and turns it over, reads the back cover. 'I know someone whose husband is really into all this,' she says. She looks at the book again and presses her lips together as she reads. 'Well, I don't really know him. He's married to one of Samir's American friends. I think he's written lots of plays, had them published or performed or something. You might have met him, at the party. Can't remember his name . . . Dom or Tom or something.'

She glances across at Mira, who is kneeling on the floor sorting through clothes she wants to give to charity. Mira hears Dominic's name and looks up. She sees Hana frown, and then watches as her eyes suddenly widen in understanding.

'What?' Mira says to Hana, defensively.

'Mira, is he the Dom . . . the Dominic you were telling me about—'

'No,' she denies, getting up from the floor.

'Mira, Dominic from your playwriting group. Is he the same Dominic who was at my party, the one married to—'

'No,' Mira says, more firmly. She dusts her knees and her palms and takes the book from Hana's hands.

'He is, isn't he?' Hana persists.

Mira picks up an old jumper from the floor, pretends to examine it.

'Mira.'

She can feel Hana watching her. Mira looks at the floor and then she drops the jumper. 'I know what you're thinking. I didn't know he was married, okay?'

'Why would you say that?'

'Because I know you! I know you're thinking, "typical Mira, making mistakes, choosing the wrong kind of guy, always creating drama".'

'No. I'm not thinking that at all, Mira. What is it with you? Why do you always assume I think the worst of you?'

Mira lets out a long breath.

'If you must know, I'm thinking he's a shit. And all I want to know is if you're okay. What will it take to convince you that I care about you? If I didn't, would I even be here?' Hana takes a step towards Mira.

Mira looks up. 'No,' she says quietly.

'Well, then.' Hana glares at her. 'So, are you still in touch with him?'

'God, no.'

'Do you want me to say anything—'

'Hana! No.'

'All this,' Hana flicks her hand in the air, 'all your writing. Those notes you took down. What are you going to do with them?'

'What?'

'Mira, are you giving up on your writing?'

'What are you talking about? No!'

Hana looks at Mira sternly. 'Good. Don't let this distract you.'

She looks around the room. 'Right then. Let's carry on, shall we?'

When, finally, they finish packing and they arrive at Raef's flat, Mira unlocks the door and Hana says, 'You're right. This place is gorgeous.'

She walks around the space, admiring the artwork on the walls, pointing out the furnishings around the house she recognises from magazines, picking up a vase, an hourglass, small pieces of pottery.

'He's got such good taste.'

'His sister did it all,' Mira says, then adds, 'You'd like him. He's very handsome. Very preppy. And neat.'

'Right.'

'Younger than you, though. I think he's, like, twelve. Just very rich.'

Hana laughs. 'Toyboy. Maybe that's what I need.'

She looks out the sash window into the courtyard. Two children are on their scooters, their mother or nanny trailing after them. Hana watches them.

'Hana,' Mira says, after a pause. 'Are you sure you're okay? Is everything . . . okay?'

All morning, there's been something different about Hana. Mira can't put her finger on it. She's been pensive, less frenetic, stoic almost. Hana turns away from the window. 'Ask me tomorrow.'

Mira smiles at her sadly and reaches out to touch her arm. Hana lets her. And then she starts to cry.

'Oh, Han.' Mira puts her arms around her, hugs her. 'Oh, Han,' she says again. In that moment, Mira doesn't need to know the details. This is about Samir. She wonders whether Samir has said anything, about that awful kiss the night of the party, but she dismisses the thought as quickly as it appears: Hana wouldn't be here if that were the case, and Samir wouldn't tell her; he wouldn't dare. And even if Mira wanted to tell her, which she doesn't, she wouldn't do it now, not with Hana crying like this.

Hana pulls away, sniffing, dabbing at her cheeks with her fingers.

'I'm just being silly,' she smiles. When she leaves, she says to Mira, 'I'm really happy that things are working out for you.' And Mira believes her.

Later, when Mira is unpacking by herself in Raef's flat, she looks for the picture frame with the childhood photo of her and Hana, the one Hana hates. She searches all her bags, all the boxes, but she can't find it anywhere. Did she leave it at Lili's, put it somewhere and forgot to pack it? Or maybe Hana really did throw it away. No, she wouldn't do that, Mira thinks, not really. She's annoyed she can't find it. But there's nothing she can do now. She figures it will turn up eventually and, if it doesn't, in time she'll forget. And perhaps she won't even miss it.

Thirty

Early on Saturday evening, Hana goes upstairs to her room to get changed. After some deliberation, she chooses a knitted dress with tights and knee-high boots. She looks at herself in the mirror critically, wonders if the boots are too much. Downstairs, Samir is waiting for her. He's wearing a smarter shirt than normal with a pair of dark jeans, and is, for the first time in a long time, clean shaven. It touches her, that he's made an effort. When he says, 'Right, shall we go then,' she can't help but feel sorry for their whole situation.

Outside, as she locks the door, he asks, 'Where are we going again?'

Hana tells him the name of the restaurant.

He looks confused. 'Why are we going all the way into town? Why don't we just go local?'

'But I've made a reservation. I told you where we were going, remember?'

'Yeah, but I didn't check the address.'

After a pause, Hana says, 'So do you want to—'

'No, it's fine,' he says. 'You've booked, let's go.'

They walk to the station. It's awful, not talking, so Hana tries to think of something to say, but making idle conversation has never been her strong point.

'The menu looks good. People at work say it's a really nice place.'

'Great,' he says.

'I took Mira to her new flat today, the one you helped her find. It's amazing. It's small, but the decor is just gorgeous. Wasted on her,' she laughs, even though she knows it's not funny. She wills herself to stop talking.

Thankfully, a train arrives quickly, and it's too noisy to talk, the sound of the brakes screeching and the carriages rattling. When they get off at Bank, Hana spends a while frowning at the map on her phone, trying to figure out which exit they need.

'I thought you knew this place like the back of your hand,' Samir says. 'You do work round here.'

'Yes, but—'

He starts walking, and she follows him, trying to keep up with him, but it's hard in her stiff, heeled boots.

'Can you not wait?' she calls. It's hard to hide her irritation.

He looks over his shoulder and stops. 'It's here somewhere,' she says, catching up with him, her voice less impatient, but he doesn't respond. When they get to the restaurant, he pushes opens the door and gestures to her to go first, touching the small of her back with his fingers. She feels herself take a little breath in. She looks over her shoulder again but Samir is looking past her and she realises the touch meant nothing.

The restaurant is ornate and old-fashioned, glass-topped tables close together and dark wood panels, shiny brass light fittings. It's nearly empty. There's only one other couple in there, older than them. They look like tourists, the wife wearing heavy lipstick and trousers cropped at the ankles, the husband in a baseball cap with a digital camera, the kind no one uses anymore, draped around his neck on a black cord. Hana feels sorry for them, pictures them wandering the surrounding streets with their phones held up to check for signal, trying to figure out if there's been a nationwide catastrophe – the City is always eerily deserted at the weekend. Suddenly, she realises she's made a mistake. This is a restaurant designed for suited business lunches and Champagne on expenses. It doesn't lend itself to any kind of intimacy at all. What was she thinking, asking the trainee to name a restaurant, just like that?

'I'm surprised this place is even open,' Samir says while they wait for a waitress to show them to their table. The table is laid lavishly with more cutlery than they need, plates stacked on top of each other. The waitress brings their menus, huge, padded leather folders with pages and pages of food inside.

'I'm sorry,' Hana looks about her. 'I didn't think it would be like this. I should have chosen somewhere else.'

She thinks of the gift she tried but failed to buy for Samir yesterday, and feels tears spring stupidly into her eyes. She covers her face with the menu, pretends to be studying it.

'No,' Samir says. 'It's fine.'

She hates this, hates how they're like strangers who don't know what to say to each other. *What are we doing here*, she wants to say, *how did we end up here?*

The waitress comes to take their order. Samir orders a steak tartare, Hana asks for the spinach ravioli.

'We don't have ravioli today,' the waitress replies. 'Do you need another minute?'

'You should have said that first,' Hana says crossly. 'When you brought the menus, you should have explained what you had.'

'Okay,' the waitress says, disinterested. 'When you've chosen something else, I'll come back.'

Samir looks at the waitress apologetically and she turns away.

'She should have said it first,' Hana repeats to Samir. 'That's what they're supposed to do. They give you the menus, they say what the specials are, they say "sorry we're out of whatever today". She didn't even say sorry. *I'm* sorry for her. It's bad service.' Hana doesn't know why she's still talking.

Samir says without smiling, 'It's okay, Hana. It's fine. Do you know what you want?'

When the waitress comes over again with their drinks, Hana orders a tomato and avocado salad instead.

'Is that all?' Samir says.

'What?'

'A salad?'

'Do you suddenly care about what I want?'

He doesn't respond, and she regrets it.

When their food comes, there are pale greyish brown streaks in the avocado and the tomatoes taste like water. Still, she forces herself to smile politely. 'So I went out at lunch yesterday to try and buy you something.'

He pauses. 'But I thought that we said no gifts.'

'We did.'

'But Hana, I thought you meant it, I mean, given everything.' He wipes his mouth with his napkin. 'You can't say one thing and mean another entirely—'

'I only said I went out to try and buy you something. My mission was unsuccessful. In the end I didn't know what to buy you, so I didn't get you anything.'

'Okay,' he frowns. 'You didn't have to do that but thank you for trying anyway.'

'I felt bad after,' she says, looking down at her plate. 'I wondered what it meant, if I couldn't find anything to buy for you.'

'Does it have to mean something?' he asks. The tone of his voice is flat.

'I think it does,' she says quietly.

Samir puts his cutlery down and looks at her. 'Go on then. What does it mean?'

'It means I don't know what you want.' She shrugs. 'We don't know what the other one wants. We don't know how to make each other happy. We make bad choices.' Her eyes turn glassy and, this time, she hasn't got the menu to hide behind.

At this, Samir reaches out for her fingers. He plays with them lightly for what feels like a long time. She doesn't know what this means. He's not looking at her face. Then he takes his hand back and pushes his plate away and clears his throat, motions for the bill. While they're waiting, he starts speaking so low that Hana has to lean forward to hear him.

'I don't know if you thought this might fix things. I appreciate the gesture. But I don't know why we're here. I don't know what we're doing.'

She nods. She scratches the thick white tablecloth with her nail. Everything has gone blurry.

On the way home, they sit next to each other on the train because it would be weird not to.

She leans her head against the window and closes her eyes, pretending to be asleep. They walk back without speaking. He keeps his hands in his pockets. Hana has the sensation that she can see two minutes into the future in her peripheral vision. She can see it, out of the corner of her eyes. She can already see him unlocking the door. She can see herself standing behind him. She can see him going upstairs. She can see herself waiting, not knowing what to do. She can see him coming back down again, a bag in each hand. She can see him, leaving. And then she blinks, and time has caught up, and they are in the house and she sees the bags, and then he is gone.

Thirty-one

Early morning, late autumn. In the small flat on the square, Mira is writing. She's dressed in leggings and a long-sleeved top, the yellow-striped blanket folded across her lap, her hair scraped back off her face. She's sitting at the desk in the narrow room, in front of the window. There's half a cup of tea next to her on a coaster, along with a glass of water, a notepad, a spare hairband. At the far end of the desk sits an antique lamp, the neck angled slightly downwards, the light dim and soft. A cork board leans against the wall to her right, neat squares of pale-coloured card pinned to it like a patchwork, each covered in small handwriting. Outside, the light is pale and the leaves on the cherry tree have turned to shades of red, gold, bronze. It is quiet. In the distance, bedroom lights come on in different houses, little rectangles glowing in the lifting dark.

Mira doesn't notice the rest of the square waking up, or the early morning birdsong drifting in through the thin windowpanes. She is focused only on her laptop, her face drawn in concentration. Her lips move as she types, whispering the words as they come to her. From time to time, she looks down at her keyboard or touches her mouth absent-mindedly, pressing her fingers to her lips. Every now and again, she sits up a little straighter and pulls her shoulders down and arches her back. There is one week left until the deadline for the Hadley Prize for Playwriting. She's kept her friends at arm's length, has barely spoken to Hana, has told everyone she has to focus. She has one act left to write. She thinks she will finish.

The play is about Natalia and Adam and their marriage and how it falls apart because in the end they both want different things. Her intention is that the audience must bear painful witness to the cracks in the marriage and its final breaking, its universality lying in the concept of multiple casting. The writing is simple, the sadness wrapped up in the silences as much as in what's said. Mira wants the experience of watching the play to feel like a privilege, for it to feel like they are being allowed to watch the most private parts of a couple's relationship, even – especially – if it's uncomfortable. She doesn't mind if Natalia and Adam aren't likeable: she wants them to feel imperfect, flawed, real.

Though, theoretically, she's been working on this play for months, it's only really in the last few weeks that the writing has started to come together. It no longer feels so disjointed, now that she finally knows what the story is and can trust it. Sometimes, at night, she wakes up feeling strange, as if she is still dreaming. Her words dance and move on the page, and she loves the way they do this. She thinks about how her words might sound in an actor's or actress's voice, considers the placement of every syllable, every comma. Sometimes, she acts out the stage directions; in the kitchen she thinks about the sound of the water from a tap, about how many movements are involved in the act of making a cup of tea. Sometimes she gets carried away and begins to picture what her three sets of different Natalias and Adams might look like. But then she has to remind herself that's not entirely her job, even though she came up with the idea. Her job is just to tell the story, then to pass it on to someone else. And though she knows there are other kinds of writers – writer-directors, or novelists or short story writers – who would hate to do this, hate to hand their words over to someone else to do with them what they will, in a way, she finds this part the most exciting.

She thinks it's beautiful to create a miniature world in words, but to let someone else take it off the page. It reminds her of all that she loves in playwriting, about the impermanence of it, the magic of something fleeting. She has no idea if her play will ever make it to the stage, can only hope it might, but if it were to, she likes the idea of the lines she has written disappearing as soon as they've been spoken. She doesn't say this sort of thing out loud, aware that it might sound pretentious or precious, but to her it feels like life itself. To her a play is a moment that lasts, until it no longer does. And when it's gone the people watching are left with only a feeling lingering in the air, like the fragrance of a perfume as someone walks away. It has occurred to her that while she's writing like this, in this almost meditative state, she feels closer to her mother than she's ever felt before.

She glances at the clock on the wall and feels her heart sink. Just a little more time . . . but no, she has to stop, get ready for work. She finds it funny how, when once the hardest part of writing was simply getting started, now it's being strict with herself about stopping. Sometimes, when she's writing, she feels like she's freewheeling down-hill, exhilarated. But if she doesn't stop now, she'll miss the train, she'll be late for work. It's a fifteen-minute walk to the station and she doesn't like to rush. Sometimes she deliberately takes the longer way around. After her morn-ing writing sessions, she finds she needs time to adjust back into the world, this whole other world that exists outside of her head, and her journey to work helps her make that transition. The walk lets her slip into her body again, like pulling on socks, wiggling her toes. She feels her legs moving, her feet. On the train, she watches people and when she gets to Flora, it feels good to be in a real, tangible world again, where she can talk to people, smile at them, touch their fingertips as she passes them their cups of coffee. She feels alert to all of this, her senses coming alive in different ways. Perhaps one day she will write about the people she encounters, make up lives for them. But for now, for this morning at least, her writing work is done.

Thirty-two

Hana doesn't hear from Samir after he leaves and she doesn't contact him either. It's not like her to indulge in self-pity, and she doesn't want to hear his excuses or justifications. She does what she always does when she feels like her life is falling apart: she throws herself into her work. She gets to the office early, stays late, and every day she is efficient and brilliant and brutal.

Sometimes a particular kind of client comes to her bewildered, in denial that their partner is leaving them but not in so much denial that they won't pay for a good matrimonial solicitor. If she's honest with herself, she's never quite believed them when they say they didn't see it coming, that it came out of the blue, that their partner had given them no indication of how they were feeling. She's always doubted this, convinced the signs must surely have been there and that people chose not to see them, saw only what they wanted to. Hadn't Samir always been more blasé than most about starting a family, relieved when she suggested at first that she had wanted to wait? But she'd chosen instead to believe in something, a dream. It occurs to her that if it wasn't children that had wedged them apart, it would have been something else.

In time the ice-cold shock she felt in the aftermath of his leaving thaws. At work she's poised, but at home she's swamped by waves of despair and hurt. She composes thousands of messages to Samir, ranging from pleading – *I*

245

can't imagine a future without you – to pure hatred: *you've wasted so many years of my life, you fucker*. Though she goes as far as typing these messages out, she's not so reckless as to press 'send'.

Still, there are evenings when her anger gets the better of her and she rages through the house like a hunter, overcome by the urge to hurt him, to kill him, if she could. On one such day, she tries, unsuccessfully, to hack into his emails, violently throws all the clothes he didn't take with him into bin liners, turns down all of the framed photographs with him in the picture. As the days go by, she grows more calculated, thinking of all the clever, underhand ways she could destroy him in the courts. *You've messed with the wrong person*, she begins to type in a text, with a kind of twisted villainous glee, *I will annihilate you*. But she doesn't send that message either.

Sometimes she stares at her phone, willing it to light up with a message from him. In a heated moment, she thinks of Mira and the man who ghosted her, Alicia's husband. Meanly, she thinks how ridiculous it was of Mira to have been so upset over a man she barely knew; it's nothing compared to what she is going through. But the spitefulness cools; she knows she's being unfair, knows that, really, she's only thinking this because she misses Mira. Now Mira's gone and moved away and Samir's gone, Hana feels her loneliness keenly. She remembers that day in Flora, when Mira had been upset. All men are dicks, Mira had said then. That was the same day Hana told Mira they were trying for a baby. Hana hasn't told her yet, about what's going on. She hasn't told anyone. She can't bear to, the humiliation too profound.

One night, eating dinner alone, Hana texts Mira. She does it without thinking:

Why did you have to move?

Mira doesn't text back for two days and, when she finally does, she says:

What do you mean? You know why, Lili's boyfriend moving in, remember?

Hana doesn't reply, realising that Mira's completely misunderstood. Failed to read between the lines.

Finally, almost a month after he walked out, a message arrives from Samir.

Hey. Wondering if we could talk.

Thirty-three

On Monday morning, five days before the deadline for the Hadley Prize closes, Mira types the words: *Slow fade to blackout* and presses 'save'.

And that's it. She's done it. She's finished writing her play.

It feels so purposeful and satisfying, writing those final words. It's like walking up a hill and taking a moment to look out over the view. She scrolls back and forth through the document. Every word, so familiar. She knows them like the moles on her skin.

The relief overcomes her and she's so tired she feels like crying. But she won't cry. This isn't a sad moment. She's happy. Mostly relieved, but also happy. And so she smiles and she can't stop smiling. She throws her head back, looks up to the ceiling. And then, like a rubber band, she snaps out of her chair, lets out a childish scream of joy and stamps her feet on the floor in a drum roll.

All she's ever wanted to do, ever since she was little, was write and tell stories. And yet for so long it's felt out of reach, lost in another world where only people better than her, cleverer than her, more together than her could go. But now she's done it. She's finished something substantial, seen it through to completion, has made something that belongs to her.

She looks out the window, searching for something. A gust of wind sends golden-yellow leaves from the cherry tree scattering. She remembers how her mother had been so proud of her when she said she wanted to study theatre and playwriting at university, even when everyone else around her, Hana especially, told her it was a complete waste of a degree. 'Don't listen to her,' her mother would say. 'She's too practical, doesn't know what it is to be creative.' Mira had always felt that she had a connection with their mother that maybe Hana didn't; this shared desire to make beautiful, moving things. Her mother never once made Mira feel like she was less than Hana, even though Hana had her Oxford law degree. But when she died, and Mira dropped out of university, Mira felt like she'd failed her, even though she had no real reason to ever believe that's what her mother would have thought at all. And yet for so long, she's carried that knot of failure inside her. Everything has been so hard, for so very long. Now she feels the knot loosen, just a little bit.

Mira feels her eyes fill up with tears again, wipes them with the backs of her hands. On the way to the shower, she jumps and claps her feet together, whoops like she's in a musical. Outside, walking to the station with her headphones in, she catches strangers' eyes and can't stop smiling.

She sends a message to her friends to tell them she's finished; they respond with claps and cheers. Molly says, *does this mean I can finally see you?* She messages Hana, whom Mira's not seen since the day she helped her move.

She sends the same message to Raef, who's been texting her every day from New York, wanting to know how it's going, sending her little encouraging messages and fist bump emojis. *It's done*, she types. *I've done it.* His reply comes instantly, even though it must be the middle of the night in New York. He sends her tiny red hearts and fat golden stars and a little bouquet of flowers, ribbons and sparklers.

Hana's reply comes several hours later. *Thank bloody god for that.*

Thirty-four

Hana makes an excuse and leaves work early. She's supposed to meet Samir at St Pancras this Tuesday afternoon, at one of the busy chain cafés in the station. The meeting was his idea, but she suggested the café. She chose it on purpose, somewhere she wouldn't ever normally, willingly, go. The last thing she wants is to meet near the office, where one of her colleagues might bump into her, and she doesn't want him to come home, because she doesn't think he deserves to, and because she knows that if he does, she won't stay in control of her temper, and it matters to her that she retains self-possession. Plus, it doesn't matter what he says here, she thinks. It's not as if she has any happy memories that could be ruined by the association of meeting him here.

The café she's chosen is noisy, the kind of place where dirty, used mugs with dregs of coffee in the bottom sit on the tables for ages before being cleared, passengers coming and going. She knows that it will make Samir squirm, having to explain himself in a place like this, within earshot of strangers. But she doesn't plan on staying long. She's simply going to listen to what he has to say and then she'll go.

When she arrives, he's waiting for her at a tiny table squeezed by the window. She sees him before he sees her. He looks tired, dark circles under his eyes, and he's wearing a coat she doesn't recognise. When he looks up and notices her, he presses his lips together in a not quite smile, raises his hand. He stands when she approaches. The gesture seems silly, overly formal.

'Hey. Can I get you anything?' he says, as she unties the belt of her coat.

She doesn't reply but sits down, placing her handbag on her lap. She coolly inspects the tabletop and then opens her bag, finds a packet of antibacterial wipes and, taking one, cleans down the surface. She takes another and wipes her hands. She notices, without looking at him directly, that he is still wearing his wedding ring, as is she. But the observation is just that, an observation; it doesn't make her feel anything.

'So, how have you been?' he asks.

'Better.'

'Better as in—'

'As in I've been better. And also, I've been worse.'

He nods. He looks at her, ashamed.

'So,' she says. 'Where are you staying?'

'With friends.' He doesn't elaborate. She doesn't ask him to. 'But I think I might take some time off, you know? Go travelling. Take a break.'

She flicks a stray crumb that escaped her cleaning, pretending to be uninterested. 'You could go to Paris,' she says, quietly.

'Sorry?'

'Nothing.'

He says, 'I wanted to ask if I could come by the house sometime, if that's okay, collect some of my things.'

It's not lost on her he says 'the house', not 'home'.

'Or you could send a taxi. I put your things in bags,' Hana says.

'You packed my stuff?'

'If by "packed" you mean, threw them in a bin liner, then yes, I did.' She talks briskly, her voice professional. Every now and again, she glances at her watch.

He looks upset. His mug of coffee sits in front of him, untouched.

'Oh, come on, Samir. What did you expect, you walked out on me.' Her voice is low.

He looks at her, unsettled, as if he's trying to think of what to say. Finally, he reaches across the table. 'Hana, I . . .'

She flinches away from him. Shakes her head almost indiscernibly and shifts her gaze so that instead of looking at him, she's looking behind his shoulder, out of the window overlooking the concourse. There's so much she wants to ask. A woman approaches, sidestepping between the narrowly spaced tables, pushing a large purple suitcase on wheels, apologising to everyone. She bumps into Hana's chair; Hana tucks it in closer to the table.

Samir clears his throat. He glances about him, draws his hand back. 'Look, Han. Can we go somewhere else? Please?' He is distraught, she can tell by the look on his face. 'I just really want to be able to talk this through.'

'We can talk right here.'

A train announcement comes over the speakers. Hana watches the steady stream of people rushing past the window in a blur, wonders how many of them are alone, how many are going home to someone. A man in a baseball cap is playing Debussy on the piano in the arcade.

They sit like this, not saying anything, until eventually Samir crosses his arms and says with a cool calmness, 'Okay, fine. We'll talk here. I think you and I both know this isn't working—'

253

'And I wonder why that is. Is it because, maybe, you lied to me about wanting to start a family, wasted years of my life—'

'I didn't lie—'

'Right. No, of course. So that day, when you told me you "gave me your word" – your words, not mine – that whenever I felt ready to start a family, we would; did I just imagine it?' Her voice isn't raised, it's matter of fact; still, Samir looks about him, nervously.

'Hana.'

'What?'

'You know, I hoped we might be able to do this amicably. Like adults.' The look on his face is weary. 'You know, for what it's worth, I really thought I wanted what you wanted. That kind of life. Whatever you might think of me right now, I wasn't pretending or lying to you on purpose. I honestly thought I would want it all. You know, eventually. And maybe that's still the case, maybe one day I will. But just—'

'Just not with me,' she finishes. It surprises her how the words fall out of her mouth so easily. And then something inside her shifts. It's Hana who stands up.

'Hana—'

'I understand. We both want different things, you're right.' She takes a deep breath, steadying herself. 'There's no point dragging this out, Samir. I can take it from here. We have that advantage at least. I'll ask someone from the office to email you. It's best to get these things started in writing. Of course, you know you'll need a solicitor. It'll be easier if we make one joint application.'

These are the kinds of things she says most days to her clients, and yet saying them now, to Samir, she feels as if she's outside of her body, watching herself, the words unfamiliar on her tongue. She almost doesn't want to stop talking, afraid of what emotions might take over if she does.

'Just do me one favour—'

He's looking at her shocked, like he's still catching up with what she's just said.

'—Just, don't go to Allegra's old firm, whatever you do. Else I won't hear the end of it.'

'I won't,' he says.

'I'm sure you'll agree, we'll want to do this quickly.' If she doesn't leave now, she doesn't know what else she might say, or do.

'Hana I—'

But she's already turned, is already walking away.

Somehow, she makes it back to Muswell Hill. But when she gets off the bus, instead of crossing the road to go home, she turns left and walks in the direction of Flora. It's the only place she can think of to go. If she's quick, she might just make it before it closes.

Mira is bent over the till, punching buttons, when Hana comes in.

'Mira.'

Mira looks up, Hana sees the surprise on her face.

'What's up?' she says.

Hana goes round the counter, moves closer towards her.

'He – I . . . it's over. It's over. We're over.'

Mira looks at her, brows drawn, and then Hana just falls into her, crying.

'Han. Oh, Han.'

Hana feels Mira's arms around her and suddenly the extreme tightness inside her begins to unravel. She's unable to control the violent shaking that takes over her body as she sobs. But Mira keeps holding her tight, telling her in a soft voice again and again that it will all be okay, until eventually Hana stills, exhausted and overwhelmed, Mira's hands passing gently over her hair.

Thirty-five

Mira sits at the square white table in the kitchen in Raef's flat with her laptop in front of her. She's finalising her play entry, checking that the pages are numbered correctly, the font is consistent, the spacing is even. The deadline is tomorrow, and she intends to submit the play today. She would have done it yesterday, only she ended up spending the night at Hana's, after she came to Flora, so unexpectedly, in tears.

Mira checks the first page. Her name is absent – the competition entries must be anonymous – but there is the title. She centres the words A MARRIAGE and feels a ball of nervous energy bounce right through her. She scrolls.

Act one, Scene one. She reads through the stage directions, checking they are correct; it is night, there is a couple, couple number one as she calls them, in the kitchen, doing ordinary domestic things. They've just had friends with a new baby over for an early dinner, but the friends are gone and we don't see them. Natalia is at the sink, washing up; Adam is wiping down the counters. They are talking. It starts small, intimate; a conversation about how nice it was to see their friends, the things they said. Natalia talks dotingly about the baby, how adorable she is; how happy their friends seemed, even if tired. It's obvious that she is dropping hints. She wants to talk about having a baby, but Adam doesn't take the bait. It goes on like this for a while and a tension builds. Adam makes a bad joke about new parents in an attempt to defuse it. Natalia is annoyed at him; she wants him to take this seriously. Adam makes another joke about all the things they could do if they didn't have a baby. They could go anywhere they wanted to, he says, lighthearted. They could go to Paris! And then comes the line, the one she overheard Hana say, that's stuck in her mind ever since.

I don't want to go to fucking Paris.

And then, a few lines later, again:

Do you know what's really hurtful though? Having to beg my husband to want to have a child with me.

Mira chews her bottom lip as she reads, her fingers hesitating over the delete button. She remembers hearing Hana say this, months ago now. It's been so long since she first wrote this part that she'd almost forgotten that they came from Hana first, not Natalia. She always thought she'd change it, but the tone is spot on for the kind of character she needs Natalia to be. She highlights the first sentence, *I don't want to go to fucking Paris,* hits delete, tries to think of something else Natalia could say. But nothing else comes. She's spent so long working on her characters, she knows them inside out now; anything else would sound fake. And so she undoes the change.

It's surely not that big a deal. The story might have been inspired by Hana and Samir in the very beginning, but it became something else, its own story, a long time ago. In the final scene, all three sets of actors come together, like echoes of each other, and in Mira's head, it's like a chorus. This is her art. In *Pavements,* she had wanted her characters to all lie down on the stage, but for no particular reason. But in this, the artistic, visual element of the three couples somehow makes sense. There's meaning to it. It's true that in her play Natalia and Adam separate too, but Mira had written that months ago before Hana told her what was going on with Samir; she only found that out yesterday. And their reasons for breaking up are different. In the play, it turns out that Adam has been having a long-term affair, the woman he is seeing already pregnant with his child. Though Mira's loath to think about him, she can still remember what Dominic once said – how people write about real life all the time, but how it becomes something else when the act of writing takes over.

If Hana hadn't told her the night before that Samir had moved out and they were separating, Mira might not be feeling so concerned about all this. She was astonished by how much Hana seemed to need her. 'You won't go, will you?' she'd said again and again, gripping Mira's arm, and Mira had reassured her she would stay. In her sadness and her panic, all of Hana's sharp edges seemed to fall off her and, even though the very next day Hana was still up early and ready for work, for the first time in a long time, Mira sensed an openness, a vulnerability about her. It's unlikely that Hana will ever read the play, but Mira doesn't want to do anything to upset her, not the way things are for Hana right now.

Still, to be sure, she texts Molly to sound out her conscience.

Mira: Do you think it's okay to use something real that my sister said in my play? Like word for word . . .
Molly: Haven't you submitted it yet???
Mira: No . . . reading it through first. Got a little panicky that I might have stolen what she said . . .? It's just a couple of lines at the beginning. But it's v. distinctively Hana.
Molly: Can't believe you are stressing over this. It's actually very sweet.

Molly: OBVIOUSLY it's okay
Molly: I do it all the time. No one cares / knows!
Molly: Plus she's your sister, not like sisters don't steal from each other!!
Molly: JUST SEND IT! DO NOT MISS THE DEAD-LINE!

It's only the play that wins that will get performed anyway. All this agonising is over nothing.

Mira fills in the submission form, uploads the play and then clicks 'submit'.

Thirty-six

It's Sunday morning, the week before Christmas, and Hana is walking with Mira through the farmers' market at Alexandra Palace, both of them drinking coffees from takeaway cups. Hana asked Mira to meet her there and then come back to her house for lunch. Hana is wearing a beret and carrying a wicker basket on her arm filled with fruit and vegetables in brown paper bags, and a glass bottle of juice. It's misty and the air smells of bonfires. Both sisters are wearing gloves and boots and their breath makes little shapes in the air. They walk slowly, in no rush in spite of the cold. Hana stops at a stall to buy two slices of apple cake. They haven't seen each other in a month, since the day that Hana met Samir at the café in the station and then ended up in Flora, crying on Mira's shoulder. Mira had stayed over at Hana's that night. Since then, Hana's been busy with work and starting her divorce application.

'So, what happens now that you've submitted the damn thing?' Hana asks.

'Now I wait,' Mira shrugs. 'They announce the winners in February. I don't expect anything, though.'

'Honestly Mira,' Hana says. 'You don't have to offer little disclaimers about how you don't expect anything every time anyone asks you about your work. You've done it, you've set out what you wanted to do, it's an achievement, so just . . . be proud of it.'

Mira shoves Hana softly with her shoulder while they walk.

'Thanks,' Mira says. She keeps smiling at Hana.

'What?' Hana says. 'What are you looking at me like that for?'

Mira just laughs. 'Han,' she says. 'Oh, Han, Han, Han!'

They keep walking. Mira stops at a stall to buy herself a crepe. When they reach the end of the path, where there are no more stalls, they stop walking and stand for a moment, looking through the mist down the clearing that leads back into the woods. Some of the trees are already bare, their branches black like burnt matchsticks. There are children wrapped up in bright puffy coats and scarves and hats. They roar, kicking through piles of leaves.

'So,' Mira says softly. 'What about you? What happens next for you?'

Hana takes a breath. 'Well, mostly a lot of paperwork. I've asked Sadie to take care of the applications. It will take months. Meanwhile he's going travelling. Says he wants to see the world. But we've agreed we'll settle everything, so no one's going to court. We'll have to sell the house, though, and, well that . . . that's not really something I want to have to think about now.'

'We could live together!' Mira jokes.

Hana pulls a face. 'God, imagine. What a disaster that would be.'

'Oh, I don't know,' Mira responds, lightly. 'I don't think it would be that bad!'

'Well,' Hana says decisively. 'It's never going to happen, so—'

Mira laughs.

'—But as for the rest of it, in theory, it should be relatively simple. No grounds for adultery, at least. So I just wait, too.' She grimaces.

It's easier than Hana thought it would be to talk to Mira about these things. She was surprised that Mira was the only person she had wanted to see after meeting Samir in the station. Mira can be terribly annoying – she is still, on occasion, the absolute worst – but it is a relief, a comfort, to know she is there. It's also a relief to no longer have to pretend to Mira that she has it all together when she doesn't. It's exhausting to keep up the appearance of being perfect. Yet she's realised that's what she's been doing for most of her life.

There are days she feels like a failure, even though she always firmly tells her clients that there's no such thing as failing at a marriage. But there are other days when she feels unencumbered, when she understands that it's not impossible to be without Samir.

'Sorry, Han,' Mira says.

'It's okay.' Hana takes a deep breath in. 'You know, I'm actually okay.' She glances at Mira sideways and then says quickly, 'I've got an appointment on Monday. At a fertility clinic. It's just a preliminary consultation, to go through my options on my own. IVF, sperm donors, that kind of thing. Might be too late to freeze my eggs, but you never know.'

'God, Hana. That's . . . I'm proud of you. You're so . . .'

'Resilient,' Hana says firmly, landing heavily on the 't', in a way that suggests she's practised this, already thought of this word to describe herself.

Mira snorts. 'Modest, too.'

'What about you?' Hana asks. 'Anything happening in your love life, or are you just waiting for your landlord to come back?'

'That's not funny.'

Hana smiles and they walk back to the gates.

Thirty-seven

Mira's sitting cross-legged on her bed, on a video call with Raef. They text all the time now, and they've started talking on weekends like this too. Even though Hana has taken to teasing her about him, Mira doesn't know what this thing between them is. It's strange to her that they've become friends despite the fact they've only met each other twice in person: once when Mira came to see the flat, and again when Raef stopped by the café to drop off the keys before he left. But she likes talking to him. He's sweet and uncomplicated, ridiculously cute. He's generous, has asked several times if there's anything she needs in the flat. She always says no, but he goes ahead and orders things online that he thinks she might need, an extra blanket or batteries for the television remote. Once, she made an offhand comment about the coffee cups in the kitchen being too small; within a week, bigger ones arrived. Hana says she'd find this creepy, but Mira thinks it's thoughtful. It's kind.

She doesn't know what will happen when he returns for good in three months. He came back to England to visit his family in Oxford over Christmas, but when Mira asked if he wanted the flat back for the holidays, he said he wasn't planning to be in London. She couldn't help but feel disappointed that she wouldn't see him. She supposes when his secondment is over and he's back for good, she will have to find somewhere else to live. But the flat feels like a home, and it's the first time she's felt that for many years. She's overwhelmingly grateful to him, for the loan of his flat, for the lack of rent, needing only to cover her bills. When she thinks about how different her life is now compared to a few months ago, she can't believe it – it feels unreal, like a dream or a scene from a film.

She's telling Raef about the film she watched the night before when her laptop pings with a notification. 'Hang on a second.' And then she jumps up, holding the laptop in her hand.

'Oh my God.'

'What? What's wrong?'

'Oh my God, oh my God, oh my God,' she repeats.

'What is it?'

'It's here. The email's here.'

'No,' he instinctively understands her meaning. 'Really?'

'Yes.'

'Okay. Calm, calm. Open it. Open it. Sit down first, then open it,' he corrects.

Mira flops back on the bed with a thud, almost hits her head against the wall as she does so. She takes a deep breath, clicks open the email.

'No, I don't want to look at it.' She half turns her face away from the screen and shuts her eyes tight.

'No, no,' Raef says. 'Come on. You can do it. Whatever it says, it's fine. It's fine.' Out of the corner of her eye, she sees him shrug. 'What does the subject line say?'

She opens her eyes fully, minimises the window he's in, and clicks into her email. 'It says . . . Congratulations—'

Raef draws in his breath.

'—to all entrants.' Her voice falls flat.

'And that's okay,' Raef says emphatically. 'That's a nice thing to say. Go on?'

She scrolls into the body of the email, scanning it, but is unable to make sense of it.

'Um . . . wait.' She reads the screen impatiently. 'The standard of entries has been extremely high this year . . . thousands of entrants . . . blah blah blah . . . however,' and here she takes a breath in and her voice grows louder, 'A MARRIAGE. . . rose . . . above all others – oh my God, oh my God, oh my God. *Raef*—'

All she can hear is the sound of Raef laughing.

The prize organisers want to meet with her straight away, they want *A Marriage* to be on in early July. They want to introduce her to their partnership theatre and the woman who'll be directing the play. It's only a small theatre, hidden away on a residential road near a park in Friern Barnet, an area in north London she's never been to before, but the theatre is known for showing original work that is fresh and exciting.

When they invite Mira to visit, her first thought is that the theatre is too tiny. She finds it impossible to believe that people have heard of it; the only reason she has is because of the prize. But then she considers the small empty stage and how close it is to the audience, and she can immediately feel how intimate a performance here would be. It's perfect. At her first meeting, the prize team explain that they'd like her to be involved with the production so that she can have some experience of what it's like to creatively direct a play, which is not something she's done before beyond a few small-scale shows at university in her second year before she dropped out of her course, twelve years ago when she was twenty. With everything happening at once, she hardly has time to process the significance of winning the Hadley Prize and what this might mean for her career, as a playwright. It's exciting but overwhelming. She's suddenly so busy that it doesn't immediately occur to her to worry about what Hana might think, about those lines in the play that Hana had said and which Mira had thought she would change but never did.

Then, Hana texts Mira asking when she might be free for dinner, and that's when Mira starts worrying, just a little bit, about the play and Hana's part in inspiring it, all over again. But whenever the worry rises, Mira remembers what Molly said – what Dominic said, much as she still can't stand to think of him – about life inspiring art, how it's part of the creative process. With the prize behind her now, she feels emboldened, her story has earned validation.

And so much has happened since she started writing this play. Hana's changed. She's so much more supportive of Mira's writing. And so Mira decides that if it comes up in conversation, she'll say something about how she got the idea for the play. And if it doesn't, it doesn't. If it doesn't, she won't.

At Hana's suggestion, they meet for dinner at a Mexican place in Shoreditch on a Tuesday night. Mira is late. When she runs into the restaurant, she notices Hana, sitting straight-backed with a blazer on, busy typing on her phone. The walls are bright pink and the music, an eighties' playlist, is very loud. Everyone else is much younger than them. Mira looks around, bemused at Hana's choice.

'Why did you pick this place?' Mira asks, as she slides into the seat opposite Hana and starts to unwind the scarf around her neck. She grabs a tortilla chip from a basket in front of Hana and pops it in her mouth.

Hana looks at Mira with a blank expression. 'Because I thought you might like it,' she says, as if it's entirely obvious. She takes a pointed sip from the bottle of lemonade she's already ordered. 'You're late. As always.' But then she smiles, takes a handful of tortilla chips and stuffs them into her mouth. She looks funny. It's so nice to see her happy.

'You look good,' Mira smiles.

'Do I?' Hana says, with her mouth deliberately open. Mira laughs in surprise. This version of Hana; Mira likes her.

While they wait for someone to come and take their order, Hana talks about her day, and when their food arrives, Hana picks up her bottle of lemonade and raises it in Mira's direction. 'Well, congratulations then.' Mira clinks her bottle with her glass of sparkling water. Then Hana says, 'So? Are you finally going to tell me what this play's about?'

Mira nods, swallowing a bite of burrito at the same time. She pauses, taking her time over her words, aware that an opportunity has objectively presented itself. 'Hmm, so . . . it's about this couple and they both want. . . different things—'

'Different what?'

The music is so loud, it's almost impossible to talk normally.

'*Things*. Different things.'

Hana grimaces but then her expression changes and she starts laughing. 'Tell me about it,' she says, with an eye roll.

Mira feels encouraged. 'Yeah, exactly,' she says. 'That's the point I'm trying to make, you know, like we've *all* been there. So I want it to feel like this couple could be anyone. Anyone.' She takes a sip of her drink and before she can change her mind, she adds with a conspiratorial smile, 'Actually, you know, I came up with the idea one night when I was round your place—'

Just then, Hana's phone buzzes loudly. She sighs dramatically and picks it up, holding her phone directly in front of her face, and then starts typing.

'God. This trainee! He is so infuriating. He can't seem to understand the most basic of instructions. I don't even know how this generation's getting training contracts these days, I don't know what's wrong with them. They're like children. Anyway. Right, give me a second. Nearly done.'

Mira waits. After a couple of minutes, Hana sets her phone back down on the table impatiently. 'So, what were you saying? How long did you say the play is on for again?'

'Oh, that's not what I was saying, but two weeks. It'll be on for a fortnight. Early July. But what I was saying was—'

'Two weeks?' Hana says, again. 'All that work, for two weeks? You should really find some other calling. And July? Really? Does it really take that long to take a script and find some actors to learn some lines?'

'There's a little more to it than that—'

'By the way,' Hana speaks over her, 'you don't have to run off after this, do you? Because I've ordered something and I need to pick it up.' This time Hana picks up her phone again and taps into her inbox, and then holds the screen up so Mira can see. It's an email confirmation for a new top-of-the-range laptop. Mira looks at it, confused.

'It's for you.' Hana is smiling brightly. 'I got it for you.'

'What?'

'You've had that old laptop for years. It's the one Samir gave you, right? It's barely working. And it's filthy—'

'But Hana, no, this is too expensive,' Mira says.

269

'It's nothing, I got a good deal.' Hana shrugs. 'I wanted to do this for you.'

An unexpected emotion comes over Mira as she begins to understand that this gift is Hana's way of showing her she's proud of her achievement. She tries to say something, but Hana cuts her off.

'You can write your next play on it. And besides, Samir might ask for his laptop back in the settlement.' At this, Hana throws her head back and laughs and laughs and it's at this precise moment that Mira purposefully forgets what she was about to tell Hana. And anyway, Mira thinks on the way back home, she can't even remember the things she said yesterday, let alone almost a year ago. Because who remembers things like that?

Raef will be back from New York for good in August, but he keeps saying that he's sure they can figure something out, that he's sure Mira could stay a little longer in his flat if she needs to, until she finds someplace else. Mira's nervous about all her prize money being eaten up by rent, when really what she'd like to do is use it as a way to allow her to reduce her hours at the café and spend more time writing. The prize money is a fraction of what people like Hana and Raef earn, and it's not as if she can just stop working, but, to Mira, the money is everything, an acknowledgement that her writing is important, something she's never allowed herself to believe before. She checks her bank account every morning just to make sure it's still there.

Weeks pass, time moves quicker than she thought it would. There are days of auditions and recalls, and finally, a cast is confirmed. When Mira is invited to meet the six actors playing Adam and Natalia, she can't stop looking at them, feels like poking them with her index finger to check they are real. One day, she's asked if she'd like to sit in on a table read and this is when suddenly Mira feels a distance between her work and the work of the actors sitting around the table. As she listens, the lines stop being merely lines that she typed on a laptop; they become alive. Mira is hooked on every word, gasps at moments of tension even though she was the one who wrote them.

One night, a Thursday, she finds herself walking past the bookshop on the Broadway and she stops to look in, peering through the railings down into the basement window. There are fewer people there than when she used to go, maybe just seven of them sitting in a circle. She only recognises one or two of their faces. Dominic's standing up, leaning against the desk, gesturing with his hands as he speaks. He looks so wholesome, so unbelievably earnest. But it's all just an affectation, she knows now. There'll always be men like him. And she didn't need him to write the play, anyway. She did that all by herself.

Then, finally, on a warm Friday evening in the first week of July, it's opening night at the theatre in Friern Barnet. When Mira arrives, she has to make her way through small clusters of people gathered in twos and threes in the small courtyard outside the entrance, sipping drinks in plastic glasses. Slowly, it dawns on her that they are here to watch *A Marriage*, that they have actually bought tickets for her play tonight, and she's filled with a confusion of excitement and pride. She hesitates on the threshold, and then steps through the doors and into the small foyer, where the ceiling is low and suddenly the light seems darker. A woman in dungarees stands behind a tiny counter of a bar and smiles at her. She buys a bottle of cold water, presses it against her neck.

Mira is wearing a short black dress with little flowers scattered all over it, with a belt and bright red lipstick and a bag hanging off her shoulder. She stands in the foyer, one arm crossed against her body. There's a framed poster for an old play and underneath it a ledge with little piles of programmes, cheaply printed on pale yellow paper cut down to A5, but with Mira's name listed first, next to the word 'writer'. She smiles to herself when she notices this, takes a handful of programmes and puts them in her bag.

Slowly, people begin to move inside and now the foyer fills up with people talking in murmurs, fanning themselves with their hands. A man and a woman from the Hadley Prize see Mira and come over to her. They greet her, ask how she is feeling, hope that she's not too nervous. She's not really nervous; after all, it's not as if she's the one performing on stage. But it's hard to explain how she is feeling. She feels that the play is both hers and not hers. The sense of detachment she first felt at the table read is so much stronger, now that her play has become something else in the hands of the director, and the bodies and the voices of the actors. She likes that they have, in a way, made it their own. Tomorrow, the play will be slightly different, it will move people differently. She loves knowing that. But she doesn't tell the people from the Hadley Prize any of this. Instead, she just makes small talk and smiles a lot, as they carry on talking between themselves, catching up on the lives of shared acquaintances and industry gossip.

She takes a step backwards, so that she's standing slightly apart from them. She checks her phone. Raef has sent her a text to say break a leg, four-leaf clovers and crossed fingers.

She smiles. Her friends are going to watch the play with her on Saturday night, they've all booked tickets for the front row, and afterwards they're going to go out for dinner; she wishes Raef could join them too. Hana's meant to be coming tonight but she hasn't arrived yet. Mira told Hana repeatedly that she didn't have to come, but Hana insisted, saying she wanted to and that it was important. It's not that Mira doesn't want Hana there, if anything she's touched by how Hana's finally taking her work seriously, but still, there's a tiny part of her that's nervous about how she might respond to the play's subject matter. A bigger part of her feels certain she's worrying about nothing, what with her concept of the multiple actors and the ending, with Adam having cheated on Natalia. More and more, Mira truly believes that her play has distanced itself from its beginnings in reality.

But Mira's not thinking about any of this right now. Instead, she's looking around her, taking in every little detail; the early evening sunlight falling into the courtyard, the soft hum of other people's conversation. She's struck by the urge to want to remember everything about tonight. Because Hana's right, it *is* important. She suddenly feels overwhelmed by an emotion; not quite happiness, not quite excitement, but something in between. Something that almost feels like a promise fulfilled, or relief.

A little bell rings, stirring her from her reverie. A staff member opens the doors through to the rows of seats. Mira joins the slow-moving line. The woman from the prize team squeezes her arms and grins with her teeth and says, 'Ready?' Mira almost wishes that the woman wasn't here, wishes she could continue to have this moment to herself, but she knows that only makes her sound ungrateful.

Without the prize, the play wouldn't be here at all. So she grins back gamely and gives the woman a thumbs up.

Inside, the set is simple, with a dining table and a fake kitchen unit, a kettle on the counter. It looks like a room from a dolls' house, only at life-size scale. Mira scans her eyes over it like she's doing a stock take. Everything is where it's supposed to be. She's seen her play in rehearsals but only broken up, an act at a time or individual scenes, never the whole way through uninterrupted. Tonight, she will watch it like everyone else, as a member of the audience.

The stage lights are on, beams falling in shafts, dust motes turning. She takes her seat. People shuffle into the rows behind her, coughing and clearing their throats, talking low. But these sounds feel softer to Mira than they do in the world outside, and also far away, as if she has earplugs in. Every now and again, Mira looks over her shoulder to see if Hana has arrived yet. The woman from the prize team tugs her sleeve and whispers something in her ear. Mira leans towards her, keeping her eyes on the stage; she doesn't catch what the woman says. The lights dim. There is a hush.

But there's a small commotion in the front row as Hana comes in whispering to everyone, 'Sorry, sorry.' Mira smells her perfume before she sees her, strong and woody. And then, she's there. She sits down in the free seat next to Mira and pulls a face. 'Sorry!' she whispers loudly. 'Work!' Mira nods to say she understands, then presses her finger to her lips. More fiddling as Hana turns off her phone and pushes her handbag under her seat. And then, finally, the lights go up and the play begins.

It's like watching a very realistic dream, seeing her play on stage. The stage is small, and not especially raised, so there's barely a separation between stage and audience, and because of this, it almost doesn't feel like a play. It feels like walking along a pavement, glancing through a window, seeing a couple gesturing to each other – and somehow knowing all there is to know about them. It feels like life. It feels private, as if the audience is intruding. Mira senses the uneasiness in the air, as the tension builds, as Natalia and Adam say hurtful things to each other, things they'd never dream of saying in front of other people. She's lost in it, the flow; she's no longer conscious of ever having written it, it doesn't feel written, it feels lived and spoken and true. And then, towards the end of the opening scene, just before the couples are about to change, Hana bends down for her handbag, picks it up and puts it on her lap. She stands up. She walks quickly along the row of seats, her back straight, without even trying to stoop so as not to block the view.

Mira looks behind her, confused, and sees Hana open the door that leads to the foyer. She looks back at the stage. It takes a moment for the realisation to hit and then she feels her whole body go cold. She knows she should go to her, but her legs feel heavy, like they are stuck in plaster, and it's not easy for her to move out of her seat. She drags herself up, without coming to standing, and then she half crouches and moves quickly, smoothly, until she's up the steps and through the door.

The moment she's in the foyer, she feels her heart beating faster. A thick strip of sunlight falls through the glass doors, the effect so intensely blinding, Mira has to raise her hand to shield her eyes. She looks around for Hana, to ask if anyone's seen her sister, but the foyer is empty, there's no one there. Then, she sees her – Hana is across the street by the old walled gate to the park, walking briskly in the direction of the main road. Mira rushes through the doors.

'Hana,' she calls after her.

'Hana!'

Mira runs until she catches up with her, until she is just behind her, just within reach.

'Hana,' she calls again, 'Hana—'

'What?' Hana turns around. 'What? Why aren't you in there, watching your precious little play?'

'I . . . you just left. I—'

'You what?'

Hana looks furious, the tendons of her jaw clenching. Mira feels lost. She gestures with her hand, not knowing what to say.

'No, go on, tell me,' says Hana. 'You what? You thought I wouldn't notice? You thought I wouldn't figure it out, that your pathetic little "play" is supposed to be about me? Have you just been taking notes on my breakup all this time? Listening in to things I've said in private?'

'It's not . . . no, you've got it all wrong, it's not about you at all.'

Hana laughs bitterly. 'Right. Of course. Let's see, shall we?' She brings a yellow piece of paper up to her face and Mira realises it's the programme. She reads it out. '"A play about the breakdown of a modern marriage. Or are they already broken?"'

'I didn't write that. I had nothing to do with that part, I didn't even see the programme until today—'

'So all this time you've been writing, you've been making fun of me? Playing games with my life?' Hana shakes the paper.

'Playing games?' Mira says, bewildered. 'What do you mean? I'm not playing games with anything, Han, you've got it all wrong, why would I . . . no, you've got this all wrong—'

'Oh, really?' Hana looks at the programme again. '"A painful study of a modern relationship falling apart. What happens when a couple can't express their emotions?"' She reads it out in an exaggerated voice, in the style of a presenter, only it's not at all funny. 'Do you think you know so much about marriage just from watching mine collapse? Do you think you're so clever that this kind of thing would never happen to you?'

'No, I . . . I just—'

'What would you know about marriage, anyway? You just go after other people's husbands—'

Mira is so startled, it takes her a moment to understand that Hana's talking about Dominic.

'—All I want – all I wanted was a child. And you get to turn that into this?' Hana's face is screwed up in disbelief, her voice trembling.

'Hana, no . . . I see why you're angry, I get that.' Mira holds her hands up, asking Hana to calm down. 'I understand why you're angry. I just found it interesting, that's all—'

'You found my life *interesting*? Am I supposed to be flattered by that? You think just because your life is shit, you get to crap on everyone else's?'

'No, no! I just needed an idea. I found the idea of wanting children interesting. That's all I meant. I needed one idea to write about, and yes, you gave me an idea—'

'I did not "give" you anything.'

'But it was just an idea, the tiniest speck of an idea, and then I made it into something else. I made it into *something*

277

else. That's all I did. If you just come back, watch the rest of it, you'd see. The actors, they change, it's meaningful, it's something bigger than just—'

'I've seen enough,' Hana says.

'I tried to tell you.'

'When?'

'That night, at that restaurant, when you got me the laptop. I tried to tell you but—'

'I have no memory of you trying to tell me anything about this. I think I would have remembered.'

'But I did. Try, I mean—'

'Clearly not hard enough.' Then, after a pause, Hana says, 'I know what you think of me. You think I can't express my emotions.'

Mira has no idea what Hana is talking about. She searches for something to say. 'I don't . . . I never said that. I didn't write the programme.'

'Yes, but you've always said it. You and Samir, always joking about it behind my back. I wouldn't be surprised if he had a thing for you all along—'

'That's not . . . It doesn't even make sense. I would never. If you'd just come back and watch the second act—'

'You think that your sadness is special. That because you cried and cried when your mother died and because you just couldn't carry on with your bloody university degree, you feel more than the rest of us? And my feelings are nothing?—'

'Hana.'

'—Well, guess what? She was *my* mother too, Mira, but I've never gone around acting the way you do—'

'Hana,' Mira half laughs in disbelief, 'this has got nothing to do with her, you're turning this into something it's not—'

'You think I don't talk about my emotions? Well, maybe that's because I never got a chance. Some of us don't just get to drop out of life and have everyone else pick up the pieces.'

Hana turns around, starts jabbing at her phone and looking around, squinting for her taxi.

'That's not fair. I'm not doing this,' Mira says.

Hana turns back. 'You know, I'll never forgive you for this.' She turns, walks away.

'I made it up!' Mira shouts in frustration. 'I made it up!'

Hana stops walking, looks back and says, quite calmly now, 'Of course you made it up. You and your little "play".' She makes the speech marks with her fingers in the air, carries on walking.

'He did have a thing for me, actually.'

Hana looks over her shoulder.

'Samir. Yeah,' Mira says. Now she's started, she can't stop. 'Yeah, he kissed me.'

'Oh, please,' Hana says coldly. 'I don't believe you.'

'Fine,' Mira pulls her phone out of her back pocket as she approaches Hana. 'I've probably still got all his text messages from after it happened. I kept them.' Mira scrolls through her phone furiously. 'Oh, look. Here they are.' She tilts her head and smiles at Hana meanly.

For a second, Hana doesn't say anything. Then she swipes the phone out of Mira's hand. She reads the words on the screen, her face at first expressionless, until something changes in it. Mira's heart is pounding, echoing in her head. The fabric under her arms feels damp. She immediately regrets what she's done. She knows that the way Samir has written those messages, the things he's said, makes everything sound a whole lot more extreme than it was.

When Hana looks up, her eyes are shiny. 'How could you,' her voice so quiet Mira barely hears her. She thrusts the phone back at Mira. Mira takes it.

A car pulls up. Hana runs forward.

'Hana, wait—'

But she's gone.

One year later

Hana is kneeling on a whitewashed floor, surrounded by brown packing boxes. She's wearing a pair of blue jeans and a white shirt half tucked in at the waist, her feet bare, her hair tied back in a ponytail. She is holding a pair of scissors, which she uses to cut through the Sellotape sealing the top of the box closest to her. Outside, the sky is light blue, threaded through with thin white clouds, and there is a steady and not insignificant breeze. It isn't warm, exactly, but it's not cold either. The French doors which lead to the small garden are wide open to let in the fresh air. Through the doors comes the faint sound of traffic and also children playing in the distance. Somewhere, someone is playing a piano.

Hana moved into her new flat yesterday. After the divorce, she found a new job at a family law firm in Highgate. The firm is much smaller than her old company. The work is no less demanding, but it is more accommodating, her workload more manageable. It's also much closer to this new flat, which to Hana is more important than anything else. Later this year, she's scheduled to start donor insemination, and the consultants say her chances for a successful pregnancy are high. Hana likes knowing that in the future, when she goes back to work after her maternity leave, she won't be far from home.

Hana paid extra for the removers to do her packing, but she wants to do the unpacking herself, so that she can put things exactly where she wants them. She opens the box in front of her. There's a layer of tightly packed scrunched-up newspaper. She removes it and starts unpacking the contents of the box, placing various items, books and picture frames, a ceramic painted bowl she bought on holiday in Greece, a pair of candleholders, on the floor next to her. When the box is empty, she cuts the remaining tape and then flattens it with her feet and gathers up the newspaper for recycling. She is about to throw the paper away when something catches her eye in one of the crumpled sheets, the side of a face, half a chin, one eye, printed in faded ink. She makes out a face, thinks it can't be. She quickly smooths the paper on the floor. It is. It's Mira.

The photo is only small, her face distorted by the print, and most of the article is missing, but it isn't hard for Hana to find the rest of it online, on the website for a London newspaper. She reads the article on her phone. It's old, from a month earlier. It's a piece about the new faces of theatre, featuring small profiles on and interviews with ten up-and-coming playwrights, directors and producers. Mira is one of them. On the website the photos are clearer. Mira is looking away from the camera and up towards the light, the effect is almost as if she's been sculpted. She's had her hair cut short, in a thick, heavy bob, a Parisian look. She looks older, more serious, neater.

Mira is introduced as a 'quiet but important new voice in theatre writing' and also 'an astonishing, perceptive talent'. It mentions how her first work, A Marriage, won the Hadley Prize for Playwriting and talks about how inventive it was, how the effect of multiple actors could have been shambolic or gimmicky but was instead piercing and haunting. Hana pauses, confused. The piece goes on to say how her second play, a one-woman piece she will perform herself, will be at the Edinburgh Fringe this summer and then later at the Soho Theatre. When asked about her creative influences, Mira explains that she's inspired by all kinds of storytelling, whether through paintings or plays or films, novels or short stories. She mentions all the writers she admires, playwrights, novelists, short story writers: Alice Birch, Virginia Woolf, Bernardine Evaristo, Alice Munro, Jane Austen. She comes across as knowledgeable, confident but not pretentious. Halfway through, there is a brief mention of a boyfriend in New York. Hana's mouth falls open, stunned. She has not spoken to Mira since she left her outside the theatre in Friern Barnet. In her interview, Mira says her playwriting voice comes to her naturally. 'It's just the way people speak,' she says. 'I'm obsessed with listening to people, hearing people talk, how they try to make sense of things in words.'

Hana puts down her phone. She stares intently into space; for how long, she can't say. Eventually she carries on unpacking.

Mira is on an overground train, leaning against a carriage door, talking on the phone. She is wearing a patterned silk scarf tied loosely round her neck and, as she talks, she plays with the ends of it with her free hand. She's speaking to Raef, who is calling from New York. He's coming back to London next week to visit for a fortnight, he does this every two months. It's the first time in months that Mira won't be working, so they've made plans to hire a car and drive to a cottage they've booked by the sea in Cornwall.

Mira is just about to get off the train when Raef says something she can't hear, so she takes the phone away from her ear and peers at it, checking her signal. Raef is always telling her to get her phone sorted out, it's old and is always dropping calls, but she hasn't yet got around to it.

'I think I'm getting cut off,' she says. 'Yep, it's going to cut—' and then the line goes dead. She shrugs, slides her phone into her back pocket. He'll call her back.

She gets off the train, walks down the path that leads from the station to the main road, humming a piece of music to herself without realising she's doing it. She stops at the Turkish greengrocers, buys a box of cherry tomatoes and a bag of apples. She's walking back to the flat when her phone rings again. She answers it without looking at the screen.

'There you are,' she says, 'I must have lost you.'

There's a pause and she frowns and says in a sing-song voice, 'Hello? Can you hear me? Raef?'

'It's not—' comes a clipped voice. 'It's me. Hana.'

Mira stops in the middle of the pavement.

'Hana?'

'Yes. It's me.'

'What's . . . Are you okay?'

'I saw your piece, in the paper. By accident.'

Mira is so stunned, she doesn't immediately know what Hana is talking about.

'My piece?'

'Correct, yes.' Hana's tone is abrupt. 'It sounds like things are going well for you.' She speaks flatly, practically monotone.

'Oh. That.' Mira closes her eyes and shakes her head quickly, as if to gather herself together. She opens her eyes again. 'I . . . yeah. That was a while ago.'

Someone brushes past Mira's shoulder and this brings her back to her surroundings. Slowly, she begins walking again, turning into the square. For a while, neither of them says anything. Mira opens the gate into the courtyard and sits on one of the wooden benches by the rose bushes.

'Anyway,' Hana says. 'I—'

'I thought,' Mira's voice is soft, slow, 'I thought I must have lost you.'

There's a pause. 'No, no, I can hear you okay. Can you hear me?'

Mira laughs a little at Hana's misunderstanding, then makes a fist with her hand. She covers her mouth and starts crying, noiselessly. Hana is saying something about how she's moved and, if she wants to, Mira can come round for a coffee sometime, only if she wants to, only if she has time, of course, and Mira nods and nods and nods, her fist still against her mouth until she takes it away, takes a breath and says yes, yes, she'd like that. She covers her eyes with her hand like a shade, crying, nodding at whatever it is Hana is saying.

It's a Friday afternoon, and Mira is walking down Hana's road, looking for her door number. Mira recognised the name of Hana's road when Hana texted the address to her. It's around the corner from where Mira used to live with Lili, although Hana's road is much quieter and prettier, overlooking the nicer edge of the park. It occurs to Mira that if she still lived there, they would have been less than five minutes' walk away from each other.

Mira is carrying a bouquet of wildflowers wrapped in thick brown paper, roses and larkspur and little white daisies. She hopes Hana will like them. She rings the bell and then steps away from the door. She is ten minutes early. She brushes her hair behind her ears while she waits.

When Hana opens the door she says, 'You're early.' There is a curious lilt in her voice. She is unsmiling, serious. Hana tells Mira to come in. Mira hands her the flowers as she does so. She says quietly, her hair falling forward, that she didn't know what else to bring. Hana takes them from her, saying she only had to bring herself.

Mira takes off her shoes without asking and then follows Hana down the hallway, into the open-plan kitchen and the lounge. Light spills in big triangles onto the whitewashed floor. Thin white curtains, almost transparent, hang at the partly open French doors, blowing with the breeze. There are two candles burning on the mantlepiece, filling the air with the scent of oranges and lemons. Above the mantlepiece hangs a picture, a still life of a vase of tulips against a pink background.

'Isn't that—'

'It's one of hers, yes,' Hana says in a hurry, not meeting her eye. 'By the way, you can take the rest of her paintings that you wanted to keep. Presumably you have room for them now?'

Mira's eyes brim with tears. She thought she'd lost all of that too. She nods. She tries to say thank you, but only a funny, stifled noise comes out.

Hana fills up the kettle at the sink and sets it to boil. She reaches for a vase on an open shelf, fills that up with water too and then places it on the old farmhouse table. She starts unwrapping the flowers, snipping the ends, and then positions them in the vase, one by one. Mira stands on the opposite side of the table. Neither of them knows what to say.

Then Mira says, 'This place. It's lovely. It's so light.'

Hana doesn't say anything for a moment. She is still busy with the flowers. Eventually she says, her expression tight, 'It's not as big as the last place, but then we won't need it so big.'

'We?'

The kettle switches off and so Hana turns back to the counter and makes the coffee.

'Oh.' She fills the coffee pot with water and then reaches into a cupboard for two mugs. 'I suppose I might as well tell you.' She moves around the small kitchen, fishing a brown paper bag out of an enamel tin, emptying pastries onto a plate, fetching two more plates from another cupboard and then milk from the fridge. Without looking at Mira, she says, 'I have a sperm donor. With any luck, I might get pregnant.'

'Hana,' Mira says, blinking hard. 'That's amazing.'

'Well, nothing's started yet.'

'Yes, but . . .'

Hana looks straight at Mira, directly into her eyes. An expression of sadness flickers momentarily across her face, the air between them crowded with questions: how did we get here? Where do we go from here?

They stand like this looking at each other until Mira says in a quiet voice, 'I didn't mean—'

Hana moves, puts the brown paper from the flowers in the bin, washes her hands. She turns back and taps her nails impatiently on the tabletop.

'Didn't you?' Hana says coolly.

Mira lowers her eyes. Then, after a pause, she says, 'I didn't mean to hurt you. I didn't mean to not tell you about—'

'About what? Samir? Or the play?'

'Both,' Mira blurts out.

'Both? Really?' Hana raises an eyebrow. 'So does that mean you regret writing it?'

'Hana,' Mira says pleadingly. She stretches her arm across the table. 'Hana, it really wasn't about you. If you'd just stayed to watch the rest of it . . . you'd have seen, it took on a life of its own and—'

'So you don't regret it.'

A small breath escapes from Mira's throat. 'I know I could have done things differently. That night, when you took me out for dinner in Shoreditch. I could have tried harder. . . I should have told you before what the play was about—'

'See, I've been thinking about that. Because when we were outside the theatre, that awful evening, I remember you said you tried to tell me at the restaurant. But I have no recollection of that.' Hana pauses, takes her time to press the plunger on the coffee pot. 'But let's say you had tried to tell me. Let's say you did things differently. What if I'd said to you, "Actually Mira, I'm not comfortable with you using my circumstances as your 'inspiration' or subject matter," then what would you have done?'

'I don't . . .' Mira makes a helpless face. 'What you're asking is impossible for me to answer.'

'But what would you have done?'

Mira glances at her hands. 'I'd have . . . I'd have found a way for you to understand,' she murmurs. She looks up at Hana and her voice is slightly more certain. 'I think if you'd seen it all, you'd have understood.'

Hana nudges the plates with her index finger. 'Well, personally I think you handled the whole thing terribly. And, to be clear, I'm still not happy about it. I didn't particularly enjoy reading about it in the paper. But it's done now. Your play is "making waves". There's nothing I can do about it. Is there?'

'It's not unusual,' Mira says quietly.

'Sorry?' Hana says.

'It's not unusual, to write about family or real life. To be . . . inspired by it.'

Hana doesn't reply to this. She picks up one of the mugs and pours the coffee, spilling some on the tabletop. She sets the mug back down in a deliberate movement.

'I read something else about you, by the way,' she says, turning to the sink to dampen a dishcloth, 'a very gushing review on some website, with all these details about the staging. You know, if you had told me that there was some kind of "bigger picture" going on, commenting on the "nature of intimate relationships" or whatever, with the different actors playing the same couple, then maybe I *would* have understood what you were trying to do, that this wasn't just about my marriage and my life as a plot line.'

She starts to wipe the table, mopping up the coffee spill.

Mira stares at Hana, confused by this switch in direction.

'Wait? What?'

Now Hana's rinsing the cloth out. Mira wishes Hana would just stand still; it's too hard to concentrate with her moving around.

'I might have understood, Mira.'

Mira shakes her head, attempting to follow Hana's meaning. 'Then . . . why, I'm sorry, why . . . are we doing this? Why would you ask—'

'I wanted to hear what you would say,' Hana says, simply.

Mira touches her forehead with her fingers, slowly absorbing what Hana is telling her, that she would have listened after that first burst of fury, that she might have accepted Mira's explanation; that things didn't have to be this way for this long.

Hana continues, 'And as for the other thing, I spoke with Samir about it. Because I had to. I didn't *want* to have to talk to him. But during the divorce there was a lot that needed to be said, and he told me—'

Mira looks at Hana, with a wincing expression. 'God, Han, I swear, it wasn't even, it barely—'

Hana finally pushes the mug in front of Mira. She pours another coffee for herself.

'—And I know that you had very little, if anything, to do with it.'

'I didn't,' Mira says, in a rush. 'I was so angry and I made it out to be a lot worse than it was. It was honestly nothing. I'm sor—'

'But you should have told me as soon as it happened. There's no excuse for that.'

Mira hunches her shoulders forward, cupping the mug in her hands, and says, helplessly, 'I didn't know what to do. I thought it would do more harm than—'

'However,' Hana dusts her hands, 'it should never have happened in the first place, and that wasn't your responsibility. So, there's not a lot either of us can do about that now.'

'No,' Mira says quietly.

'And believe it or not, I didn't actually ask you here just to argue.' Hana's voice is still firm, but the look on her face has changed to something softer. 'I'm moving on with my life. I don't want to be miserable anymore.'

Mira covers her face with her hands. 'I messed everything up. I should have called you, I should have explained, but I genuinely thought you'd never want to speak to me again.

And I was scared of somehow making it worse. The more time went by, the harder it felt to try and sort things out. I didn't know where to even begin.'

She drops her hands, holds on to the edge of the table. She focuses on a knot in the woodwork. She reaches out to touch it with her finger, stares at it until it turns blurry. 'This year's been so hard,' she says, slowly. 'Without—' Hana clears her throat, pours milk into her coffee. She stirs it slowly, the sound of the teaspoon hitting the sides of the mug filling the silence between them. Eventually, Hana sets the spoon aside.

'Can't have been that hard. With your "astonishingly perceptive talent" and your "boyfriend" around.' Hana raises her eyebrows, takes a croissant and drops it on a plate and then slides it across the table to Mira.

When Mira looks at her, she sees a trace of a smile on Hana's face, but it isn't haughty, as Mira might have expected, it's gentle. Hana picks up her coffee, helps herself to a pastry and heads to the sofa. She sits down on one side of it, her legs curled up under her. Unsure of what to do, Mira follows, holding her mug in one hand and her plate in the other. She hesitates before perching on the other side of the sofa.

'You said,' Hana continues, taking a bite, 'that he looked about twelve.'

'I'd only met him once then,' Mira mumbles. She picks at the croissant with her fingertips.

'You're dropping crumbs everywhere.'

'Sorry,' Mira says. And then she bursts out crying, covering her face again. 'I really am sorry. I'm so sorry for everything—'

At first, Hana doesn't say anything and Mira feels like an idiot, crying uncontrollably. Then Hana lets out a long breath, and Mira hears her put down her cup on the side table. Hana turns sideways towards her and puts her hand on Mira's shoulder and then, in one quick movement, pulls her into a tight embrace. 'All right,' she says, a slight quaver in her voice. 'It's alright, it'll be all right.' Mira nods into her and Hana lightly strokes her hair.

They sit like this for maybe three or four minutes and, in those minutes, they each understand that they still have this, will always have this, even if they came close to losing it, even if one day they might come close to losing it again. Then Mira lifts her head and Hana shifts and they both pull away, and the moment is gone.

'So go on then,' Hana says, helping herself to a tissue from the box on the side table, before passing the tissues along to Mira. 'Tell me about him. He's not married, I take it?'

Between laughing a little shakily and wiping her cheeks and blowing her nose, Mira eventually confirms he's not married, no. And though there are some silences, and though at times the conversation is stilted, the sisters keep on talking. When it gets cold, Hana gets up and closes the French doors. She comes back to her position on the sofa, reaching behind Mira's back for a throw and shaking it out, spreading it lightly over both of their legs.

While Hana is tidying up, Mira spends a while looking around the living area. It's so different in style from Hana's previous home. It's simpler, more relaxed, reminding Mira of a summer house. She takes in the books on the shelves, running her fingers across their spines. She's surprised to see so many authors she loves – Virginia Woolf and Jane Austen, Alice Munro and Bernardine Evaristo. She can't remember ever seeing any books in Hana's old house that weren't just about the law. She never imagined Hana would ever have any interest in these books, stories about women, mothers, daughters, lovers, sisters. Then she stops, frowns. These books are all so familiar to her. These are *her* favourite writers, the ones she mentioned in that newspaper interview. Could it be that Hana paid that much attention to what she'd said? When she takes one of the books off the shelf and flicks through it, she sees the corners turned down, passages underlined. It unexpectedly stirs her to think of Hana here, alone, reading, starting over again. She glances away from the books, looks about her at the pieces of Hana's new life. I should have been here for you, she thinks. I should have been here for you, she wishes she was brave enough to say.

As she moves to return the book to its place, something falls out from between the pages and flutters down to the floor. Mira bends down to pick it up, still holding the book in one hand, and when she turns it over and sees what it is, she lets out a surprised little laugh. For here it is, the old photo that Mira had kept for so many years, the one she thought she must have lost or that Hana had thrown away when she moved from Lili's to the flat on the square.

It's the photo of Hana and Mira as girls, the one their mother took, back when she was alive and Hana and Mira were too young to know what complications were yet to come, too young to really know anything of love or loss or the vastness of life. For how could they have? They were just little girls. They had no way of knowing. Mira feels a tug inside her, an ache. She shakes her head, feeling silly for being so sentimental. But then, she's always been so. She smiles, wipes the skin under her eyes with her fingers, then slips the photo between the pages and places the book back on the shelf.

Acknowledgements

I don't even know how to begin to say thank you to my literary agent Laurie Robertson at Peters Fraser and Dunlop. When I signed with you, I had no idea that I was gaining not just an agent but also a friend. Thank you. For the WhatsApps, for the long phone calls, for the reading that you always do, for never saying you're too busy, for your thorough notes, for lending me your make-up bag that time my under-eye concealer ran because I'd been crying in Waterstones. For all of it. Remember when I joked that I'd dedicate this book to you 'if' I ever finished? Well. You've been with me on this journey with Hana and Mira since the very beginning. I hope you're proud of who they've become.

To Charlotte Humphery, my editor at Sceptre, and Nico Parfitt, my assistant editor. I've *loved* working with you both. I'm kind of sad that it's come to an end. Thank you for everything – your editorial notes, your excellent perspective, our frank discussions, the way you pushed me to elevate my writing and kept me focused. I feel like I've grown as a writer with you, and there is so much that I have learnt from you along the way that I want to remember for all my writing. Also, Charlotte, I can't not say it – thank you for introducing me to Crazy Ex-Girlfriend (which makes a cameo on p.33)! I will forever be indebted to you for making me laugh by sending me funny links when, at times, I felt as if I might break down over my manuscript.

To all the team at Sceptre, everyone who has had eyes on my book, from copyeditors to line-editors to proofreaders to design and publicity: thank you. I'm very proud to have had two books published by such an elegant publisher; at times, I can't quite believe that I do. Charlotte Ager, you were on my wishlist from day one for the cover. Thank you for bringing Hana and Mira to life in your beautiful composition.

The last time I had a book published was in 2021 and it was still partly lockdown, so I wasn't able to connect very much with other authors. How nice it is for things to be different now. I'm so grateful to have had the opportunity to talk about writing with Lucy Caldwell, Natasha Lunn, Nikesh Shukla, Sara Nisha Adams and Chloë Ashby. I hope to have many more such conversations.

Thank you also to the Instagram book readers in my phone; if I start naming you, I might (accidentally) leave someone out, so I won't – but you know who you are, and thank you for your generous support of all my books. Our exchanges bring a smile to my face. I really hope you like *Playing Games* too. The same goes to all my writing students and subscribers to my newsletter, Dear Huma – you have no idea how much you've kept me going whilst writing and editing this novel. I'm always delighted to write to you and to hear from you.

Thank you to my lawyer friend Laura, for guiding me through legal profession timelines so that I could get it right for Hana; and to Hugo at Perk Coffee Bar, for patiently explaining the ins and outs of Mira's job.

Thank you to my very first reader and very dear friend, Liz Rees; not just for reading all my books before anybody else but also for years of understanding. To Lindsay, thank you for your cheerfulness and long chats; for your friendship. Parul, our Saturday night dinners are the best; it means a lot to have a friend like you who understands what it is to take risks, to choose to do things differently, creatively. hadn't left. To Sarah K, I wish you'd stayed in London. The shorthand between us is everything, you just *get* it, and I wanted so much for Hana and Mira to have that too.

I was inspired to write this story partly because I find family relationships and sibling dynamics fascinating. I'm so thankful for my Qureshi and Birch families, and my own siblings (who are neither Hana nor Mira, incidentally!) Though we all now have our own families, once upon a time we were the only family we knew. How lucky we are to have had that. And a special thank you to my sister-in-law Toki, for supporting me through tricky times and helping me find my energy when I was struggling.

Claire Jakobssen, as a family, we'd be lost without you. Thank you, for being such a grounding, soulful presence in all our lives and for making the stressful times feel less intense and more manageable. Please don't go anywhere.

I love writing, it is the only thing that makes sense to me and there is nothing else in the world that I would rather do; but the truth is, at times, it *hurts*. And when it does, there's really only one person who gets me through. Thank you, Richard, for your gentleness, your love. For bringing the sun to me, after the cloudy days have passed.

And to my three super smart boys, Suffian, Sina and Jude. Look, I know you're getting tired of me writing soppy things about you in my book acknowledgements; I know, it's not cool. But maybe one day it will mean something to you. Guys, listen, I love you. And I know it's not easy, having a mum who writes books because sometimes I live in those books in my head all the time, and sometimes I'm distracted, even when I'm with you. I'm sorry. But thank you, for yanking me by the hand and guiding me back to you. I'm so lucky that I get to hang out with you.

And Sina – thank you for letting me borrow your beautiful simile on p.262 about the branches of the trees being black like burnt matchsticks. You should definitely move your name up to gold for that.

Boys, this book is about sisters, not brothers, but still I hope that if you ever read it one day, you'll know that what I'm trying to say is: take care of each other. Be patient, be kind. Try to forgive. And if you can, try to remember this time, the way you each are right now, aged ten, eight and six, because it's really rather wonderful.

Read an extract from
Things We Do Not Tell the People We Love

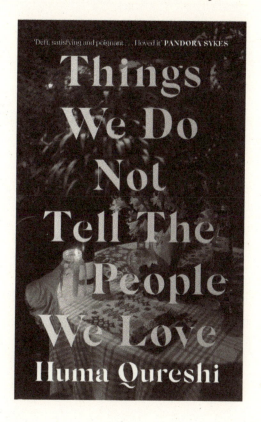

'A deft, satisfying and poignant collection of stories . . . I loved it'
Pandora Sykes

'[Qureshi] has a wonderfully luminous, understated style of writing'
Diana Evans, *Evening Standard*

'Huma Qureshi is a writer I know I'll be reading for years and years and years'
Natasha Lunn, author of *Conversations on Love*

Premonition

My mother had mentioned offhand to me that you were engaged to be married to a girl who had studied medicine at Oxford and I had thought, *but of course*. I remembered how exceptionally picky your mother was about these things. I had been on my way to meet Cameron at the time so I was not paying much attention to what my mother was saying and was in a rush to end our call but after I had caught my breath from running for the bus, I remember thinking it was not so surprising that you had ended up following convention and doing things so traditionally after all.

I had little reason to think about you or your wedding again until Cameron's birthday several months later when we went out for dinner at Mildreds. It had been raining thickly and we squeezed through the door to join the back of a huddle of warm bodies waiting for tables, everyone's coats smelling like bonfires and damp leaves. Cameron turned to kiss me and as he leaned in, I thought I saw you behind him, standing in line next to a girl with a head full of tight curls golden at the tips. I couldn't be sure, for it had easily been ten years or perhaps even more since I had seen you, but I recognised something. It was there in the way that you stood slightly slouched and in your face, which had not changed so much. I must have been staring at you because when Cameron moved away again, he squeezed my hand and laughed, 'Hey, who are you checking out on my birthday?'

When we moved to our table and sat down, I stole a better look. Shadows flickered across your face from the low-hanging copper lights and perhaps you had that odd feeling of being watched, for you looked up right then and caught my eye. And that's when I realised it really was you, because that was exactly what we used to do.

*

I had first felt you looking at me when I was fifteen years old. We had known each other as children, which is to say we did not know each other at all. Our parents had been friends since before we were even born but you and I barely spoke to each other. Though my mother had told me once that we played together at each other's houses when we were very small – something I certainly did not and still do not remember – by the time we reached secondary school certain lines had been drawn and I understood that I was not supposed to talk to boys and it was, I imagine, the same for you with girls. But then you started looking at me.

The first time it happened, we were at a dinner party at an uncle and aunty's house, or so we called them though they were not blood relatives, but just another Pakistani family we happened to know. All of our parents did this back then: hosted dinners for sixty or seventy people at a time, squeezing more guests than they could comfortably accommodate into each other's houses every single Saturday night. Back then the English girls from my girls' school went to real parties, teenage house parties with boys and alcohol and no parents at all, and it embarrassed me how boring my life was. Our dinner parties were our parents' idea of a good time. They loved these parties; they lived for these Saturday nights, when all the men, all the fathers, sat around on long sofas discussing politics and the state of the NHS, in which they all happened to work, uninterrupted, while the women, our mothers, helped each other in the kitchen and laid dining tables and stacked paper plates with bought-in-bulk napkins, gossiping. Actually, perhaps that is unfair; to this day, I have no idea what our mothers talked about, but I can guess now that some of it might have been about the lives they had left behind to make this country their home.

Meanwhile, we sat upstairs in separate bedrooms, girls in one, boys in another. All of us girls sat on the floor watching films while you boys were across the hallway fighting over computer games or football. Like the other girls, I had to dress up for these dinners in fancy silk shalwar kameez, brightly coloured and embroidered but mostly badly-fitting outfits that smelt like the suitcases in the loft and which I hated because they made me feel like a Christmas tree, but you got away with just tee-shirts and jeans. It bothered me that none of the boys were required to make an effort, that our mothers didn't collectively look you all up and down and scrutinise you the way they did us, assessing the fairness of our skin, the curve of our pubescent waists, the early signs of our marriageability.

Sometimes, the older girls whispered about crushes they weren't supposed to have. They talked about you especially, because you were considered the best-looking one, with unusually creamy skin, gold-flecked hair and deep-set chestnut eyes. I admit this was a novelty for all of us. 'He doesn't even look Pakistani,' they used to say, awestruck, in spite of your scruffy clothes. I had heard the other boys sneer at you and call you pretty, because you were also very skinny in a runner's sort of way, but you just laughed and shrugged it off like the rock star we all thought you were.

That first time I felt it – your eyes upon me – we'd been summoned to the dining room for dinner. It was customary to call the children down for food after our fathers had been served but before our mothers, and we would help ourselves to paper plates that dented in the middle under the combined weight of rice, chicken and shop-bought pizza brought out especially for us kids, and which we carried back carefully to our designated rooms, the bedroom carpets protected from potential spills with crisp white sheets sellotaped to the skirting boards. At this particular house, the dining table had been pushed back against the wall to make space for the guests and we were ushered in by some of the aunties, queued as though we were at an all-you-can-eat buffet. But you stood out of line, slouching against a sideboard, clutching a paper plate to your chest. You always had this attitude about you that seemed to say you were better than all of this and I liked that, because inside I sort of felt the same way too. I saw you from the corner of my eye, stood there, and all of a sudden, I realised you were watching me, even though there were other people around. I don't remember how I knew, only that I felt it, only that I could sense I was being watched because my skin tickled and I became aware of my own breathing. When I realised it was you watching me, somewhere inside of me a series of synapses sparked. I looked up then, shy and unsure, and though I caught your eye and though we both looked away again, it was not before you held my gaze just a fraction longer than was appropriate.

Later that night you were all I could think of and yet I'd never even spoken to you in my entire life.

*

It went on for months, at every Saturday-night dinner we went to: a private symphony of glances that varied in intensity, movement and pace. It made me uneasy but not in an altogether unpleasant way; I felt brighter, prettier, stranger, by which I mean closer to unique, under the hold of your gaze. I quickly understood, of course, that this was something that was just between us, something only we did, something we didn't need to talk to anyone else about and certainly not to each other. It was our secret. But still, sometimes, I convinced myself I was imagining it because you were older than me and the best-looking of all the boys and there were plenty of prettier girls with long shiny dark hair in our group for you to consider. I was thin and flat-chested, quiet and bookish, short and bespectacled. I played the piano and this was the only thing I could think of that made me different. You knew this because my parents always made me play for our guests when dinners were held at our house. But apart from that, there was little reason for me to stand out. There was no logical expla- nation for your interest in me.

*

I began to feel you like some kind of premonition. Somehow you appeared at the same time I did across landings and in hallways and dining rooms, as though you were waiting for me, as though you knew I'd be there. You'd hold my gaze; I'd look away but when I looked back, there you were again. It progressed. We'd pass each other on the stairs, me going up, you coming down, and in the space between heartbeats you'd brush my hand or my arm, once or twice even the small of my back as you followed me, and I knew it was intentional because it kept happening. Your touches were tiny, seemingly accidental – sometimes your fingers pressing the tips of mine as you wordlessly passed me a glass or a plate – but they cracked me open, like lightning across the sky. Our star-crossed moments may have lasted only milliseconds, but they filled the whole of my small schoolgirl world and kept it turning, like shafts of dust dancing gold in a splinter of sunlight.

Though once I was bored by them, now I could no longer wait for Saturday nights. They always seemed so far away. The weeks passed slowly; I used to spend every break time desperately trying to catch snatches of what the other girls at school were saying, making mental notes on their conversation so that one day I might have been able to join in, but now I preferred being on my own because it gave me time to think of you. I'd sit in a stairwell with my Walkman and I'd replay our latest exchange of secret looks to a soundtrack of love songs and every beat made my heart ache because I yearned for you. I began to care more about my appearance, begging my mother to let me swap my glasses for contacts and pluck my eyebrows, asking her to alter my shalwar kameez – the only clothes you ever saw me in – so that they might be slightly more flattering and she humoured me, I guess, because she thought it meant I was interested in my roots or something. But all I wanted was to find a way to keep you looking at me, to not have you drop your gaze or swap your attention to someone else.

When Saturday evenings finally came around, I searched for clues to find out whether your family had already arrived at whosoever's house we were invited to next, scanning the long line of cars parked all the way down to the end of the road looking for yours, seeking for a glimpse of your trainers in the rubble of guests' shoes discarded untidily in heaps by the front door. Sometimes you weren't there and on those nights I felt my heart sink. On the drive home I would slump, sullen in response to my parents when they asked if I had fun.

I found dinner parties at your house especially thrilling, overwhelmed by the notion that I was right there, in the place where you lived and dreamed and breathed, knowing that my hands might pass where yours had already been. Every little thing inside your house took on meaning; sipping from a glass, I found myself wondering if perhaps you'd drunk from the same one, washed it yourself and left it on the draining board, and this alone left me feeling lightheaded. More than once I slipped inside your bedroom without anyone knowing while you boys watched the football in your TV lounge. I remember your room smelt like musk or warm bodies or clothes left out too long in pale rain, a smell that later at university I came to know was what the inside of most boys' bedrooms smelt like, and the crevices of their skin first thing in the morning. But I was an only child so back then this was all still a mystery to me. The sight of your bed sheets crumpled made my head spin though I did not fully understand why. I never stayed long but I caught glimpses of your books by writers whom I did not yet know like Solzhenitsyn and Sartre, and I sifted through your CDs, surprised to find you liked the same sort of music my father kept on twelve-inch. The Carpenters, Cat Stevens, Lou Reed. I began to search for you in the lyrics of my father's songs, repeating them in my head. *Hello my love, I heard a kiss from you.* Sometimes I thought about taking something, a book, perhaps a paper from your desk covered by your handwriting, just to have something that belonged to you, but in my awkward shalwar kameez I had no pockets to put things in.

*

At Mildreds I made no conscious effort to look at you but I felt you there like a faint shadow, glancing across at me while I laughed with Cameron or covered his hand with mine or when he lifted his spoon to my mouth so I might taste his dessert. While once I might have cared that someone from the small place where I grew up, which now felt a million miles away, had seen me with Cameron, it had stopped bothering me a long time ago. When my mother asked where I was or who I was with, I was not completely forthright and spared her the finer details but at least I did not lie about it completely or pretend that Cameron did not exist. She knew his name, had deduced herself, I think, through a process of elimination that I was more or less living with him. But for all it might have pained her, she had not yet confronted me about it so I took her silence as a sort of begrudging acceptance after all these years. Though I did not bring him up unless she asked, I was done with the secrets and the lies. I had spent my life at university living like that, hiding boyfriends like crumpled love letters, and now I was too old for it. I briefly wondered who the girl you were having dinner with was, the gorgeous girl with the tight gold-tipped Afro curls whose wine you poured and whose hand you held. She was obviously not the good Pakistani girl who had studied medicine at Oxford and thus not the girl your family had proudly announced you were engaged to.

Cameron had left the table for the bathroom and I was shrugging on my coat, still damp and nubby from the rain, when our eyes locked again. You nodded in my direction by way of acknowledgement, as if the years that had passed hung there suspended in the fine particles of air. The girl you were with was looking down at her phone, her features illuminated softly by the glow, ethereal. When he returned, I let Cameron guide me to the door and as we walked past outside

I could just about see you, hazy and unclear through the mist of shadowy condensation that had gathered on the inside.